HERO *of a* HIGHLAND WOLF

TERRY SPEAR

sourcebooks
casablanca

Published by Sourcebooks Casablanca, an imprint of Sourcebooks, Inc.
P.O. Box 4410, Naperville, Illinois 60567-4410
(630) 961-3900
Fax: (630) 961-2168
www.sourcebooks.com

Printed and bound in Canada.
WC 10 9 8 7 6 5 4 3 2 1

To my best girlfriend, Diane Stokes Kupfer,
who sneaked the first two romance books
to me when I was thirteen.
She'd picked them up from her sister
who was a librarian and ten years older
than we were. I was shocked and wowed,
and didn't read another romance for years.

And now, I can't get enough of them.
Thanks for your friendship all these years.
When we managed to hook up
at the RWA national conference in Orlando,
it was as if we had never been apart.

To everlasting friendship, love, romance,
and many more years.

Chapter 1

INHERITING A SCOTTISH CASTLE HIGH ON RUGGED cliffs overlooking the North Sea might have been appealing, if not for Grant MacQuarrie, the man managing it. Unfortunately, Colleen Playfair couldn't just fire him. Not when he had taken the reins to care for the property, following in his father's and grandfather's footsteps. She planned to go easy on him, but as she drove from the airport in Edinburgh to meet up with him in the Highlands, she dreaded the confrontation.

Just from the brief talk she'd had with Grant over the phone—in which he had grunted more than he'd spoken—she assumed the terms of her inheritance had pissed him off royally. Colleen tried to see it from his viewpoint: having the absentee landowner pop in to tell him what to do when he had been there day in and day out. And she was a woman and American.

She tapped her thumbs on the steering wheel as she considered the countryside. The ancient stone walls had meandered across the land for centuries, dividing it, and the sheep dotted the bright green grasses covering the hills. Like a pastoral scene of ancient times.

She loved everything she'd seen so far: the people, the old buildings, the vast uncluttered landscape now before her, the rivers and streams and trees. She would love it here, if Grant didn't give her too much grief.

She sighed.

The terms of her inheritance weren't her doing. One of the biggest problems she foresaw was that she didn't know when she'd have a chance to run as a wolf. As a royal, she had very few human roots, which meant she could choose when she shifted—as opposed to the more newly turned, whose wolfish drive was dictated by the moon. But she would have to run and she was already feeling the need, the tingling urge to stretch her…wolf legs.

According to her father, Grant and his staff were human. She would have to get used to the layout of the land to learn where and when she could safely run.

She could just imagine someone seeing her as a wolf, alerting the rest, and starting a massive wolf hunt. Or worse, someone witnessing and then reporting her shifting. Then she'd have to change not only the person who had witnessed her shifting, but everyone else at the castle as well. Her whole visit could be a disaster of epic proportions.

But she wasn't giving up *her* castle for *anything* or *anyone*.

———

Grant MacQuarrie swore he would rather fight a clan war, battling in the glen like they had done in earlier times, than have to deal with this.

For seven centuries, courtesy of *lupus garou* genetics and their ability to live long lives, he and his ancestors had administered Farraige Castle for the Playfair family. The family included a John Playfair, a noteworthy Scottish mathematician, geologist, and physicist, and his younger brother, who was a famous architect with a son even more famous. Colleen's direct ancestor, the youngest of the Playfair brothers, was the inventor of statistical graphs.

Then there was Colleen's own father, Theodore Playfair, whose mother, Neda, owned Farraige Castle. He had fought with his mother and left, mating an American and inheriting Farraige Castle upon his mother's death. But he had left the management in the MacQuarries' capable hands and returned to Maryland. Thank...the heavens. The man had been a thorn in Grant and his brothers' arses for as long as Grant could remember.

Now Theodore's daughter was arriving to take over.

Grant folded his arms as he stood on the castle walk towering over the stone drive that led into the inner bailey. Glad to see that his friend Ian MacNeill and fifteen of his pack members had arrived to help him out today, Grant smiled.

His triplet brothers, Enrick and Lachlan, joined him as they watched the men gathering in the inner bailey. Everyone was dressed in kilts and no shirts. Grant had figured they would look even more fearsome that way when the lass arrived. Their muscled shoulders and torsos were oiled, their skin glistening—making them appear as though they'd been fighting for some time previously. Their swords and dirks were at the ready as they waited for word to start, joking and laughing with each other in the meantime.

Grant and his clan had no trouble overseeing the estates and would continue to do so, just the way they had been. Some slip of an American girl had inherited the castle and properties, and she would arrive to tell him how to run things. For a year and a day as part of the legal terms of her inheritance. Just like her father before her.

Two years earlier, they'd had to deal with her resentful father, which had been a trial in and of itself. Theodore had dictated new terms, ordering Grant and his people to change a lot of their procedures. Implementing the changes had caused a lot of strife, so Grant and his clan had gone back to the old ways of doing things once the tyrant left. Grant hoped the daughter would not be as difficult to deal with.

One hand resting on the hilt of his sword, Enrick, the middle triplet, shook his head, his tawny blond hair tousled by the wind as he stared down at the gathered men. "Seems you're going to a lot of trouble to make the lass think we're warlike barbarians in an attempt to scare her away. Or make her think she has no say in what we do."

"I'm hoping this will be enough," Grant said, giving Lachlan a scowl as his youngest brother—by fifteen minutes—grinned, his dark brown hair curlier than Grant's and Enrick's, his eyes the darkest brown of the three. He was also the most lighthearted, not as serious as the rest of them. Except in battle.

"So, if Lady Colleen Playfair doesn't turn around and run out of here shaking to the tips of her toes, what will you do then?" Enrick asked, casting a look in the direction of the long, winding drive that led up to the open gate.

"Have you not heard?" Lachlan raised his brows. "Grant has given her the White Room."

Enrick looked from the men in the bailey to Grant. "Nay, you did not."

Grant let out his breath. "You know the trouble the

MacNeill brothers faced when American she-wolves invaded their castle, aye?" He looked back at the MacNeill men, waved at Ian, and headed to the tower stairs to join the men below. "Besides," he said, clomping down the centuries-old stone steps, "she won't last that long. Once she sees all those sharp swords and dirks, and all that fighting and mayhem, she'll turn around and leave realizing she really didn't want to stay here after all. I've made reservations for her at a nice bed and breakfast two hours from here."

"Surely not for a year." Enrick snorted.

"Nay, for two weeks."

"Duncan MacNeill warned me the lasses from America can be as stubborn as us. So we might have a real fight on our hands. Especially since this means she could lose her inheritance to her cousins. How are you going to keep up the ruse that we are unruly barbarians for a year and a day?" Enrick asked.

"She won't last more than a day or two," Grant assured him. "And from what I have gathered, her cousins are betas, so they would be easily swayed. If they inherit the properties, everything will go as planned."

"Are you sure you want her to stay in the White Room?" Enrick asked.

"The chamber is one of the nicest rooms we have at the keep. It overlooks the sea and has a delightful view of the gardens. I'm just trying to be hospitable. Besides, her grandmother wished it. Who am I to go against the woman who had a heart of gold?" Grant said, thinking fondly of Neda Playfair and saddened that she had never met the granddaughter she would have doted on if she'd had the chance.

Enrick grunted. "And if Colleen doesn't want to stay there? You know the bad blood that existed between Colleen's grandmother and her father. If he poisoned Colleen against Neda, then she might not want to stay in the room for that reason alone. Not to mention the accommodations are rather…lacking."

"No other rooms are available. She can stay in the village, then. One of the men can escort her there," Grant said.

He was determined to keep the castle running as smoothly as always—*his way*. He didn't like change. He guessed it was because Neda, who had essentially raised him and his brothers, loved to change things— from reorganizing to adding new stuff and getting rid of old things. He loved constancy in his life. Most of all, he didn't like the idea of an outsider coming in and telling him how best to do his job when the person didn't have a clue about the operations.

Enrick frowned. "How are you going to make the two adjoining chambers that are free for guests to use suddenly unavailable?"

"Lachlan is having them painted as we speak. The furniture is all moved out, and paint fumes are ghastly for our sensitive sense of smell." Grant smiled a little.

Lachlan bowed his head a bit. "As his lairdship wished."

"I still think you're going to extremes on this," Enrick said. "You could have waited until you saw her. Maybe she's not anything like her father. You could have given her a chance."

"If she was only going to be here for a few days, we'd treat her with kindness and hospitality, agree to everything she said, and then send her on her way. Afterward, we would conduct business the way we've always done. End of story. But she's not going to reside here for only a few days. So we need to find a way to cut her stay short," Grant said, determined to get the upper hand with the lass right away. "You remember how it was with Theodore, do you not? We didn't think we'd ever last through *his* stay."

They exited the tower and greeted Ian, leader of both his gray wolf pack and the MacNeill clan, and several of his clansmen. "Where are your brothers?" Grant asked, surprised that they wouldn't be here. They all loved a good skirmish.

They were all great fighters, and Grant's brothers had looked forward to taking on Ian's in a mock battle. When it came to swordsmanship, Ian, the oldest, really had no match, except for Grant. As it should be. Pack leader against pack leader. Clan leader against clan leader.

"My mother had some activity planned and needed their help. My wife actually was pushing me out the door to come here with some of our men to help you," Ian said, wearing a blue-and-green kilt of the more muted, ancient variety. He smiled, his dark brown eyes lighting up with amusement. "So where is the lass?"

"On her way. We checked with the airline and rental car agency, so unless she's had unforeseen trouble, she should be here soon. We'll conduct the fight in the inner bailey as soon as she arrives. Or…start it, actually, as she drives up the road." Grant motioned to the wall walk where two lookouts were posted. "They'll warn us well beforehand. Then after the practice fight, we'll have a feast in the great hall. I've set it up so that she can see what it was like to eat in yonder castle during medieval times."

"Us all sweaty and oily, and I take it you mean to have her sitting between some of the hulking brutes during the meal?" Ian asked, sounding amused.

"Aye. Roasted boar—the whole thing, apple in mouth and all—no silverware, a bard telling bawdy jokes, the dogs underfoot." Grant smiled. "Good thing we took some of those pups of yours off your hands a couple of years back. They're unruly and love new guests. She won't know what hit her."

Ian shook his head. "I forewarned you that Americans can be...odd. And do the unexpected. You might not get rid of her that easily. How old is she?"

"She's twenty-six. Not too old that we might give her a heart attack, or too young we could scar her for life."

"Have you considered that she might like all that you're going to do? That she might want to stay even longer? Not that you could keep the charade going for all that long. Have you thought, perhaps, that if you went about your routine lives, she might be so bored that she'd leave? Visit the surrounding countries while she has a chance? I doubt her inheriting the properties is contingent on her being here every minute of the day for three hundred and sixty-six days," Ian said.

"Aye. I've thought of it. But you know me. I'm not a patient man, and the sooner I can get us back to doing things as usual, the better."

"Car approaching!" one of Grant's men shouted atop the curtain wall.

Grant gave Ian an evil smile. "As the Americans would say, it's showtime."

Chapter 2

COLLEEN KNEW SHE'D HAVE TROUBLE WITH GRANT MacQuarrie and his men as soon as she contacted him to tell him what she was tasked to do to earn her inheritance. She truly thought an outside pair of eyes—hers—could help see where improvements could be made in the management of her properties. After she had lived there for a while.

From Grant's reluctance to speak with her about any of it, she knew she would have difficulties with the old goat. Not that he was that old. Thirty, she thought. But his stubbornness made her think of him in that way.

It wasn't *her* idea to live at the castle for all that time. Like Grant and his people, she also had to make the most of it.

As soon as she turned into the winding, private drive that cut through a forest, she felt a shiver of excitement and a hint of trepidation. "Okay, you can do this."

She kept reminding herself that the castle was her family's, and Grant was only its manager. Not its owner. She was certain he'd try to intimidate her into not wanting to stay. But she could do anything for a year and a day if it meant keeping the family legacy that she would someday pass on to her own descendants. How many Americans could say they owned a castle in Scotland? Who were also wolves?

She spied a waterway where ducks and swans swam.

She smiled. Then frowned. She was glad to see so many trees where she could run safely as a wolf, but she would have to avoid disturbing the birds' habitat.

Her good friend Julia Wildthorn, now mated to Ian MacNeill, called her on her cell. Colleen stopped the car, thinking that if Julia had anything else to warn her about before she reached the castle, she'd better hear her out.

"Ian and some of his kin should already have arrived at your castle to battle it out with the MacQuarries in an unscheduled fighting match. But my mother-in-law has ensured the rest of the brothers and their kin remain busy. That will keep them away from Farraige Castle, so you'll have fewer men to deal with if they mean to give you a hard time," Julia said, a smile in her voice.

Colleen had never met Julia's mother-in-law, but she already loved her.

"Ian wouldn't let me come this time—though that would have been a hoot when they realized we are best friends," Julia said, chuckling.

Colleen smiled. "I'm almost there, I think. I just reached the canal-like pond where the swans are swimming."

"Okay, just a couple more turns, and you'll be there. I can't wait to hear how they react when you arrive. Keep me posted when you can," Julia said, sounding excited about the prospect.

Colleen suspected Julia would use her story in a future werewolf romance she would write.

"I will. I suspect Grant and the others had the notion that a little rough swordplay would scare me off." So Colleen had come prepared.

"Oh, yeah, typical macho-male ploy. Love ya, Colleen. Don't let them give you any guff."

"I won't." Colleen had every intention of having a little fun with this. "Talk later."

She opened the car windows before she drove around the last two bends in the road so that she could listen for the sound of fighting. She heard none.

When she saw the great gray wall and the four corner towers, she held her breath in awe at the sight. *Her* castle. It was beautiful. Then she saw movement on top of the wall walk and heard a man shout down that a car was coming, warning of her impending arrival.

She wanted to laugh.

Even so, her heartbeat accelerated. She was certain they were getting ready for her. She had two male cousins who had always teased her growing up, and she was used to dealing with them. She would have no problem dishing it out where Grant and the others were concerned. Except her cousins were betas. Grant was human, but he was still all alpha, from what her father had said.

She didn't know all that they had planned and she didn't know them, so she was somewhat apprehensive, though she hated to admit it.

She drove into the inner bailey and saw the sight she had tried to envision on the way here. But nothing had prepared her for this. Hot, hot, hot men in kilts with oiled abs, pecs, and bare legs, and wearing leather boots—some ancient, others more modern. The men were absolutely drool worthy! The only thing she regretted was that *she* hadn't been given the opportunity to oil them down.

She even considered stopping some of the sparring men and offering to rub oil on any spots they had missed, just to show they didn't intimidate her.

She parked and just stared out the window, jaw dropping as she watched the men slashing at each other with humongous swords, the metal clanking and the sound reverberating off the castle walls. She was dumbfounded and enthralled. This was nothing like the movies, or even the Renaissance fairs or Celtic fests she'd attended. The battling men were so close up and real. And so many of them. Maybe thirty?

She took in a deep breath and her heart began skipping beats. She smelled *wolves*! Not humans. *Wolves*. *Oh…my…God*. Her father had lied to her. Why? This changed *everything*. Butting heads with an alpha human was a lot different from taking on an alpha male wolf. He could smell everything about her that she could about him. She thought she'd have the advantage in dealing with him. Not now.

The hot testosterone poured off the men in waves. And their wolfishly delicious scent was a real turn-on. She doubted anyone could smell her interested scent, considering how much the men exuded.

Focus! She sat for a while just watching from the car as the men mostly ignored her, although a few glanced her way, checking her out. Probably trying to determine if she was quaking in her low heels yet, afraid to leave the car. That worked well for her. Let them believe what they would about her. She'd prove them wrong when she was good and ready.

She wondered which one was Grant, or whether he was even out here fighting with the men. Taking in a deep, admiring breath of all that gorgeous Highland wolf flesh, she dug through her bag and pulled out her camcorder. Armed, she left her car and began videotaping the scene. Once she was back in the States, she'd view this whenever she wanted to enjoy some really hot Highlanders in action.

A few stopped to watch her then, smiling, which surprised her because she assumed their fearless leader had ordered the men to put on the show of a lifetime to discourage her from staying. Smiling at her wouldn't have the right effect, unless they thought she was a timid beta wolf and their interested smiles were meant to scare her off.

Or maybe her skirt whipping around in the wind had caught their eyes. The gypsy-like floral, silky, partly sheer fabric was a tease, allowing the viewer a glimpse of legs, but the built-in very short underskirt stayed put, hiding all the important parts. Still, they seemed to be waiting to see her skirt fly above her ears. They would be disappointed. Or maybe they thought watching her would cow her. She concentrated on looking for Ian MacNeill, at his wife's request.

Most of the men were still fighting. From the pictures Julia had shared with her of Ian and Grant, Colleen recognized the MacNeills outfitted in their predominantly blue-and-green kilts. The MacQuarries wore red-and-green plaid.

She continued to shoot the ones who battled it out, while scanning all of the men, looking for Ian. The men worked their gorgeous muscles as they swung their swords, tensing, parrying, and thrusting. Oh my heavens, the sight was dazzling.

Then she caught sight of Ian fighting Grant MacQuarrie. *Sure*. The pack leader of the MacNeills squaring off with the pack leader of the MacQuarries.

She couldn't get over the notion that her father had lied to her about them being human. What did he think? That once she learned they were wolves, she would hot-trot across the ocean to meet them? And date them, or something? Though if she'd known they looked this hot, she might have.

Colleen smiled slightly. Ian was angled more so that she could see his face, while now Grant's back was to her. His shoulders were muscled and tanned, his legs the same—well-sculpted and sexy. The breeze ruffled his light brown hair, but she'd only managed to get a glimpse of his face and now she couldn't see it.

Julia would be thrilled to get this video of her husband helping Grant to play this trick on Colleen. She and Julia had lost contact with each other over the last couple of years, both of their lives having been so hectic. Colleen still couldn't believe that Julia had mated a Highland wolf, and she intended to see as much of Julia as she could while she lived here.

She noted that a few more men had stopped fighting and were watching her and grinning. She tried to concentrate on the men in combat and couldn't help smiling herself. *Impressive*. Oiled to a fare-thee-well, they were trying to look like they'd been sweating for some time, which made their muscles all the more magnificent. She knew the shouted warning of her approach meant the men had just begun their fight when she arrived.

As Ian and Grant lunged and parried, she observed their impressive footwork, too. Every slicing blow sent a hint of unease through her, though, as she worried that the men would accidentally injure each other. She loved the way the wind whipped their kilts about. She caught a gorgeous shot of Grant's very toned, hot ass. That would teach him to go without any briefs on a windy day! Maybe he thought she would be so shocked to see him naked beneath the kilt that she'd run off.

Not her.

She just hoped she wouldn't catch too much of *Ian's* exposed body parts as she continued to film the men in action. With a smile, she focused on Grant's kilt, just in case it lifted again. She'd snap a couple of still shots this time.

A man approached her, but intent on her mission, she didn't turn to face him. She took in a deep breath to smell his scent, like all wolves would do, sensing whether the other wolf was dangerous or interested. He was interested. He would check her out, too. Just a natural tendency among wolves.

"You, lass, must be Lady Colleen Playfair."

Her skirt whipped around the Highlander's bare legs, but he didn't seem to mind.

She was indeed titled. The barony had passed down from generation to generation, though in America she had never been referred to as a baroness, so she wasn't used to hearing anyone call her by that title.

"I am." She wished he'd go away because now she had to divide her concentration between Grant and Ian and the man standing next to her. Even if the men had meant the training as a ruse, the two pack leaders seemed to have something to prove to their respective clans—if not to her.

"That's my brother, Grant MacQuarrie. And the one he's fighting is Ian MacNeill," the Highlander said.

"Nice," she said, not quite ready to reveal that she knew who the two men were.

"I'm Lachlan, Grant's younger triplet brother. Glad to make your acquaintance." His voice hinted at kindliness.

"Thanks. Nice to meet you." She wondered then if Grant would be the only source of trouble here or if his brother sought to feign friendship, slip under her armor, and work on a way to get rid of her in a different manner. She didn't trust him.

Arms folded across his muscled chest, Lachlan stood way too close to her.

"Did you get tired of fighting?" she asked with a hint of a smile.

"I'm a lover, not a fighter."

She wanted to groan out loud at the cliché, but she managed a small smile instead. She imagined he loved to fight as much as any of the other Highlanders in the bailey today.

"You don't want to film any others sparring?" Lachlan asked, sounding curious.

"I promised Ian's wife, Julia, that I would film Ian if I could and email the recording to her later."

Lachlan drew in an audible breath, and she couldn't tell whether he was amused or worried. "You *know* Ian's wife?"

She loved his reaction but hesitated to tell him the truth, still not sure if she should let the proverbial cat out of the bag…yet. Then she decided she would so she could see what happened when he told his brother Grant. "Yep. Good friends for years. I never expected her to end up living in Scotland, mated to Ian like that. When she learned I was coming here, she immediately contacted me. We intend to get together as soon as we can."

"You know Julia MacNeill," Lachlan said under his breath as if the truth was sinking in.

Did she ever. Girls' all-night slumber parties—and she was game to have one with Julia and her new sisters-in-law and mother-in-law as soon as she could—cooking parties where they baked only the most decadent chocolate concoctions, movie night… You name it, they had a night for it. She fought the urge to laugh evilly.

"Did Julia happen to tell you her husband was coming here to spar with Grant and my kin today?"

"Yep."

Lachlan burst out laughing. She smiled then. She couldn't help herself. No way could Grant pull the black-faced Highland sheep's wool over her wolf eyes.

Another man lowered his sword and glanced at Colleen and Lachlan. He motioned to his opponent that he was done, bowing his head slightly, and moved in Colleen's direction. "I'm Enrick MacQuarrie, Grant's middle brother, and you must be…?"

"Colleen," she said, annoyed at the pretense, as if he wasn't sure who she was. She was certain they didn't let just anyone onto the castle grounds. "I'm enjoying the fighting. What a delightful…" She caught her breath as the wind swept Grant's kilt upward again and she got another toned-butt view. *Snap, snap.* She took some hot shots that time. Omigod, if only she had such a gorgeous gluteus maximus. "Beautiful…show," she finished. She was certain she wasn't playing the game the way they had intended.

"She's good friends with Julia MacNeill, Ian's wife," Lachlan said, as if Enrick wouldn't know who he was talking about.

"Julia MacNeill," Enrick said.

She wanted to laugh, but she managed to keep her mirth under control. The brothers' surprise at learning of her connection to Julia was just too rich.

"Julia *knew* about the sparring," Enrick continued, not asking a question.

"Aye," Lachlan said.

"She told you?" Enrick asked Colleen, still sounding surprised that no one had fooled her. Maybe they even wondered what else she might be aware of.

Like…they planned to put her in the White Room. She didn't know what that was all about—nor did Julia, because even Ian didn't know—but Colleen suspected some murderous ghost lived there. Julia had told her about Ian's ghostly cousin, Flynn, and how he caused mischief for some of the lasses at Argent Castle.

So what kind of a ghost lived in the White Room? A scary one to help change her mind about staying, she assumed. It wouldn't work on her. She didn't believe in ghosts.

"Yes. We're the *best* of friends," Colleen said.

If she demanded that Grant give her another room, she suspected he would tell her no others were available. If they thought she was a pushover, they had another think coming.

Chapter 3

ENRICK DIDN'T LAUGH LIKE LACHLAN HAD DONE WHEN Colleen mentioned she knew Julia. He seemed a lot more serious as he watched Grant and Ian slow down, looking as though they were beginning to grow weary. She wondered how long they'd continue with the ruse. She was tired of filming them, but she would keep shooting them as long as they continued to fight.

Many of the men had quit sparring and now watched the two pack leaders in their bid for dominance.

She loved it. In her world, men just didn't do that. Maybe a couple of men battled it out in a show at clan gatherings or Renaissance fairs. But not gathered about in an ancient castle's bailey, or with everyone wearing kilts, bare chested, and beautifully greased down—and with all of them also part of a wolf pack. She noticed then that no women were about. None watching. Not even from the ramparts and out of harm's way. Was this usual? Or did Grant think having only braw males in attendance would intimidate her further?

His plan wouldn't succeed. She loved observing them in battle. She wished Julia could be here, too. She knew her friend would take copious notes to use in writing her Highland werewolf romances.

Finally, Ian conceded. "We could fight all day, you and I, Grant MacQuarrie, my good friend. But I'm famished."

"Aye, to the feast." Grant glanced in Colleen's

direction as if he finally had time to acknowledge her as she stood there with her camcorder in hand. He also noticed his brothers standing on either side of her. His brows rose marginally to see them there. Although he was in charge, his brothers seemed to have other notions.

She finally turned off the camcorder, right after she got a nice smile from Ian and an equally captivating scowl from Grant, directed at his brothers. She was enjoying the brothers' reactions.

Grant's gold-flecked brown eyes squarely held her gaze. His wolfish expression was stern, typical of a pack leader, his light brown hair caught by the breeze.

Grant stalked toward her, joined by some other men who wore the same plaid, while Ian watched from a distance.

All pack leaders inherently had the wolf's stare down to perfection—judging a newcomer's threat and whether the new arrival was a beta or, even worse, an omega. He wouldn't intimidate her as much as he might like as she met his gaze with a smile. She didn't have any delusions that a smile would win him over. But she hoped she might befriend some of the betas in his pack. She counted on it.

"You must be Lady Colleen Playfair. We were in sparring practice—" Grant said, sounding very much in charge and as though he couldn't be bothered rearranging his schedule to accommodate her arrival.

"She knows Ian's wife," Enrick said, cutting his brother's comment short.

Grant looked from Enrick to Colleen, his expression surprised as his brows rose in questioning and his jaw dropped a little. She was having way too much fun, and it killed her to have to stifle a laugh.

He glanced at the camcorder in her hands and said, "You don't plan to share that with the world, do you?"

She suspected his sudden change of subject had to do with being unsettled to learn that she'd known about all this beforehand. He sounded more like he was telling her than asking her. Of course, she wouldn't share the video with the world. She'd need the men's approval, and she was certain this wolf wouldn't give it.

"Oh, I'd love to. I'm sure it will remain mostly mine for private viewing. But Julia"—Colleen waved at Ian—"wanted me to send her a copy of it. She's a romance writer, you know. The video will be great for visuals to use in writing scenes for her next story." And Colleen would most likely send her girlfriends back home some of the special shots of Grant.

Though she wouldn't say whose hot buns they were, in case her girlfriends shared them with social media outlets. And she would only send shots of that special part of his anatomy so no one could actually identify him. What were girlfriends for, after all?

Ian then joined them and Grant said, "Lady Colleen Playfair, meet Ian MacNeill."

Before he could finish formal introductions, she smiled brightly at Ian. "I'm one of Julia's best friends. She has told me so much about you. You're the hero in nearly all her books." She shook Ian's hand.

"*Nearly* all?" he asked, a glint of humor in his dark brown eyes, his mouth curving upward.

"Sure. Before you came into her life, she had to make up fantasy heroes," Colleen said very seriously. She'd read some of Julia's recent releases, and she could see a real difference in the look of her heroes.

"She...never mentioned *you*," Ian said, sliding a half-guilty, half-amused look at Grant.

"Ah, why would she talk about me? I'm sure that once she arrived here, you occupied all of her thoughts," Colleen said breezily.

"This way," Grant said, motioning to her and Ian to join him in the keep. He did not look very happy.

Ian smiled at her as he displaced Enrick, while Grant took his brother Lachlan's place beside her. Ian shot Grant a look that said whatever Grant had planned wouldn't work on Colleen. He nodded in sympathy, as though he had faced the same issue with his wife as Grant now had to deal with—a headstrong American she-wolf.

Knowing Julia, Colleen could just imagine. She wondered what Grant had planned for her next. The feast, yes. Haggis? Blood pudding? She had acquired a taste for them already, preparing for her stay here. So he wouldn't make any headway with getting rid of her in that way.

She was famished.

Grant couldn't believe the she-wolf had known about the mock fight before she arrived. What else did she already know about? What else had Ian shared with his pretty wife that she, in turn, had shared with Colleen?

The White Room. Grant had mentioned that to Ian earlier in the week. Though no one but Grant's people knew the significance of the chamber. He was glad he had not revealed more to Ian. But before today, Grant hadn't told Ian about the feast they had planned.

Colleen's dark brown hair curled over her shoulders,

some of it whipping in his direction and tickling his shoulder, while her silky, sheer skirt slapped at his bare legs. He would have moved out of the fabric's path, but he stayed in close proximity in an attempt to intimidate her. His skin was oily and sweaty, and he didn't believe any prim and proper young woman would want to share the same space with him. She, on the other hand, smelled of a soft floral fragrance—jasmine, he thought—and all she-wolf. He had a devil of a time not breathing in *her* scent in a much-too-interested fashion. He just hoped she hadn't noticed.

The lass had not looked the least bit intimidated. He couldn't believe his brothers had been standing on either side of her like bookends. Maybe they had made her feel safe from all the men's fighting, but they should have left her alone. He would have to learn what else they had discovered about her.

Then again, she'd seemed so intent on capturing the action on her camcorder that maybe she wouldn't have felt unsettled if his brothers weren't guarding her. He couldn't believe she'd captured him and Ian fighting on video. To share with Ian's wife!

As much as he hated to admit it, Grant wondered if his brothers might be right about the difficulty of this task he'd taken on.

She held her chin high and worked hard to keep up with his and Ian's quick, long-legged stride. He couldn't help but witness her pert breasts bouncing in the clingy top she wore. He attempted to keep his eyes averted, straight ahead on his target—the keep, the great hall, and the feast that was sure to shock her.

His damnable gaze shifted twice to take in the

appearance of her nipples pressed against the fabric, as if he had no control. If that wasn't enough to catch his attention, her skirt was semi-sheer, allowing the viewer glimpses of her naked legs from about thigh high to her heeled shoes.

He tried his damnedest not to show any interest, though his wolfish side was ruling his human half at the moment. He needed to concentrate on his goal: running the Playfair properties without interference from the lass. For a year and a day! Two weeks, he could handle. A month, maybe. But a year?

He shook his head, saw that his brothers had already entered the keep, and hoped they ensured that everything for the meal would be just as he had ordered.

As soon as they entered the keep, he heard the sound of his dogs racing to greet them, their toenails scrabbling over the stone floor, out of sight, but they would be here momentarily. Did Colleen like dogs? They sounded like horses stampeding.

Grant smiled, ready for the next phase of his plan to work.

Before Colleen and Grant and the others reached the dining room, three monster dogs that looked as big as horses sprinted toward her. She thought they would attack. They did—in a wet, slobbery, loving way. Thank God, she *loved* animals. All kinds and shapes and sizes. Though she wasn't ready for the assault of the giant, woman-licking hounds that dwarfed her and would be taller than their master when standing on two legs. They were Irish wolfhounds, with big, doe-like brown eyes;

huge, wet, warm tongues; and bristly chin whiskers that made them look like little old men. They were adorable, but they needed some obedience training. And she knew just how to go about it.

She'd need some treats. And a clickable pen.

She wanted to scowl at Grant, who didn't make a move to quiet the dogs as they nipped at her in playful exuberance and jumped all over her. If they ripped her skirt, she would take it out of Grant's salary.

His men watched, smiled, chuckled, and waited to see her reaction when she couldn't take one footstep toward what she suspected was the great hall. She greeted the dogs, attempting to calm them and showing she wasn't scared of them. Frustratingly, she couldn't hide from the men that she felt a bit overwhelmed. If she couldn't show the wolfhounds she was in charge, she wouldn't be able to establish to anyone that *she* was the owner of this castle.

She had to remind herself that these things took time, and she couldn't expect to change things overnight.

The dogs finally "escorted" her to the great hall, as if the wondrous aroma of roasted pig was too much for them to withstand. They didn't forget her. They kept returning to her, or looking back to make sure she still followed them. Which she thought was cute of them.

She belatedly realized that the men taking her to the feast were half-naked. She almost smiled. All these men seated at the tables, bare chested, some as hairy as the hounds, would make it appear that she was at a nudist-colony feast. As long as *she* didn't have to be nude, she didn't care.

And Grant? He might think to intimidate her with his

nakedness and his sweatiness, but hey, she was a wolf, and he smelled *divine* to her—all that hot, yummy testosterone rolling off him in delectable waves. She took another deep breath of him, while she attempted not to let him know how much he interested her. She admired him strictly as an art form—like Michelangelo's sculpture of David in a kilt, rather than totally in the raw. Though she couldn't help wondering how Grant would look standing on a pedestal like that, totally in the raw. She smiled a little to herself.

When she finally managed to reach the great hall, where rough-hewn boards were set up as trestle tables with benches next to them, she thought she'd landed in the medieval period. Julia must not have known about this or she would have warned her. Colleen was dying to say how quaint it was for them to live in the past. But she bit her tongue. She didn't want Grant to think he'd gotten her goat, as her father used to say.

At least the tables were situated like a comb, the spine serving as the head table, and she wouldn't see beneath the lower tables and witness how well-endowed—or not—the men were in their kilts, in case they hoped to shock her.

She thought of pulling out her camcorder and taking a picture of the medieval setup for Julia to use in her writing, but then Colleen saw the main course. She hadn't expected to observe a *whole* roasted pig sitting on the serving table displayed right in front of the head table. She had the sneaking suspicion she would be sitting fairly close to it with a bird's-eye view of the beast.

Sure, she had eaten a roasted pig, apple in its mouth and all, in Hawaii at a luau, though when they served the meat, she didn't see them carving it from the poor pig. And she'd been a *long* way from the table where the pig was. The night had been upon them, torches wavering in the oceanic breeze, and the pig not even visible.

Everyone observed her, waiting to see her reaction. She had to put on a great show, though this would be tougher than she'd thought.

"Over here," Grant said, guiding her to the head table, and yes, he sat her right in front of said pig. The only good thing was that she was seated smack dab in the center of it, not at the tail end or where she had to look at its snout.

Then she noted she had a huge portion of blood pudding and haggis sitting in the middle of her...*trencher*? A piece of brown bread was being used for a plate as in early medieval times. *Come on*. They couldn't be living that far in the past. Where were the plates? The silverware? She was dying of thirst and was looking forward to drinking a cold glass of water. She hoped Grant wouldn't serve honeyed mead or ale on top of everything else.

A servant carved slices of pig for Grant and her.

"We bring our own knives," Grant said as if he could read her mind and handed her his sharp-looking knife. "*Sgian dubh*," he said. Then he took another knife, stabbed his slice of pork with it, and began to eat off it like a barbarian!

No forks. No spoons. No napkins. No plates. And no glasses of water.

Tankards of... She sniffed at her drink. Whisky. *Great*. She didn't drink anything harder than sweet, syrupy, fluffy drinks like margaritas, daiquiris, and on occasion, a minty green grasshopper. And no straight-up alcohol.

She'd never get through a meal if she had to drink from a huge tankard of whisky, especially with as many hours as had passed since she'd last eaten and the jet lag she was suddenly feeling. She'd be under the table in a flash.

—⁓—

Grant almost felt sorry for the lass when he saw her eyeing the pig. Colleen put on a face that said it didn't bother her, but her scent told him a different story. Yet he couldn't back down now. He hadn't expected her to be so…accepting of him and his attempts at unsettling her. She really was remarkable in the way she had handled the fighting, him, the dogs, and now the pig. He couldn't help but admire her for it.

His people watched him as much as they did her, judging for themselves if he could go through with this. As their leader, he had to lead by example. Yet, he was already feeling somewhat guilty. When did he get to be so indulgent?

To her credit, she'd eaten some of the blood pudding and haggis. Not even he could eat as much as was piled on her trencher. Had he told the staff to use trenchers of bread? He hadn't recalled going that far.

One of his clansmen, serving as bard, told bawdy jokes that would shock any woman to the core. Colleen smiled and laughed with the rest of them, not acting as though any of it disconcerted her.

She'd enjoyed the pork, pretending that the sight of the dwindling pig didn't bother her. But the whisky seemed to give her pause. If she thought she'd come to tell him how to do *his* job, then she should be able to hold her whisky, just like anyone who had been in charge in the past. Even her grandmother, Neda.

He motioned for the carcass to be taken away. Men carried it off, and the dogs ran after them, interested in the scraps they dropped on the stone floor as they headed for the kitchen.

"You don't like our whisky?" Grant asked, sounding as though she was insulting him by not drinking it.

She'd taken a small sip and then tried hard not to choke on it. Her eyes flushed with tears, and her cheeks grew red. He wanted to slap her on the back, treating her like one of the warriors, and say, "Well done." But he kept his hands and his words to himself.

"It's good," she said, her voice a little rough.

"Do you not drink it at home? Any Scotsman worth his salt drinks whisky. Or…" He gave a dramatic pause. "Do you drink it with water? No good Scotsman dilutes his whisky in such a manner." He had figured she wouldn't be able to drink any of it.

It was the smoothest brand they had, so he would rather not waste it on the woman if she couldn't manage it. He just wanted her to admit that she was not a true Scotswoman and, though she owned the castle, she would never be one of them.

She kept sipping it, taking a lengthy break, then clearing her throat and trying again. He had to admire her for keeping up the pretense. Then he frowned at her. He didn't want her to feel bullied into drinking the whisky and become sick over it. She was supposed to acknowledge he was right and leave well enough alone. What if she never drank any liquor and had a fatal overdose? That wouldn't do.

"Bring the lass a tankard of water," he ordered one of his men, not wanting to sound desperate, but he must have because all of a sudden every eye was on him and the lass.

"Are you all right?" Ian asked Colleen.

Grant noticed then that she was no longer sitting up tall and straight. In fact, she listed to the side. *His* side.

Without warning, she fell over and planted her head in his lap. No one said a word, wisely, as all eyes remained on him, waiting to see how he would handle the matter.

Bloody. Hell.

He hadn't expected her to pass out. Why couldn't she have just admitted she couldn't handle the liquor and given up the deception that she could?

He sat there for the longest time—at least it seemed that way to him—as he tried to decide what to do next. Her head was resting on his groin, which had a mind of its own as it began to react to the woman's touch.

Trying to get his mind on how to rectify the matter, he realized someone would have to stay with the lass to ensure she didn't become ill in the middle of the night. Yet, he'd sent all of the women away.

Bloody. Hell.

He should have had one of his men carry her to her room, but he couldn't. Not without worrying about her health. She was Grant's responsibility. As much as he hated to do so, he would have to make a minor change in chamber assignments. Just for tonight, though, and he wasn't about to share this with his people.

"Ian, thanks for coming and helping us out," Grant

said, not moving the lass from his lap, wishing to say his good nights before he left the great hall and unable to think of much else but her head resting against his groin.

Ian smiled at him knowingly. "We enjoyed the sparring immensely. But next time, Julia will insist on coming to take notes."

"She will have a video of the action," Grant said, not altogether pleased that Colleen had recorded them, or that the two women had known what the men were up to and kept them in the dark. "We will have to get together again soon."

"Aye, I look forward to it."

"Tell your brothers and your cousins we missed them, and that we enjoyed it immensely."

"I will do that."

Grant rose from his seat and lifted the lass in his arms. "Good night, men. Thanks for the grand sparring practice everyone participated in."

Several raised their tankards to him, some saying, "Aye" or "Hear, hear." Many looked like they were fighting laughter as they smiled at him. And the lass.

When Grant left the great hall, he heard Enrick's quick footfall approach.

"Is she going to be all right?"

"Just passed out. But I need to be sure she won't become sick later." Grant bypassed the floor that led to the White Room.

"You're putting her in a different room?" Enrick asked, following Grant as he maneuvered up the narrow, winding stairs to the next floor and headed for the lady's chamber adjoining the laird's.

He had *not* needed his brother's assistance in this

matter, nor his questioning of Grant's actions. "Enrick," Grant said in an altogether irritated fashion, "why are you not below stairs visiting with our guests until they leave?"

"You need my aid." Enrick opened the door to the lady's chamber for Grant.

"I could have managed."

"You know what happened when Ian placed Julia in the chamber adjoining his?"

"They ended up mating." That was *not* happening between Grant and the lass. "This is only for tonight. If she becomes ill, I want to know right away."

"I don't think she is used to drinking whisky," Enrick said, stating the obvious.

"Aye," Grant said as Enrick pulled the covers aside so Grant could lay her on the lady's bed. He slipped off her shoes and laid them on the floor next to the bed. He pulled the covers over her, and for a moment, he and his brother watched Colleen as she slept, her dark brown curls covering the white pillow, her face angelic in sleep. "I had assumed she would tell me and not attempt to drink it."

"She tried to prove that she could take anything you threw at her. Remarkable, really. I had not thought she would be that determined," Enrick said.

Lachlan entered the room. "I thought she would sleep in the White Room."

Grant wouldn't continue to explain his actions to the whole bloody pack. "Watch the lass for a moment, Lachlan." He walked into his own chamber and sighed, wanting to take a shower and clean off the oil still covering his torso.

"Maybe we're going about this all wrong," Enrick said, following Grant into his chambers.

Grant was reminded of one of their wolfhounds. He hadn't remembered his brother being such a shadow. "How so?"

"If she loses her inheritance, we could have more trouble if one of her male cousins inherits the castle instead. Wouldn't a male wolf be even more difficult, demanding, and insistent than a female? Like her father was?"

Grant gave Enrick a look that asked if he was serious.

Enrick shrugged. "If one of her cousins demands we make significant changes, we'll have to. But the lass is... well, a lass. And with all your charismatic ways with a woman, I would think you could, well...charm her into seeing your point of view on running the estates."

"Nay," Grant said. He would not pretend interest in the woman. He was never deceitful about a thing like that. "Besides, from what I gathered from speaking to her solicitor, she is very much an alpha. Her cousins are betas. If one were to inherit, he would be easy to manipulate."

"I still don't understand why you chose to put her in a chamber adjoining yours and not the White Room," Enrick said.

"This is the only chamber that has an attached room not currently being painted, and since we sent the women of our pack away for the next two weeks, I couldn't just have another female stay with her."

Enrick smiled a little.

Grant shook his head. "I'm going to shower. Either you or Lachlan watch her for me in the meantime, will you?"

"As you wish."

Enrick joined Lachlan in the lady's chamber, and

Grant started a warm shower. Thinking of the way the lass's skirt caressed his bare legs and how her nipples pressed against her blouse, he instantly became aroused. He had just lathered up, glad to get the oil and sweat off his skin, when someone flushed the toilet.

Immediately, his warm water turned to hot and nearly scalded him. "What the devil…"

He pulled open the steamed-up glass door and looked from Enrick to Colleen.

"Closest bathroom," Enrick said as Colleen tossed her dinner into the ceramic bowl.

"Bloody hell," Grant said under his breath and yanked a towel off a rack, but he didn't cover himself in time before Colleen turned her pale face in his direction and got an eyeful of his aroused state.

Chapter 4

"ARE YOU READY TO RETURN TO BED, LASS?" ENRICK asked Colleen, offering her a hand up from Grant's bathroom floor. Grant was still securing his towel around his waist or he would have aided her.

What else could go wrong tonight?

"I don't think your whisky agreed with me," she said in barely a whisper. "And the room is spinning out of control." She took another gander at Grant's towel, and he couldn't help but be a wee bit amused.

She took Enrick's hand and stood, then rinsed her face in the sink and dried it with a towel as he held on to her elbow to keep her from falling.

Grant let out his breath. "Go to the kitchen and get her something to settle her stomach, will you, Enrick? I'll take it from here."

With his arm around her waist to keep her steady, Grant returned Colleen to the lady's room, which, by all rights, should be hers. Her husband—or for wolves, mate—should be in the room Grant now slept in. But she couldn't stay in the room adjoining his while she remained here, or it could signify that they were attached. Nor would he give up his bed to sleep elsewhere, which would also cause conjecture on his people's part—making them think he was no longer in charge. A night, no problem. But months, a year? He couldn't allow it.

Even if she felt that it was her right to stay in this

room, he didn't believe she'd want to cause speculation
any more than he would. He was glad that Lachlan, at
least, had departed for the evening.

Enrick brought her something to settle her stomach,
and after she drank half of it, she covered herself back
up with the covers, not looking at Grant or his brother.

She closed her eyes and didn't say anything. Neither
did Grant.

Enrick glanced at his brother's state of undress, and
Grant took a deep breath. "I've got it. Go to bed. See you
in the morning."

Enrick looked back at Sleeping Beauty, smirked, then
left the room and shut the chamber door.

Grant closed her bed curtains to keep the warmth in
and returned to the shower to rinse the soap off hastily,
in the event she returned to steal his cold water with
another flush of the toilet. He toweled off, then finally
climbed into bed. He'd barely shut the bed curtains
when he heard a woman's footsteps as she ran past his
bed to his bathroom.

He listened, heard her lose more of her supper, the
toilet flush, and the water in the sink run. Then she
hurried past his bed and into the lady's chamber. The
mattress creaked a little in the next room, then blissful
silence. He truly felt bad for how she was holding up.
But he couldn't do much more for her now.

He closed his eyes and tried to sleep, but he couldn't
with worrying about the lass.

Then he heard something different—her soft footfalls
headed toward her chamber door. What the devil?

Her door opened into the hallway, and he heard something else. Toenails clicking on the floor as they headed

out of the lady's chamber. Wolf toenails. He groaned and threw his covers aside, naked, then headed into her room. Her skirt, blouse, peach panties, and matching lace bra lay scattered on the floor. She was gone.

He hurried out of her room and down the hallway to catch her. She was racing down the stairs to the first floor.

Hell and damnation. All he needed was a tipsy American she-wolf getting herself in trouble. He headed in the direction she'd gone, then heard the wolf door squeak open and shut in the kitchen. He called on the urge to shift in a hurry, not sure how he would convince her to return to the keep. His body welcomed the change, his muscles warming, stretching, his human form turning into the wolf.

He shoved through the wolf door and listened.

Despite being drunk, she moved fast, her nails clicking on the stone walkway leading through the gardens.

Tracking her scent, he sprinted through the cool, misty herb garden and then down the stone path to the sitting garden. She wasn't there. He circled around, sniffing for her scent. Then he stared at the gate that led to the rose garden and the seawall. Either she'd come and gone this way before he reached the outdoor sitting room, or she'd jumped over the wrought-iron gate that led to the rose garden. He didn't think she could have moved fast enough to get here and leave again, racing down the garden path before he arrived.

He leaped over the gate, clipping it with his back paws. He smelled her delightful she-wolf scent in the rose garden and followed it until he reached the four-foot-high seawall. He glanced to the left and then to the

right of the moss-covered gray stones. He didn't see
her. She wouldn't have risked her neck going over the
seawall. Then again, she wasn't sober. The place was
unfamiliar and the smells provocative enough to entice
a visiting wolf to check them out.

He jumped on top of the slick wall and looked down.
Below on the jagged, slippery wet rocks, he saw the
she-wolf loping along the path he and his brothers used
when they were old enough to risk it and young enough
to chance it before they knew better.

He was angry at himself for giving her the whisky and
putting her in harm's way. He howled for her to stop, hating that his clansmen would hear him and worry that there
was trouble. There was—in the form of one sexy she-wolf.

She paused, turned, and slipped. His heart in his
throat, he watched in horror as she fell. He raced after
her. Though wolves' paw pads could keep better footing
on ice than humans', he still slipped on the wet moss in
his haste to reach her.

She stood scarce inches above the rocks where the
waves were breaking when she managed to stop her fall.
On her belly, she panted and didn't seem to notice when
he came up behind her. They were much too close to the
breakers. He had to get her back up to the path before a
wave crashed farther up the rocks and swept her away.
And him with her.

He nudged her to get to her feet. She snarled at him.
He didn't back off. He needed to get her up to the seawall and over it. Then he had to return her to the lady's
chamber, pronto.

"Grant, do you need our help?" Enrick called out,
nearly out of breath and sounding more than concerned.

Grant looked up to see at least ten of his men peering over the wall. He shook his head. At least he didn't think he needed their aid.

He was glad they had come to help him, should he need it, though he wished no one had seen any of this. He nosed her side to get her to climb the rocks to the path. He couldn't carry her in his human form. Much too slippery. They'd manage the climb better in their wolf forms.

She suddenly leaped on top of the rock farther away from the breakers. Then her legs gave out, and she was sprawled on the mossy boulders. He clambered up the rocks and nudged her again. At first, he thought she was injured. Then he realized she was still very inebriated.

Being down here made it even more dangerous for her in her current condition. And he was afraid once she was on her feet, she'd turn and head into danger again, not realizing how treacherous it could be. He continued to nudge her, getting her to stand and then move back up the path. She couldn't seem to walk a straight line over the rough-edged rocks, and she swayed a bit on her feet.

"Is she still drunk?" Lachlan called out.

Obviously, Grant wanted to say to his brother in a growly tone of voice.

Grant had wanted to keep her safe until she was over being sick, but he hadn't expected her to do anything dangerous like this. Which made him even gladder that he'd kept her in the adjoining room so he could watch over her.

When they finally reached the seawall, she just stared at it. Enrick and Lachlan climbed over it and hoisted her up to another couple of men who eased her down on the other side.

As soon as the she-wolf stood in the bailey, Grant joined her. By the time he reached her, she was sprawled out on the stone pavers, eyes closed, sleeping.

"I guess she's not going anywhere unless we take her there," Enrick said, a smile in his words as he lifted her off the ground. "Lead the way."

Grant grunted and loped back to his chamber. When he reached it, he shifted and heard his brother laying Colleen on the bed in the lady's chamber.

"Be sure to bolt the door in her room," Grant said. He heard the bolt slide closed and then Enrick joined Grant in his bedchamber.

"She's more of a challenge than we thought she'd be. Thank God you caught her before she took a dangerous dunking in the sea," Enrick said.

"Yeah, that's why I wanted her door bolted. If she opens it, I'll hear it. I'll do the same in here."

"All right. See you in the morning," Enrick said, and Grant noticed the small smirk his brother wore.

"Hopefully, she'll be feeling all right by then," Grant said, then closed the door after his brother's departure and bolted it. At the very least, if she tried to leave the chamber, she'd have to shift first to unbar the door. He hoped she'd sleep the rest of the night instead.

Now that he wasn't leaping over seawalls and trying to secure her safety, he looked at her one last time. She was a pretty wolf with a reddish-brown mask. The lower half of her face was white all the way down her throat, and the white above her dark brown eyes emphasized them. With that and red fur in a strip down her nose, she looked just lovely. Her coloring reminded him of her grandmother's, except that Neda's had been grayer.

Satisfied Colleen wasn't going anywhere, he returned to bed. This time he succumbed to a deep, bone-settling sleep.

Until a hand fell against his bare chest, giving him a near heart attack. He jumped back on the mattress, about to grab his sword, when he saw that the intruder was Colleen, snuggled under his blankets and sleeping in *his* bed! And naked.

"What are you doing in my bed?" Grant roared.

"Closer…to the…bathroom," she said, her voice hushed with sleep, and yet she seemed to have enough awareness to know her own mind and that she would have her way in this, or else.

He absolutely refused to move into the lady's chamber. He couldn't, not if he wished to keep face with his men. They wouldn't barge in on him, but the cleaning staff would smell his scent on the lady's sheets. Then again, now they would smell the lady's scent on *his* sheets.

He could not allow the woman to sleep in *his* bed! Yet what choice did he have? If she needed to reach the bathroom quickly, he had to admit that she should be closer to it.

Which meant *he* could not be here.

He quickly got out of bed as she turned to watch him, her eyes half-lidded. Aye, he was naked again. Despite her inebriated state, or maybe because of it, she seemed to enjoy looking him over. And that had the added disagreeable effect of arousing him when he shouldn't be feeling that way in the least. He grabbed his kilt, the quickest thing within reach, and belted it around his waist, then left his chamber.

Hell and damnation. First day of the lass's arrival and what happens? He's rescuing her in the middle of the night for all to see. And now this. She was naked, sleeping in his bed, and he was off to look for a place to rest for the remainder of the night.

He definitely had to rethink the eating arrangements. The lass would get no whisky for the rest of her stay here. She could drink anything she liked as long as it was not alcoholic in nature. And after this night, he would sleep in his own bed while *she* slept on the lower floor in the White Room.

Chapter 5

COLLEEN WOKE FEELING MUCH BETTER AND VAGUELY remembered a very naked Grant coming out of his shower last night, looking red-skinned, soapy, and more than heated—in a steamed sort of way. She must have scalded him. She was sorry for that, but she hadn't given it a thought when she flushed the toilet. Besides, if they didn't have another bathroom for her to use, she really couldn't have helped it.

She stretched in the bed, smelled Grant all over the sheets, and sat up quickly. What was she doing in *his* bed? Naked! Oh. My. God!

She rushed out of the room and returned to the adjoining one, shutting the door. Her skirt, blouse, bra, and panties were scattered on the Turkish rug all the way to the lady's chamber door that led into the hall. She stared at her clothes, trying to recall what had happened last night. Had she wandered around the castle in the raw in the middle of the night? And when did she end up in Grant's bed? And then she recalled—he had been in it! At the same time!

Naked!

She was burning up with mortification.

Then she paced. She needed a shower. She took a sniff. Why did she smell like the fishy sea? Then she vaguely remembered the rough surf, waves, rocks, but not much else. What had happened last night?

Thank God, Grant wasn't around. Surely she could lock the bathroom door or his chamber door and get a quick shower until someone could tell her which bathroom she could use.

She picked up her clothes off the floor and set them on a chair. Afterward, she rummaged through her bag for some fresh ones and her shampoo, then stalked through the room into Grant's. She was in the middle of her shower when she heard Enrick call out, "Grant?"

"He's not here," Colleen shouted back, hoping Enrick didn't walk in on her while she showered. She realized she'd been in such a panic to shower quickly and get dressed before Grant caught her at it that she'd forgotten to lock his door. "He slept somewhere else last night."

She hoped he had.

She smiled, thinking she had cooked Grant's goose by letting his brother know Grant hadn't been able to sleep in his own room, since she was certain he intended to move her into the White Room tonight.

"Okay, I'll…look for him elsewhere," Enrick said, sounding highly amused. The door to the chamber shut.

She hadn't planned to make any changes in the management of the place. Not right away. She didn't know why Grant thought he had to make her feel unwelcome.

Finished with her shower, she climbed out to grab a towel, which was way too far from the shower itself. That meant she was dripping water all over the tile floor when a male someone said, "My laird…"

She whipped a towel around her wet, naked body and shrieked.

───◆◆◆───

Stretched out on a plaid recliner and half-asleep in the sitting alcove of the study, Grant felt as though someone was close by. He took a deep breath. *Enrick*. Grant opened his eyes to see his brother smiling down at him, arms folded across his chest. He was dressed properly in jeans and a shirt.

"So what's next on the agenda? No White Room. No more whisky. She enjoyed our sparring, so that didn't seem to work, either. Did you sleep here all last night?" Enrick asked.

Grant shot him a look that said he did not think the situation was the least bit humorous. "We'll eat, then I'll show her the grounds." Grant stood, then started to stalk off to his chamber.

"She's in your shower."

Grant paused and looked back at Enrick.

"I didn't see her. I thought you were in the shower, but she called out to let me know that you weren't there."

"Bloody hell." Grant turned and went to the kitchen. "Let's get some breakfast, then."

Enrick glanced at Grant's kilt. "Are you…going to wear your great kilt for the rest of the time the lass is here?"

"*Don't* say another word," Grant growled, giving his brother a look that said he was serious.

Enrick just grinned.

Darby, Grant's personal valet, hurried to meet with Grant. He was perfectly dressed as always, with every red hair in place, but judging from his pinched brows and lips, Grant suspected Darby had met Colleen. Hopefully, not naked in the shower.

"A lass was in your bedchamber when I went in to change the linens. Though Iona usually does the job,

she was sent away for two weeks, and I must do it now."
Darby sniffed a little at the notion. "The woman in question screeched when she saw me and told me to leave
at once."

"Was she dressed?" Enrick asked, grinning.

"In a towel. I'm sorry, my laird. I didn't realize she
was in your room. But she is a wolf. Have you taken a
mate? That changes everything, and you will have to let
me know when to straighten your chamber from now on."

Enrick, the next most serious of his brothers, was still
grinning.

"No. She is the castle's owner," Grant said, his voice
tight with annoyance. He'd forgotten Darby had been
away the past couple of weeks, got in early this morning,
and hadn't been here when the lass arrived.

Darby's mouth hung agape. Then he glanced at
Enrick for confirmation, as if Grant would jest about
such a thing.

"Aye, she is," Enrick said, still smirking.

"Oh. I may need to look for other employment, then.
Maybe with the MacNeill clan at Argent Castle," Darby
said with great regret. He'd served Grant forever and
was the most likable valet Grant had ever had.

"Why? What did you say to upset the lass?" Grant
asked, not knowing what else could go wrong.

"She told me to tell you that you were sleeping in the
White Room tonight and for a very long time after that.
I told her she'd better watch her manners or she'd find
herself locked out beyond the castle walls."

Enrick chuckled.

"And she said?" Grant asked. He was not moving to
the White Room.

Darby opened his mouth to speak, but the lass spoke instead.

"I said…" Colleen informed Grant as she swept into the room like a she-wolf with a mission—an alpha she-wolf who was very much in charge, her gaze locked onto his, her expression combative. "I might need to find…"

"Find what?" Grant asked, standing tall and growling now.

She shook her head. "Maybe we need to speak of this privately."

If the lass thought she could send him and his pack off the properties to install some other wolf pack to manage her place, she would have a battle on her hands. He and his ancestors had managed the castle and grounds for seven hundred years. He knew everything about the place, and who to contact when anything went wrong. This was the only home they had known. And her grandmother had treated them like family. Neda Playfair would never have moved them out. Besides, the will made some stipulation to allow the family to stay here.

If they walked out today, Lady Colleen Playfair would be in a world of trouble.

"In private?" Colleen said, folding her arms as she regarded Grant with an alpha's stare.

From when she'd first arrived, Colleen did not think she had come on too strong with Grant MacQuarrie. Then again, considering he was a Highlander who probably wasn't used to a woman telling him what to do, maybe she had. Although, come to think of it, her grandmother must have been running things until she

died. Maybe she'd been easygoing with Grant and his
kin and allowed them to do as they pleased. Her cousins
had warned Colleen that if she didn't play hardball with
Grant, he'd bulldoze right over her, and she wouldn't
have a say in anything—despite the castle being hers.
She had meant to be nice, even knowing he was trying
to scare her off.

She arched a brow when he didn't agree to meet with
her in private.

"Come this way," he said, his voice gruff, annoyed,
as if she had pushed him to the edge.

She hadn't gotten that far yet. Wait until he knew her
next plan of attack. That would teach him to take her on.

After Julia warned her what Grant had planned,
Colleen had tried to go along with it—for the time
being—to show him that he didn't need to feel threatened.

She wasn't sure what had made her snap and gather
up her mental sword to fight him, but she suspected it
was because she'd been sick with no bathroom close
by when she was trying to sleep last night. No way had
she wanted to sleep in Grant's bed—with him. She only
vaguely remembered being closer to the bathroom. Like
she would have been in her own home. In her groggy
state, when she retired after another trip to the bathroom,
she had believed that *was* her bed.

She wondered how long he had remained there before
he left his chamber.

She was tired and cross, and she wasn't about to
take any more crap from the Highlander. He was probably just as fatigued and annoyed. They both needed
naps—in separate beds.

He ran his hand over his disheveled hair. His face

sported whiskers and his hair was mussed from having just woken up, making him look ruggedly sexy and just a little barbaric. He looked like he'd love to take her on in the inner bailey, to fight a duel to see just who would win. And truly? She was ready.

The she-wolf was more stubborn than any Grant had ever met.

Colleen smiled, the look pure vixen, Grant thought. Dressed in warmer clothes today because the temperature had dropped, she wore burgundy brushed-suede boots that added an inch and a half to her petite height, snug-fitting jeans that showed off her toned legs, and a mint-green cashmere sweater that hugged her breasts. She looked…edible. Not hot and sexy, but soft and tasty.

If the lass thought to tell him she intended to find someone else to take his place, Grant ought to leave her to her own devices. Order his pack to depart. She couldn't even lock the gates at night without him and his men to do the job.

She'd be begging him to return after one night.

He motioned for her to follow and headed down the hallway.

He wanted to get this out in the open with his brother present. But he decided it might be better to sequester her in his study and lay down the law there. It was killing him to do so. He had nothing to hide from his people.

When they reached the study, he let her go in first, then he followed and shut the door. Before he could utter a word, she motioned for him to be quiet.

He glowered at her, not believing her gall. She was beautiful, a spitfire, and a royal pain in the arse.

He said, "Why don't we take a seat."

"Fine." She sat on one of the leather chairs facing him. The day was misty and no sun graced the room this morning, so it seemed darker than usual with rows of books lining one wall and his desk against another. Wood was stacked in the fireplace, ready to add a warm glow to the room later tonight. "Okay, I know you didn't want me here to begin with, but you knew I had to come. So first of all, get used to the idea. I certainly didn't expect you to be so melodramatic about it," she said.

"Melodr—"

"I loved how you put on the sparring show yesterday. So did Julia. The whisky was a little much. But I could deal with that. The bedroom without a bathroom? Nah. Not for a year and a day."

He didn't say a word. Had someone told her the White Room didn't have a bathroom? Or was she referring to the lady's chamber?

"You were to stay in the lady's chamber only for the night. Beyond that…"

"Beyond that, *you* will stay in the White Room. Or some other you so choose."

His jaw dropped. He didn't know what to say. She had the right to move anyone from any chamber she wished. The property *was* hers. But he couldn't believe she'd do it. To *him*.

He folded his arms and glowered at her. How would that look to his people? He ground his teeth, attempting to keep from saying what he knew he might later regret.

"The point I want to make is that I have no intention of changing anything unless I believe it necessary once I get the layout of things here. So you are jumping the gun, to my way of thinking. If I suggest some changes later and you don't like them, we can talk about them. Civilly. Castle owner to castle manager." She smiled.

Her expression was pure evil.

"About the White Room..." he said. He couldn't sleep in there.

"You can move out of the laird's chamber by night-fall. No rush."

He ground his teeth some more and glared at her, but for the first time ever, he didn't have a good comeback. Somehow the American she-wolf had taken control.

"You said you were going to find—"

"A solution to the problem." She again smiled wick-edly, and he suspected she meant he'd be out on his ear if he didn't like it. "Now, if you don't want to deal with me, that's perfectly acceptable. Maybe one of your brothers could speak to me on your behalf and I could tell him what I'd like, and he could relay the message to you."

"Bloody hell, woman."

This time her smile was highly amused.

"You will deal with me. Not my brothers. Not my clansmen. They are all part of *my* wolf pack. Together we manage your castle, but I run the pack. No one else." He wanted to say she had no part in telling his people what to do, but he attempted to keep his temper before he said too much more.

"I completely understand."

Surprised she'd acquiesce, he was still on guard. "You and your cousins are without any other family? You are not part of a pack?" He wanted to know if she was in charge of a pack and was used to getting her way because of it. What if she moved her whole pack here to take over?

"What I do back home doesn't concern you, Laird MacQuarrie. Now, can we have some breakfast? On plates? Or do I have to buy some for myself to use while I'm here?"

He growled under his breath. He'd already ordered that the dining tables be returned to the dining hall, that plates would be used for all future meals, and that silverware would be present. "It's already set up the way I'm sure you're accustomed. As to the White Room…"

"I hear it has a beautiful view of the gardens and the North Sea. You will love it, I'm told."

How the hell did she know that?

She smiled. Then she rose from the chair and flounced toward the doorway of the study without another word, as if she owned the place. Which, damn it to hell, she did.

He would never live it down if—instead of the lass—*he* had to sleep in the White Room. But worse? That she would sleep in *his* chambers!

Chapter 6

COLLEEN REALLY HADN'T WANTED TO FORCE GRANT to leave his own room. She knew the impact that would have—the fact he might lose face with his people. On the other hand, she had to take drastic measures to show she was in charge if she was going to live here for so long.

Thankfully, before she had found Grant that morning, she had overheard two of his men discussing the fact that he had given her the White Room. They couldn't believe he would do such a thing. They'd mentioned the location, and when she had time and could check it out without anyone being the wiser, she would. Though she was just as clueless as earlier as to what made the room unappealing. Then she heard Darby, who she suspected was Grant's manservant of sorts, giving Grant an earful about that *woman* in his chamber.

Grant had really brought all of this upon himself. If she made him do this, maybe he'd cool his heels a bit and see that she was not the enemy and that she could change the arrangements in a few days to accommodate them both. Besides, if he was all hot alpha, his people wouldn't say anything to his face about the room changes. Maybe behind his back, but not be up-front. He could handle it. She assumed he'd suddenly find a more suitable chamber than the one he had planned for her to use that they probably believed was haunted. She couldn't imagine what else could be wrong with it.

Before she left the study, Darby blocked her exit.

"Pardon the interruption, my laird," Darby said over her head, preventing her from leaving, "but Laird Borthwick is here to see the lady."

That gave her a little thrill of expectation. Archibald Borthwick had been waiting for a friend to arrive at the airport, but he'd been delayed several hours and Archibald had started a conversation with her, welcoming her to Scotland with such friendliness that she had admired him for it. She hadn't expected him to see her so soon, or here like this without calling first. He'd offered to buy her lunch and to drive her from the airport to Farraige Castle, but she'd already rented a car and was dying to see her castle and what Grant intended to do when she arrived. But what a pleasant surprise to see Laird Borthwick now, and a welcome break from dealing with Grant.

"Borthwick is here, is he?" Grant started to leave the study in a gruff manner, acting as though he intended to throw the man out.

Intent on stopping him, Colleen quickly seized his arm. His hot, hard, bare, muscular arm.

Their gazes instantly collided. The astonished look he gave her amused her. She was certain *no one* grabbed him and stayed him like that. She was used to stopping her cousins in such a manner if she felt the need. She hadn't thought anything of it. Just a natural reaction on her part.

Grant wasn't anything like her cousins. He wasn't a beta. He was a warrior from a long line of warriors. And he looked at her like he wasn't sure what to do with her. Thrash her or…well, thrash her.

"I'll speak with him," she said to Darby as if Grant had no business making such a decision. Which he didn't.

Darby looked from her to Grant's arm, and she quickly released Grant, the contact making her think of manhandling him for other reasons. Like wrestling him to the ground in play, except she was *not* thinking in terms of playing—really. Why her thoughts turned so wicked when she was with him, or…not with him, she wasn't sure. Maybe it was because he wore that sexy kilt again. Bare legs and feet this time and, of course, the bare chest, though his skin was now clean of oil. That made her think of how much she'd love to oil him down again—until he spoke and got her mind back on track where it needed to be.

"He is not one to trifle with," Grant said, barely suppressing a growl and not believing the lass was interested in meeting with the man.

When Colleen had seized his arm to stop him from confronting Borthwick and tossing him off the premises, Grant immediately saw a flicker of a smile on Darby's lips. The man was the most serious of wolves. He rarely smiled, though he was a happy sort. He just didn't wear his expressions for all to see. So when the lass grabbed Grant, he was surprised to see Darby's reaction. But no more so than Grant himself was shocked at the lass's action.

He should have been angry with her, but instead, her touch made him think of more carnal pursuits. He'd never had a woman treat him in such a manner. He instantly had the notion of throwing her over his shoulder and marching up the stairs to *his* bedchamber, where he would have *no* interruptions while they continued to iron out the details of her stay. Thinking of tossing her on his bed brought to mind how he'd been with her in that same bed earlier.

Which is why he'd left the bed so quickly. No sane, naked man could sleep with an appealing, nude she-wolf and not want to do much more than just sleep.

"Your family and mine have always been at odds with those of the Borthwick wolf pack," Grant informed her. Didn't she know anything about her family's history?

"Well, maybe it's time to bury the hatchet," she said, sounding like that would be an easy task.

"Over my dead body," Grant said.

She frowned at Grant, as if she hadn't expected him to be so vehemently opposed. "I'll see him."

And with that, Colleen brushed her breasts—her heavenly, very appealing breasts covered in the softest sweater—against his naked chest as she squeezed by him and Darby. She left the study as Darby gave Grant a raised-brow look, as if inquiring what Grant intended to do about the out-of-control American she-wolf.

Damned if Grant knew. He hadn't won one battle with her yet. He and Darby quickly left the study to catch up to the lass.

In the front entryway to the castle stood both Enrick and Lachlan, arms folded across their chests, not allowing Archibald Borthwick to go any farther. Normally, they would have taken a visitor to the sitting room to wait for an audience with Grant.

As much as they all hated the man, they wouldn't let him go anywhere until Grant said so. Unfortunately, the lass was the one who would have the final say this time.

Wearing black dress pants and a pin-striped shirt, Archibald appeared to be on a date. Not to mention that his blond hair looked recently cut, and—Grant rubbed his own whiskery chin—he'd had a fresh shave. To Grant's consternation, Archibald's gray eyes focused first on Colleen, as if she was leading the pack. Archibald was careful not to look her over like a hungry wolf, or he would have gotten a fist in the jaw—Grant's fist.

The woman might be giving Grant a bountiful amount of grief, but she *was* his landlord and he would protect her at all costs from the avaricious advances of a wolf who was only interested in the properties she held. Even if she didn't think she needed his protection.

Archibald's gaze shifted to take in Grant's appearance, including the fact he wore nothing but his kilt, his face was unshaven, and his hair was a bit unkempt. Even his brothers smiled at Grant's current disheveled look. They, on the other hand, were both dressed in jeans and sweaters, freshly shaved, and much more presentable. Damn it to hell.

"May we speak in the gardens?" Archibald asked, smirking at Grant but then holding Colleen's gaze, his smile brightening. "Alone?"

Grant could not believe this. What was Borthwick up to? Not that he didn't have a good idea. How did he know about her coming here so soon? The lass could not fall under the Highlander's seductive charms.

"Of course. If someone would point the way," she said.

"Darby will take you there." Grant nearly choked on the words and then gave his faithful valet a nod.

When the pompous Borthwick left with Colleen, Enrick said, "She is not what I expected."

"After speaking with Ian's brother Duncan about his American mate and hearing what Ian has gone through with his, she is just what I thought she'd be like. Their brother Cearnach is too newly mated and wouldn't reveal all the trouble he's had with his mate. But I'm certain it was considerable if we can judge her based on the others." Grant grunted. "What is Borthwick about?"

"Isn't it obvious?" Enrick said, looking cross. "He is intent on wooing the lass. Just think, if he succeeds and ends up mating her, what will happen then?"

"I will kill him first," Grant said.

"Aye. But if you don't, you can see how, as her mate, he could end up taking charge of the castle. What if he lived here and began giving us orders?"

"I would kill him," Grant repeated.

"Aye. But if you couldn't, you know what he would be like. If he mated her, he'd install his own family in all the key positions. They could make life miserable for us. And we have no place else to call home," Enrick said.

"Aye," Lachlan said. "Which means you have to win her over first. Don't you see?"

Grant wasn't about to play some game with the lass. Not that he wasn't interested in her in a purely physical way—how could any wolf not be? And he couldn't help but admire her for her feistiness. But that wasn't the role he was meant to play. She would return to America, sooner rather than later, and he had to get things back on their regular schedule.

"Unless you want me to try my hand at it," Lachlan

offered in as sincere a way as possible, though Grant swore he heard a hint of humor in his brother's tone of voice.

He shook his head at his youngest brother and walked into the kitchen to see what was transpiring between the lass and Archibald before they disappeared into the gardens. His brothers joined him and they peered out the window. Colleen smiled sweetly and promptly dismissed Darby. He didn't look happy and quickly glanced back at the keep as if checking whether Grant watched and approved. Grant did not approve, but the woman was not in need of a chaperone, as much as he wanted to ensure she had one with the likes of Archibald on the prowl.

Darby stood at the entrance of the gardens, looking perplexed.

A low mist cloaked the area in a film of white, and Colleen and Archibald laughed as they entered the gardens and disappeared from the brothers' view.

"You are suggesting I act in a romantic way toward the lass?" Grant had no intention of tricking the she-wolf into believing he was interested in her as a mate prospect. He certainly couldn't do it for a year.

"You're not seeing anyone else at the moment, which would be your only obstacle. And I assume the lass is not with anyone, either. You might even find you like her," Enrick said. "She's good-natured as far as not getting upset about our charade yesterday. You don't have to really mate her, just act attracted enough that she gives up the notion of being fascinated with anyone else."

"It's either that or Borthwick attempts to make some inroads with her, and if he does, we're in trouble. By the way, what will you do about the sleeping arrange-ments?" Lachlan asked. "I understand she was in your bed already. Sounds like a start to me."

Grant figured he might as well be up front with his brothers. They'd know what went on soon enough. "She has decided she wants to stay in the lady's chamber."

The brothers first looked a little surprised, then both grinned at him.

In absolute exasperation, Grant let out his breath. "She wants *me* to sleep elsewhere."

Neither of his brothers said anything as that bit of information sank in, and then they had the audacity to laugh!

When they saw Grant's deadly serious expression, Enrick said, "Seriously? I thought you were sharing the chambers with the lass." He shook his head. "All the more reason to get in her good graces. Where will you sleep? Surely you don't mean to oust anyone out of their own rooms."

"I don't. I'd never do that to any of our people."

"I suspect someone might offer for you to take his chamber," Lachlan said.

"And have to sleep in the White Room instead?" Grant shook his head.

The brothers laughed again.

"You won't sleep in the White Room, will you?" Lachlan asked.

"Until the spare connecting chambers on the third floor are painted, I will," Grant said.

How could his plans have been so disrupted by one little American lass, when he thought he had this well under control?

Chapter 7

COLLEEN SUSPECTED GRANT WOULDN'T LIKE IT IF SHE made the effort to be nice to Archibald Borthwick, since he was also an alpha wolf. She didn't know the man, but he had been so pleasant to her. That was so different from the way Grant was treating her that she intended to keep seeing Archibald—as a friend. He had even offered to take her on several tours of Scotland. And she thought she'd take him up on it, once she was more settled.

She'd thought at first that Grant and his people were humans, so naturally she'd loved it when Archibald realized she was a wolf and wished to make her acquaintance, not bothered at all by the fact she was an American. Because of the natural inclination to meet another of their kind, and the fact that fewer she-wolves existed in wolf packs, she could understand his interest when he learned she was free and available.

After she had discovered what Grant and his pack intended to do to persuade her to leave sooner than the time she was required to be here, she figured what the heck. Maybe Archibald would make Grant change his mind, and he and his men would be more civil toward her while she stayed here for the rest of the year.

She hadn't expected Archibald to jump quite so quickly at the chance to get to know her better. She should have realized it. He probably was afraid Grant or his brothers might try to sweep her off her feet first. As if that would ever happen. But Archibald was interested in moving this along a little bit faster than she wanted. For one thing, she hadn't intended to stay in Scotland.

"We could go boating," Archibald finally said.

"I'd love to. Later," she said. She really was tired after the long flight here and then all that had gone on during the night that kept her from sleeping much of it. She'd prefer to take him up on his offer once she'd rested up a bit more and could really enjoy seeing the sights. She sighed. She had never expected that Grant and his people would know Archibald and dislike him so much. Why did people hold such grudges? She didn't. As far as she was concerned, she didn't know him and she would treat him like a friend, just like he treated her. She definitely had no plans to mate the wolf.

"I understand. Jet lag. You're probably tired still."

"Yeah. Give me a week and I'll be ready to see some sights." Really, a couple of days would have been enough, but she hated to leave things so unsettled here, almost afraid if she left the castle, she would lose what little control she felt she'd gained.

She glanced back at the castle and swore she saw Grant and his brothers watching her through one of the windows. Then she noticed movement on top of the wall walk. Two men were observing her. Was it a case of curiosity? Or concern for her or that she might fall for the wolf and put them all out of business?

It was misty and damp out. She could barely see to the end of the herb garden and only glimpses of the gardens beyond through arbor-covered gateways.

She wished she could tell Grant that she had no intention of changing the management. His pack had been managing the estate for eons, and she expected it to stay the same for eons more. But she thought this might keep him on his toes. As for Archibald, she'd be as friendly as he was, but if he thought she wanted more, she'd let him know in a heartbeat that she wasn't interested. Then again, maybe she would be. Only time would tell. But she wasn't jumping into anything right away. She had a whole year to live here first.

She understood Grant's concern that she'd come to make a lot of changes he couldn't live with. A last-ditch effort would be to have her cousins come stay with her and be her backup if this didn't work out. They were both ready to join her anytime.

"So tell me all about your life in America," Archibald said.

She smiled at him, liking how he would ask, unlike Grant who only wished she'd return there. She started talking about her home in Maryland, about the Inner Harbor in Baltimore and trips to Annapolis. She loved the water.

"I love the water, too. My manor house has a nice-sized lake for a view."

"I bet it's lovely." She loved the ruggedness of being on the ocean, though. The tumultuous sea, the ever-changing view, the force and power of it. She loved lakes, but they usually just—sat there.

"Did your friend ever arrive at the airport?" she asked.

"Uh, yeah. But his flight was delayed by four hours. You and I could have had something to eat." He smiled.

He had such a charming smile compared to Grant's scowls. "Oh, I *couldn't* have. Grant and his people were eager to show off their fighting skills and celebrated my arrival with a grand feast right afterward. It was the experience of a lifetime."

"Grant did?" Archibald said, frowning.

Yeah, but not in exactly the way she had made it sound—as if he'd done so to welcome her. But she didn't want to let anyone outside the pack know that Grant was trying his darnedest to change her mind about staying here. She smiled. It was like a secret pact between them. Grant would act all growly and stubborn, and she'd smile back and have her own way.

"Oh, yes. They were delighted to have me here and couldn't have done anything further to make me feel more welcome." Could Archibald tell what a phony she was? She could understand Grant's concerns and figured this was the only way he knew how to deal with his frustrations.

They continued to stroll through the herb garden, while Archibald remained quiet.

She didn't know enough about the area to ask any questions, and walking in the damp cold without a coat was chilling her to the bone. She was certain she'd acclimate to the varying temperatures and weather conditions eventually, but she was having a difficult time enjoying this. She sighed.

Well, if he couldn't come up with another topic, she might as well ask him about Grant. "I take it that you and Grant know each other fairly well?" She couldn't imagine that Grant only saw Archibald as an alpha male wolf who was trespassing on his pack's territory. It had to be something that went deeper.

Archibald smiled this time, but the look was not pleasant.

"Not what you would call friends?" Certainly not from Grant's perspective.

Archibald shrugged. "I don't really feel comfortable here, speaking with you. The gardens have ears."

She raised her brows, then glanced around and noticed a gardener studying the roses. A teen who had been watching them from another garden turned red-faced and quickly looked away. Were Grant's people spying on her and Archibald? She wasn't sure whether to be annoyed or amused.

"I would love to take you to a village and offer you breakfast, and we could really visit," Archibald said, sounding hopeful.

"I'd love to. Later," she said, feeling she was too tired to be the best of company. Even now she wished to put on a cheery face, but she couldn't conjure up the warmth to back her smile. She was still thinking about dealing with Grant and what would be next as she butted heads with the man.

Footsteps headed in their direction, and she turned to see who approached. They'd only been walking in the chilly fog for about ten minutes, which in itself seemed ridiculous. Then again, the Highlanders were probably used to the weather. If she was back home, she would have found something else to do with her time. She was getting damp and chilled, and she hoped whoever approached would get her out of this predicament in a way that wouldn't hurt Archibald's feelings.

Grant's man, Darby, hurried to catch up to her and said with urgency, "My Lady, Laird MacQuarrie says the morning meal is ready, if you'd like to join us."

Hearing her referred to this time with a title, she was

taken aback. So politely now, instead of the way he had taken her to task in Grant's chamber. She wasn't used to being referred to as "lady." In America, she didn't use any title. She was just Colleen, as far as she was concerned. In Scotland, it was different. Maybe using her title would ensure that some of the wolves in Grant's pack treated her with more respect. Though she didn't think she'd ever get used to being referred to in that manner.

She hesitated to speak. The preparation of breakfast seemed to have occurred awfully fast. Why didn't Grant say they were getting ready to eat as a reason she shouldn't take a walk with Archibald? She suspected they'd thrown breakfast together in a hurry in an attempt to whisk her away from him.

Was Grant trying to make amends with her, then? She doubted it.

A light breakfast might settle her stomach, but she didn't think inviting Archibald to eat with them would help. She could imagine the tension escalating in the dining hall. Darby's interruption was just what she needed. She didn't even mind knowing Grant was attempting to get her away from Archibald.

At least for this morning, the way she was feeling, she much preferred Grant's disheveled, kilted appearance to Archibald's polished look, because she was feeling a little disheveled herself. Not in appearance, but psychologically. And, at least while conversing with Grant, she felt she knew the ground rules, somewhat. Annoyed, gruff, angry—all of it was fine with her as long as she knew where he was coming from. With Archibald, it was more of a courtship game, she thought. And she really wasn't ready for it until she was settled and refreshed and could act more like her normally enthusiastic self.

"Thanks, Darby. I'll be right there." To Archibald, she said, "Maybe we can do this again sometime later. After I'm more settled at Farraige Castle."

Archibald's deeply knit brow softened a bit. "Of course. Would tonight be too soon?"

"Later" meant later. Much later. "How about at the end of the week? I can get in touch with you. I have your number."

His brow tightened again. "I will call on you then."

She got the distinct impression that he wasn't waiting for her to call him. Maybe believing she wouldn't. Or that Grant wouldn't allow her to. She wondered if she'd bitten off more than she should. Yet, at the time, she had thought it was a brilliant idea.

So much for her brilliant ideas.

She walked with him back to the castle as Darby followed in their wake, not stealthily like a wolf, but noisily like he wanted them to know that he was listening in on their conversation. He would probably report everything that was said back to Grant. Not that anything much was said.

"I will call," Archibald said again, his gaze steady on hers, ensuring he was getting his point across—that Grant wouldn't stop him from seeing her.

She totally agreed with Archibald there. And then he left her at the back door and took off around the side of the castle to the front where his vehicle was parked.

Darby pulled the door open for her, his expression somber. She wanted to talk with him, with anyone, about how she felt, but she seemed to be the enemy in this situation. Shouldn't "don't bite the hand that feeds you" come into play here?

This time when Darby escorted her to the main dining hall, mahogany tables were set up. Instead of benches, they had olive-green and gold embroidered chairs with cushioned seat backs. Plates and silverware were set out, too. Much, much better. Really nice, in fact.

She smiled at Grant, who was scowling but attempting to moderate his expression a bit.

She fought chuckling. Something appealed to her about that great, growly Scot. Maybe it was because she wasn't used to men like him. Her first two mates had been even-tempered betas. She'd loved them, but they had been predictable, and when she had lost them many years ago, she didn't think she'd ever take a mate again. Not that Grant was a mate prospect, but she did wonder how being mated to a wolf like him would measure up. She couldn't even imagine.

She took in a deep breath, recalling the smell of him in his bed.

He was one hot Highland wolf.

That she had taken a walk with the "enemy" in the gardens had probably killed Grant. He'd shaved, in a rush it appeared, having nicked himself in a couple of spots. He would heal quickly because of their wolf genetics. But the bloodied spots made him seem so much more human and lovable. He wore jeans and a T-shirt. She missed seeing him bare-chested while he wore only his kilt.

"We have an assortment of items for breakfast. Sausage, pancakes, bacon, toast, jams, eggs anyway that you like them, porridge. Tea. Or…coffee," Grant said, walking with her to their new seats.

Same location. No roasted whole pig to eyeball while eating the meal.

"Thanks," she said, meaning it. She appreciated how he had changed to accommodate her. The walk with Archibald had been well worth the effort.

As soon as they took their seats, Colleen asked for some toast, a little grape jelly, one egg over easy, and sausage. Grant looked surprised when she asked for tea.

"I always drink it. Never acquired a taste for coffee," she said.

Grant nodded, but then he got right down to business. "What did Borthwick want?"

She figured he would ask and was surprised he'd waited this long. "He wished to welcome me here to Scotland." She hoped that Grant would realize that was a barb at him for not welcoming her properly to her own estates.

In ye old days, if she had been the owner of a castle and returned to it, the estate manager would have been careful to welcome her home in a proper manner. Grant would learn soon enough that she wasn't leaving.

"Oh, and by the way," she said, wanting to let him know just what she had in mind to do if he had any notion to give her further trouble, "my cousins may come to stay also. Just wished to give you a heads-up in case I feel I need their help."

"Help with what?" Grant quickly asked, his tone of voice close to a growl.

She smiled. "We're...close. They're like brothers to me. They just said they'd be on standby if I needed their help with anything." *You*, she wanted to say. But she kept her mouth shut and just smiled again—a wolf's smile, indicating neither he nor anyone else would push her around.

"We can make accommodations for them. We'd be pleased to set them up anytime they'd like to come," Grant said, as if realizing he'd better shape up or else, even if it killed him to do so.

"Okay. Sounds super. They said they have bags packed and ready to go. I just have to give the word."

"Great." He didn't sound like he meant it at all.

She enjoyed her meal this time, served up with tea and a glass of water, no whisky. She suspected no one would ever serve it to her at a meal again. Which would be fine with her.

"What did Borthwick want?" Grant asked again, his growly tone still audible.

She would love to tell him Archibald wanted to have wolf pups with her, but she curbed the wicked urge to say such a thing. Grant might believe her and try to have the man murdered.

She didn't believe in holding grudges, especially since she didn't recall her father discussing any problems her family had with the clan. Not that her father had talked about much concerning family, except how much trouble her grandmother had been and that dealing with Grant and his people had been a chore because they were human. But maybe Grant and his family had experienced real difficulties with Borthwick and his people. She sighed.

"What happened between you and Archibald that would give you reason for not liking the man?" she asked. She swore everyone around them stopped eating to hear what he had to say.

"I would think you would know best."

She waited while he finished eating his eggs. "Well, I don't. If you wouldn't mind enlightening me, I would appreciate it."

He put his fork down. "My family has managed the Playfair estates since the keep was built. Archibald's grandfather, Uilleam Borthwick, murdered my grandfather, John MacQuarrie, while he was serving in the capacity I do now. My father, Robert MacQuarrie, took over the management and my mother, Eleanor, mysteriously died in a fall from these very cliffs when my brothers and I were three. Your father was living at Farraige Castle at the time."

Her mouth gaped. She was shocked to the core to learn that Archibald's grandfather had murdered Grant's. How could Grant insinuate her father was responsible for Grant's mother's death, though? Her father was despicable, but she couldn't imagine he would do anything so horrible.

"You're not saying my father had anything to do with it," she said, wanting to clear up any misconception she might have.

"Your father felt he should manage the castle. After John died, my father took over the role as my family has done for centuries. But Theodore was furious. He swore he'd get back at his mother—your grandmother—by marrying a young American she-wolf and left for the States. He shunned your grandmother, refused to answer her letters, and didn't care what she did with the castle."

She noted Grant had avoided saying he believed her father had anything to do with Eleanor's death, but he hadn't denied it, either. Had her father been capable of murder? She couldn't believe she'd been so clueless about all of this.

"But my grandmother willed it to him anyway," Colleen said softly.

"Aye. Theodore was still her son. She had another, but he, too, left. And that one was the younger of the two."

"My cousins' dad. He died young also."

"Aye. Theodore did return home on occasion, maybe to ensure she didn't give the estates to his younger brother, or maybe so that she didn't will them to my father. Your father was visiting Farraige Castle when my brothers and I were twenty and away at college. One dark and stormy night, Robert MacQuarrie fell to his death from the same cliffs."

Colleen couldn't help the tears that filled her eyes. She looked away. Grant didn't say it—just like he didn't come out and tell her that her father was responsible for Grant's mother's death—but the implication was clear.

"Did my father still want to…manage Farraige Castle?" she asked, not wanting to hear the answer.

"Aye. Theodore and Neda had a big row. Instead of her installing him in the position, she called me home right away."

"And you were only twenty." She took in a deep breath. She could imagine her father wanting to kill Grant for the slight.

"Theodore returned to America, and years later, Neda left the castle to your father. Like you, he came here for a year and a day to observe and then he returned to Maryland to be with his mate, leaving the castle in my care. In the will, knowing the bitterness between your father and my people, your grandmother ensured the MacQuarries would continue to live here. Theodore could have replaced me as manager, but he would still have been stuck with us living here and so he left it in our hands, though he made every change possible while he was here. I think he realized at that point, he really couldn't have managed the properties himself or found a replacement for me who would have done as well. Then you inherited the castle when your parents died."

"I'm so sorry about your grandfather's and your parents' deaths. But I really don't see what Archibald has to do with his grandfather killing your grandfather."

If her father had been at the heart of it, she hated him for it. How could Grant or his pack feel anything but animosity toward her? She wasn't like him, but she hadn't lived here like Neda had. She didn't know them. And she hadn't wanted to come in to displace Grant. Yet she'd pushed him out of his bedchamber, which could make it appear she was doing just that.

"From what I understand, Uilleam wanted to manage the estates," Grant continued. "Not that many wolf packs have the honor of such a task. Often, the owner of a keep would have his own pack to run it. But your grandfather, Gideon Playfair, was a lone wolf and earned the right to build the castle after fighting in battles for the king. He also had his own barony. What he didn't have was his own pack. Gideon mated Neda, and they had the castle built and needed a wolf pack to manage the estates.

"Uilleam Borthwick, Archibald's grandfather, had his own family, but not a pack to run the place. John MacQuarrie, my grandfather, had a title and his own pack, but no land to call his own. Your grandfather gave the job to John, and Uilleam couldn't accept it. When my pack learned he had killed John, they hunted him down like the dog he was."

She couldn't believe all that she was hearing. She was glad that Grant's family had resolution in the case with his grandfather, sad as it was that he had to lose him in such a way. But what about his parents? She felt sick thinking her own father could have been involved.

"I take it you never learned who killed your parents."

"My mother had no reason to be on the cliffs in the dark of night. Neither had my father. Your grandmother adored me and my brothers, and Theodore hated us for it. Your grandmother was like a mother to us, doting on us. Theodore felt she loved us more than she had him when he was that age. According to my father, it wasn't so. Theodore had been a moody and perverse child and teen. Without her mate to help control Theodore, Neda dealt with him the best she could. He showed her no love or respect like my brothers and I did. I apologize for speaking the truth to you, lass, when he was your father, but I feel the words need to be said."

"I'd rather know the truth of the matter," she said, not wanting to divulge that she had never gotten along with her father. She knew all about the moodiness. She had experienced it firsthand.

Taking the news in, Colleen poked at her egg. She'd never known the details of why her father hadn't gotten along with her grandmother. Her father had only said he and his mother had never seen eye to eye and when he mated Colleen's mother, they had left and he had never gone back. Until he inherited the castle and was forced to. Just like Colleen was. Only she had thought she would enjoy the experience if she could get past Grant's defenses.

Now to hear her father had returned to the castle on occasions unbeknownst to her? How many more lies had he fed her?

She had never even met her grandmother. Her father had said she was a hateful woman who despised having to raise a couple of kids. He had never said anything about Grant or his brothers. She would ask Grant more about her grandmother later, feeling bad she hadn't gotten to know her before she died.

How had her father acted toward Grant and his brothers when he came to live here for a year and a day? She had been away at college and couldn't take time off to visit. Not that she would have. She had avoided her father as soon as she was old enough to do so.

Her father's relationship with Grant put a whole different spin on the situation. Her gaze steady on his, she said, "I take it when my father came to stay here, the experience was rather...tense."

"Aye." Grant didn't expound.

She wasn't sure she wanted to hear all that had gone on. She suspected her father had been awful to live with. Just as he had been while she had to live with him. Mainly because of the drinking. Since he already held bad feelings toward Grant and his brothers, she could only imagine how well that had gone over.

He wasn't one of those happy drunks, either. No. When he'd had too much, he'd been surly and mean.

Was that why Grant had been wary of her staying with them? She had to dispel any notion that she was anything like her father. She was more like her mother—even-tempered, cautious, and to her way of thinking, great about considering both sides of an equation before she made any decisions. She did appreciate that though she owned the place, she didn't live here. She certainly had no intention of making a bunch of changes at the castle unless they would improve its financial state or conditions for the people who lived here.

Still, she didn't understand why Grant had taken such an aversion to Archibald.

"I understand why you would have a lot of animosity against Archibald's grandfather since he murdered yours, but why Archibald? He's just the grandson."

"Like grandfather, like father, like son," Grant said simply.

"How so?" she asked. What Grant revealed said nothing.

"You know why he shows interest in you?" Grant asked.

She thought about what Grant had remarked on. It all had to do with running the estates. Like grandfather, like father, like son. So they had all wanted the job and would do anything to get the position?

She stiffened at the insinuation that Archibald wouldn't be intrigued with her just because she was... *intriguing*. She didn't believe he was up to no good. Grant was projecting that Archibald would be just like Uilleam Borthwick because they were related. When it could be the furthest thing from the truth.

Guys liked her. Normally. They became interested in her if she showed any interest back. She had to admit Archibald's attention had flattered her. She didn't believe in love at first sight, but something might develop between them. Given time.

Though she had to admit when she saw Grant fighting

Ian in the inner bailey, working that hot body of his, she did believe in lust at first sight.

She sighed. She could never be accused of being gullible. "Of course, I know why Archibald is interested in me. He wants me to have his babies."

Enrick choked on whatever he was drinking with his breakfast.

Lachlan glowered at her. Grant stared at her as if she'd turned into the Loch Ness monster on a bad day.

"Well, in truth, I didn't tell him that I owned the castle. Just that I was visiting for a year."

"You don't think he knew who you were? That he was there only to meet you and attempt to win you over?"

No, she hadn't suspected any of that. "So you think he believes he might get his hands on the castle, even if he has to mate with me to do it." She smiled, amused at the notion. But that changed the rules a bit where Archibald was concerned. She would be more careful with regard to dating him, having fun but ensuring he understood she was leaving in a year. And not mating a Highland wolf who would lay claim to her properties and stay here while she returned to Maryland.

"You can't be serious," Grant said, his face red with anger.

"What? That I'd go along with such a farce? Or that he intends this charade?" She noted the hall was completely silent.

"Then you realize what he's up to," Grant growled.

She smiled. "I think it's too early to say about anything."

"Why did you have him come here?"

"I didn't have him come here. He took it upon himself to see me here. But I would like to know why you think he's such a problem." She still didn't see the correlation between Uilleam killing her grandfather and the grandson.

"Archibald tried to tell your father what a poor job my clan and I were doing. He hoped to get rid of me when your dad stayed here before."

"Ah." Though she was surprised to learn that Archibald had latched on to her father. Maybe there was some truth to him having a motive for why he was now so friendly with her.

"What do you mean by that?"

"You believe I will be just like my father." She wouldn't tell Grant otherwise. She wouldn't expect him or anyone else to take her word for it. She'd have to prove it by showing just who she was.

He grunted.

"Well, suffice it to say, you have nothing to worry about—for the moment. I am really easy to get along with and don't intend to make any changes for the present without seeking your consideration. So, do you have someone in mind who can show me the properties today?" she asked.

"I will," Grant quickly said.

Truly surprised that he would offer, she wondered why Grant hadn't thought of trying to seduce her. If they mated, he and his family would never have to give up their home. If he hadn't tried so far, she didn't think he was interested. And yet she swore from the way he was looking at her now, he wasn't acting just as her manager, but like a Highland wolf desiring a wild and sexy romp with a she-wolf.

In her dreams.

Chapter 8

GRANT WASN'T SURE WHAT TO THINK OF THE LASS. HE *had* thought she would be just like her father. That she would have the same superior attitude and the same disagreeable personality, and hold the same grudges. But she didn't seem to be anything like him.

Grant had a hard time believing she could be so different.

He'd relaxed some after they'd had their talk at breakfast, and he was sorry to hear she hadn't known how much her grandmother wished to meet her. He took her on the grand tour, showing her the castle grounds and the farmland connected to the property. But the highlight of the tour seemed to be the Highland cows grazing in their grassy pasture. She was fascinated with the "cute" woolly cows and had to get out of the car for a closer look, which couldn't help but amuse him. She was just as enthralled with the vista of the North Sea. Unlike her father, who couldn't have cared less about anything but the finances and his next drink.

"I think I was a sea sprite in my other life," she said wistfully, breathing in the sea air. "I love being near the sea."

He stared at her, surprised to hear her speak about something so personal. "At home where you live, are you land bound?"

"I am. I love visiting Annapolis, and the Inner

Harbor in Baltimore, but otherwise, I live way inland.
This is beautiful."

"It can be bitterly cold and stormy." He didn't mean
to ruin her impression of the area, but if she had romantic notions that it was always this way, he wanted to
dispel them.

"Yes," she said, as if the notion pleased her.

The weather had been nice since she'd arrived, except for this morning when it was so cold and foggy
and she'd taken the walk with Borthwick in the gardens.
Grant wondered then if really bad weather would faze
her—her father had hated the wet weather and cold.
Though Grant didn't remember anything that Theodore
had actually liked.

Grant drove her to the last stop they'd make, where a
white, frothing burn poured over moss stones in a quiet
glen. Green, grassy hills surrounded them, and sheep
wandered near the top of one of the hills.

"Can we climb them?" she asked, prompting him to
pull over into a car park.

He was surprised to see her smiling face, her eyes
sparkling with fascination. He hadn't expected to see her
this enthralled with the land. Of course she'd appreciate
what the land could mean financially to her, but to treasure it like he and his kin did? Definitely unexpected.

She was out of the car in a flash and climbing the
nearest hill before he could hurry to catch up. The grass
was like velvet and the climb easy as they made it to the
top. He pointed to a waterfall cascading down one of the
hills way off in the distance.

"It's beautiful," she said. "I wish I had my camera."

"I can bring you here again," he said, not sure why he

said so. She could come here on her own any time she wanted and didn't need him to escort her. Dark strands of her hair whipped across his shoulders, and he was reminded of his first encounter with her when he wore his kilt and how her hair and skirt had whipped at his bare skin, tantalizing, teasing, tickling him.

Her lips parted in awe as she surveyed the surrounding lands. She turned to see the hills behind them that stood even taller. "Can we climb those?" She spoke with such enthusiasm that he smiled.

"Aye, if you wish it."

"I do." She hurried down the incline like a sure-footed sheep, then raced across the narrow footbridge built over the burn. When she reached the other side, she began the climb.

Grant nearly laughed at her exuberance. He hadn't expected to enjoy the outing, just assumed it would be a grueling duty, nothing more. He could envision her racing up and down the green hills in her wolf coat, with him in hot pursuit. No one lived out here for miles around, yet even then, visitors to the area might see them, and running at night would be a better choice.

He had no idea why he was even thinking along those lines. Why would she want to run with him through the hills at night as a wolf?

He always joked and played with his clansmen when they were through with their work for the day. Well, even *while* they worked. But being with Colleen here like this felt different. For a moment, he didn't feel like he served as the manager of her estates while she was the owner and taskmaster. He felt like a man with a woman on a Sunday jaunt in the glen. Except she wasn't just any woman. She was a she-wolf, her cute little arse jiggling ahead of him as he climbed the hill to join her.

When he reached the top, she was trying to catch her breath and swayed a little. He grabbed her arm, and he didn't know *what* came over him. But suddenly he was looking down into her smiling face, as if she was smiling at *him*, and he wanted in the worst way to kiss her.

She didn't pull away from him, either.

He shouldn't kiss her, but damn, he wanted to.

Still breathing hard, her heart beating fast, she placed her hand on his chest. He expected her to push him away, but she didn't. She just stood there looking up at him, waiting for him to do something. He breathed in her scent, all woman and she-wolf and...interested.

They stood high on top of the hill overlooking the glen, the water rushing by, the sheep grazing on the green grass across the burn, and white clouds passing overhead against the blue sky.

He still had hold of her arm, but then he released her, cupped her face with both hands, and kissed her.

When his lips met hers, he knew he shouldn't do this. He intended to make it sweet and unassuming, to quench some damnable need that he had to satisfy. He didn't presume it would go anywhere, and he almost imagined it would be lame and unappealing—after having built up the expectation that kissing that sweet mouth of hers would make his world spin and topple over. He hadn't thought she'd crave the intimacy as much as he did. Yet when she wrapped her arms around his neck and kissed him back, she exhibited an eagerness that turned his world on end.

She was more than willing.

He held back, not wanting to frighten the lass. From her response, she didn't appear to be the kind of she-wolf who frightened easily. Her soft lips pressed against his, her body caressing his own, when he was only thinking in terms of lips and kissing and *not* of rubbing their bodies together as if in preparation for something even more intimate! Despite the cool breeze sweeping around them, he was burning up. He should end this now, not wanting her to think he had designs on her to gain her properties. Yet, just from the way *she* wasn't pulling away, *he* couldn't either.

She had to feel what her body was doing to his, the vixen, as she brushed against him. She continued to kiss him until they both had to come up for air—as if she was unwilling to give up first. She smiled at him. He was so shocked at her response that he couldn't control his own. His body was eager for more. He stared at her dumbfounded, which made her smile broaden even more.

He had worried she might regret what had passed between them. What *had* passed between them? He felt unbalanced. But she only smiled wickedly at him as if she was perfectly fine, though he swore she was just a little breathless.

"I'm hungry," she said, throwing him for a loop. "It must be about lunchtime."

Lunch. He couldn't get his mind off the kiss they had shared, and she was thinking about lunch?

But she was right. He hadn't realized how long he'd taken to show her around. He wanted to say something about the kiss they'd shared, but she had already pulled away from him and begun making her way down the hill.

When he reached her on the bridge, he again wanted

to explain himself, but she hurried across it as if nothing had happened between them. And that bothered him more than he wanted to concede.

Hell, he'd been a fool to leave his bed this morning. He should have stayed in it—*with her*.

He opened her car door for her, and then they were off.

"Thanks for showing me the properties," she said, her cheeks a little flushed. "You've done a lovely job maintaining them."

He respected her for appreciating how he had managed the properties, but more than anything, he wanted to speak about what had just happened between them. He didn't want her reading more into it than what it was—just a spur-of-the-moment reaction to being close to a bonny lass in a beautiful glen...

So then why couldn't *he* quit thinking about it?

"We've always taken pride in managing the properties," Grant said, trying to focus on the real world and not his passion for the lass. Despite the fact that his body still craved her touch and he'd had a devil of a time making it down the hill wearing trousers when he was fully aroused. A kilt would have made it so much easier to manage.

Colleen felt all tingly and hot and deliciously sexy after the kiss she and Grant had shared. He'd obviously been just as affected as she had, only she'd managed—*somehow*—to control her evident reaction better than he had. Which she was glad for. She didn't want him thinking she melted under any old Highlander's kisses.

She'd loved seeing the sea and the castle grounds, but the glen where they'd shared that magical kiss...she would remember that forever.

He was quieter now than when they started the tour, maybe because he didn't have anything more to say about the properties. She didn't believe he could still be thinking about the kiss—like she was.

After praising him for a job well done, she couldn't think of another thing to say. She should tell him she didn't kiss men like that, ever, but she thought it might be better if they didn't discuss it. He probably kissed all the lasses like that and didn't give it another thought.

She shook her head at herself and watched out for the castle, but she couldn't see it for the trees and the long winding road that led up to the castle walls.

When it came into view, she smiled. The four round, gray stone towers stretched to the blue sky, and she saw three men on top of the wall walk watching their approach. She couldn't imagine they'd have guards posted all the time like in ye old days.

Grant parked the car in the inner bailey and she said, "Well, that was a lovely tour. Thanks so much for taking time out of your busy schedule to show me around." And then she fled into the keep.

—⁓—

"How did the tour go?" Enrick asked Grant, who watched Colleen hurry off.

"What?" Grant asked his brother.

"The tour? Did she act bored and give you grief like her father did?" Enrick asked as they headed for the keep.

On the one hand, Grant was thinking how much he'd like for her to stay longer. On the other hand, after what just happened between them—though he was still unsure what had occurred—he thought she needed to leave sooner rather than later. How could he even look at her now without thinking of that kiss and the way she had pressed her body against his? And how he wanted more?

"Grant?" Enrick looked back at the castle and said, "You didn't have words with the lass, did you? She seemed a little flustered and looked to be in a hurry to leave you behind."

"She's hungry," Grant said.

Enrick frowned at him.

Grant hadn't expected to still be so rattled when he sat down to the meal. All he could do was take deep breaths to smell her scent. He could tell she was just as interested as she had been earlier. Not good. He had no designs on her or her property, and he didn't want his brothers or anyone else believing he did.

"Where's the whisky?" she asked, buttering a slice of bread.

"You can't be serious," Grant said, shocked. Maybe she did have a drinking problem. Hell, maybe she was just like her father...only her drinking problem was more insidious.

Colleen was surprised at Grant's reaction. She was trying to touch on inane subjects, just to make a bit of conversation. She couldn't stop worrying about whether Grant had told his brothers he'd kissed her in the glen and was making headway with seducing her. What if that was the only reason he had done so? To heel her with a kiss—very much like training the hounds with bits of meaty treats, which was on her agenda.

"I don't want to drink any of it unless maybe it's

made into a whisky sour. Certainly not for a few weeks, if that," she said, not intending to drink anything that contained alcohol for a very long time.

Grant looked at her like she had to be crazy to even think of ruining good whisky in such a manner.

"I just wondered why you weren't drinking any. I thought braw Highland warriors drank it at every meal."

"Not this afternoon." He didn't say anything more and cut into his fish. Then he paused. "Do…you recollect that the cold waters of the North Sea nearly swept you away in the middle of the night?"

She stared at his serious expression for a moment, trying to recall such a thing. Now that he brought it up, she vaguely remembered being drawn to the sea. Though she'd dismissed the notion of scrambling over wet, mossy rocks as just part of a vivid dream due to her inebriated state. And yet, she'd smelled the seawater on herself.

"As a wolf," he further explained.

Her body flushed with mortification. Who all had seen her like that? Exactly what had she done? Was that why she smelled of fishy water this morning before she took her shower?

"I needed to stretch my legs," she offered, thinking maybe that's why she would do such a dumb thing, or maybe it sounded like a good explanation. She was highly thankful his people were wolves. What would have happened if they hadn't been? They would have shot her, that's what.

"Aye, well, in the future, I would ask that your wolf venturing be confined to *this* side of the seawall. The trails leading to the sea are too dangerous for anyone to navigate, especially if the person has imbibed too much."

She wanted to ask whose fault that was, even though she knew very well her own stubbornness had made her careless.

"I will take your concern under advisement," she said, finishing off her bread. "I hope I didn't inconvenience anyone too much." She truly hoped only Grant had known of her escapade.

"I howled to warn you not to get too close to the water's edge until I reached you. But you ignored me."

Vaguely, she remembered him nudging her. Like in a dream. An annoying wolf who wanted her to move when she'd been too tired to. "You howled." *Great*.

She could guess what that meant. He was the pack leader, calling out to her in a distressed wolf's way, warning her to return. His kin would have hurried out to see to the matter, just like any wolf pack would.

Even if they didn't believe he needed help, they would have arrived to see what was going on—as was a wolf's ever-curious nature.

She wanted to ask how many had seen her in her drunken state, risking her neck above the breakers. But she didn't dare pose the question. She never got drunk. Ever. Which had been part of the problem with her inability to handle the liquor last night. She didn't approve of such behavior. Her own father drank way too much and had behaved badly on many occasions, embarrassing her and her mother more than once. She didn't want anyone to see her acting in such a manner.

"Thank you for seeing me back to my chamber."

Grant said, "It was the least I could do for you." He didn't comment on her saying the chamber was hers.

"Why did you leave the bed this morning?" Or last

night. She wasn't certain when he'd run off. "I needed to be close to the bathroom. You could have slept in my room. I promise I wouldn't have made any untoward advances," she said. Not like she did on the hilltop. Then she frowned. Maybe she had made untoward advances to him in bed and that was why he had left. She felt her body warm.

His mouth kicked up at one corner as if he was trying hard not to show how funny that notion was to him. What? He'd think she would have ravished him? Unable to keep her composure when she was so close to the hot Highlander? But she really couldn't remember what she'd done to make him leave.

She stiffened a little at his response. She wasn't that needy. Just because she might have seemed like it when she kissed him.

She'd been mated twice. She often had wolves interested in her. Just because she wasn't mated now and Grant and his people didn't want her here didn't mean other wolves wouldn't find her appealing.

She'd also considered the possibility that he might attempt to pursue her, mate her, and gain control of her properties that way. Then he'd never have to submit to her wishes. And he and his clan would never have to worry about losing their ancestral home.

But he didn't seem to be interested even in that. He just wanted her gone. Unless he'd kissed her as a way of changing the dynamics between them. Sure, kiss the she-wolf, make her melt under his touch, and she'd be as malleable as any beta wolf under his jurisdiction.

She didn't know why she was thinking along those lines. Maybe the feeling of being in her ancestral home, where she felt she belonged in an odd sort of way. Maybe her dad didn't, but being here felt right to her. Despite the way Grant didn't care for her presence.

No matter what, she wasn't giving in to the madness and showing him anything other than her professional side—this *was* business, after all. She didn't want to think of herself as his superior, but she had to remember that's just what she was. The boss did not kiss her employee, and she had to remember that.

And then her traitorous mind thought back to him vacating the bed in the middle of the night to leave her alone. How he'd grabbed his kilt from the bench and stalked out of the room. And that made her recall what she'd seen once again. He'd been naked. Only this time in bed with her. And she, likewise.

A recipe for disaster.

Her cell rang and she wasn't sure who to expect. One of her cousins, maybe. But it was Archibald. This was not a good time to talk. "I'll call you back as soon as I'm through with lunch."

She smiled at Grant, who looked like he expected her to tell him who had called and then he'd tell her how much he disapproved.

———⁓———

After the meal, Colleen said she was taking a walk in the gardens, and Enrick and Lachlan wished a word with Grant about the tour. Both were concerned that it had not gone well—mainly because he didn't wish to discuss it. He noted that as soon as she'd made it outside, she'd made a phone call, probably to the person who had called her during lunch. He suspected it was Archibald

and that she wanted to speak with him in private. That didn't bode well.

"Her father was Neda's flesh-and-blood son, but we were the ones who took care of Neda and her properties," Lachlan said, getting wound up about the situation all over again.

"Don't you think she did it for the lass? Her only grandchild, to carry on the family line?" Enrick asked.

Grant ground his teeth. "Colleen has never lived here before. She's not part of the heritage or the history." Even though she seemed to enjoy the tour, he suspected it was a passing fancy. Living here day in, day out would be a whole other matter. "She doesn't care anything about the place like we do. This is home for us. Always has been. She is just a visitor."

He tried to convince himself of that. What if he was to fall for the lass—not that that was at all likely—but what if he did, and she wanted to leave after the weather got bad? Or she longed for her American home?

He'd be mated to a she-wolf who would be depressed and unhappy, and then what? Would she drink to drown her sorrows? He could envision the whole situation becoming a disaster. Mating was for a lifetime and… Hell, why was he even thinking of such a thing?

"She's an *unwelcome* visitor," Enrick said, although Grant swore his brother was digging for the truth, watching his reaction, wondering what had gone on between Colleen and him.

"Aye," Grant said, not about to ever tell his brothers he had kissed the lass.

Grant noted Lachlan was watching out the window, his arms folded across his chest, listening to the

conversation but interested in something taking place near the gardens.

"What are you gawking at?" Grant asked, crossing the floor to join him.

"The lass who doesn't belong here."

Five of his men were supposed to be patching around loose rocks on the seawall. Instead, they were sitting on stone benches, arms folded across their chests, smiling as they observed Colleen. All three of his Irish wolfhounds sat in front of her. Their eyes were focused on hers, their expressions saying they were eager to please.

They never behaved. Even for him. But at least she hadn't been on the phone for long. Unless she'd just made a hasty date with Archibald. Grant ground his teeth a bit.

"How in the world did she manage that?" Lachlan asked, peering out the window beside them.

"Bribery, it looks like," Grant said. He couldn't imagine getting the dogs to mind any other way. Even so, he couldn't believe they'd behave for treats. After the way they had jumped all over her when she first arrived, he was surprised to see she had so much control over them now.

What if she had kissed him and rubbed that sweet body against his in an attempt to heel him as she had the wolfhounds, only she didn't even have to give him a treat to make him mind? *Bloody…hell*.

"Did you know her cousins are arriving next week?" Enrick asked.

"What?" Grant turned to see Enrick's serious expression. "I thought they were only coming if the lass felt she needed help in handling us," Grant said, not liking

this new scenario one bit, despite having said it was fine with him if they came to visit. Surely they didn't mean to stay too long.

"Apparently they wanted to come anyway to check out their castle."

"The properties are the lass's. Not her cousins'." Grant hadn't meant to sound so protective of her. He tried to tell himself he only worried that her cousins would try to dictate to Grant and his pack, in addition to the lass having her say. He let out his breath in exasperation. "What next?"

"Look, they're following her as if she were the Pied Piper. They're not jumping on her, but walking beside her like perfectly behaved, well-trained hounds," Lachlan said.

Grant stared out the window, not believing this. "When exactly are her cousins arriving?" he asked, wanting to take care of this issue right away. He still wondered if the lass hadn't called them and told them she needed help with the Highlanders.

"Friday after next at 9:45 in the morning," Enrick said. "Where did you want them to stay?"

"The blue and gold rooms." Though Grant wanted to have them stay in the White Room while he stayed in one of the newly painted adjoining guest rooms.

Maybe after the kiss they'd shared, she'd changed her mind about him sleeping in the White Room instead of his own chamber.

He managed a small smile.

Chapter 9

LATER THAT NIGHT AFTER COLLEEN HAD READIED HER-self for bed, she heard Grant opening drawers while he packed some stuff to vacate his chamber. She hated that he had to move, but she couldn't see any other way to handle this unless he finally and miraculously came up with another bedroom she could sleep in that had a bathroom en suite.

After what seemed like forever, he shut the door to his chamber, not banging it as she suspected he might do. He hadn't spoken a word to her at dinner, and she assumed he was seething about having to move from his chamber tonight. She also wondered if that's why he had initiated the kiss earlier today—an attempt to change her mind about where he'd sleep.

Was he also upset with her about her cousins com-ing? She'd told them they didn't have to. Even sug-gested they arrive later because she felt Grant and his people still needed to become accustomed to her being there first. But both of her cousins worried about the weather getting worse. They wanted to see the castle before that happened and then return home.

She could have said no and insisted they wait until next summer when the weather was better, but they were so eager to visit that she had agreed.

She hoped she and Grant hadn't returned to business as usual—him being all growly, and her cheerfully at-tempting to show it didn't bother her.

Hating to admit it, she much preferred him kissing
her atop a hill in a serene glen.

———

Grant toted his bag into the White Room and shut the door
none too gently. He could live with this as long as he needed
to, he told himself. He'd had an awful time trying to be civil
to anyone this afternoon, knowing that as soon as the day
ended, he would be subjected to sleeping in the White Room.

Everyone was well aware of the reason for his dis-
content and, thankfully, gave him a wide berth.

He stripped out of his clothes, then pulled aside the
white ruffled and eyelet-trimmed curtains and stared at
the white comforter and blankets decorated with pink
roses covering the bed. The *tiny* white bed.

Maid staff would be certain to give him grief about
leaving fur on the bed if he shifted and slept there. When
he'd kissed the lass on top of the hill, he had been the
alpha male to the alpha female, on top of the world, right
with the world. Now he felt like one of his Irish wolfhounds relegated to the doghouse.

He stretched his body, embracing the heat and change
in his muscles until he stood on four paws, staring at that
damnable child's bed. He growled, not that it did him
any good, and curled up on the pink-and-white braided
rug next to the hearth.

He still wondered how it had come to this. Him, the
pack leader and manager of the estates and a laird in his
own right, sleeping on the floor of the room reserved for
the now "owner" of the castle.

———

Colleen shouldn't have felt guilty for sleeping in the lady's chamber while relegating Grant to the White Room. She wondered if he slept there or had made someone else do so while he commandeered that pack member's room.

She finally closed her eyes, wrapping the blanket and covers tight to her chin, and heard a strange sound coming from the direction of Grant's chamber.

Her eyes popped open as every one of her senses went on alert. Had Grant sneaked back into his chamber to sleep, defying her order? She couldn't imagine the Highland alpha warrior-wolf sneaking anywhere. Unless he was ready to do battle with his enemy.

He might see her as his enemy, despite the fact that she paid for his services and he had free room and board, but she didn't believe he was ready to engage in combat with her.

She heard some more strange noises. She wasn't sure what to do. Make him leave? Pretend she slept right though it? Maybe he had only come back to get something out of the bathroom.

She closed her eyes, listening. Another odd sound. A creaking noise. She listened for a long time, half expecting to hear Grant climb onto his bed and the box springs to squeak.

Nothing.

She barely breathed as her ears tuned in to sounds only her wolf half could hear. A strange rumble. She ground her teeth.

She had to know what he was doing. If he thought to make noises all night long to disturb her sleep just because she made him leave his chamber…well, he wouldn't get away with it.

Dressed in a long T-shirt, she left the bed and crossed her room barefoot. She opened the door to his chamber, didn't see any movement, and walked across the floor until she reached the bed, then listened.

No sound. No breathing. No heart beating. Another rumble. It came from the bathroom.

She peeked between the midnight-blue curtains and found the bed empty. She had no desire to see Grant naked again. Well, not that she didn't admire his form or really want to see him like that again, but that wasn't conducive to conducting her mission here.

She stalked across the tapestry rug to the bathroom where the solid oak door stood ajar.

"Grant?" she called out.

No response.

Goose bumps dotted her skin. He was either in the bathroom, caught, or attempting to pretend he wasn't there... No, he would be too alpha for that.

She pushed the door open and peered in. No one. The bathroom was empty. No noises.

Maybe by the time she moved around his curtained bed, he'd slipped out through his chamber door, not wanting her to catch him here. Surely she would have heard him opening and closing his door into the hallway.

She sat on a bench by the bed and waited, thinking if Grant or anyone else was pulling shenanigans, maybe even unbeknownst to Grant, the perpetrator would return, and she'd catch him at it. As she suspected, no other noises occurred. She continued to sit there, so sleepy she was barely able to keep her eyes open.

She closed them for a moment. Or she thought she

"What the devil are you doing here, lass?" Grant growled. "Have you changed your mind about sleeping here?"

He had to be kidding.

"This is a little girl's room," she said, annoyed. She could see why his brothers didn't want to switch rooms with him. "Why in the world would you think I would want to stay here?" Not that she believed he thought anything of the sort. He wanted to encourage her to leave.

"By your grandmother's orders, *this is* your room," Grant said.

Colleen couldn't believe it. Her grandmother had wanted to see her all those years? She felt a lump in her throat, and her eyes grew misty.

"I'm sorry, lass. I thought you might have already known. She sent letters to you when she thought you were old enough to read. She had a private investigator take pictures of you while you were growing up, and she had them on display in her chamber."

She couldn't believe it. "Did she stay in the lady's chamber, then?" Colleen somehow managed to get out.

"No. Once her mate died, your grandfather, she moved into the other wing in a corner apartment and wanted my grandfather to take over the laird's chamber."

"Who stays in her room now?" Not that Colleen wanted to use it. She didn't believe in ghosts, she reminded herself, but she didn't feel comfortable with the notion of sleeping in there.

"It's been left like it was in her memory. If you want to stay there, you can. I wasn't sure you would want to."

She shook her head.

"Did you…come here for some reason? Other than to check out the room?"

The noise in the bathroom disturbing her sleep didn't seem so important now. She wanted to resolve the sleeping arrangements instead.

"Why don't you sleep in my grandmother's apartments? You can't sleep in this bed. Why didn't you say so?" she asked. She thought they believed a ghost haunted the room. She'd never expected this.

"You told me where you wanted me, and I'm fine with it." He tried to look like he was fine with it, but his expression and growly tone said otherwise.

"You can't sleep in that bed. You're too big. Stay in Neda's apartments," she said.

"The single women live in that wing and *only* the single women."

"So you're inferring I should move there?"

"Not at all."

"Fine. Do what you want." She was about to turn and leave when he reached for his pants. Was he planning to drop them right in front of her? Sure, most wolves didn't sleep in anything, but he surely hadn't been sleeping in that bed.

"What I want is to sleep in my own bed," he said, then unzipped his pants. "But since that's not an option, I'll sleep here." He pulled off his pants and dropped them to the floor, his gaze remaining on hers—she would not be intimidated—and shifted.

So that's how he slept in here. As a wolf. She thought he would jump onto the bed, but instead, he curled up on the rug and closed his eyes. He was just as stunning as a wolf, with rusty-colored fur around his face and body if maybe she should stay in a room where the bathroom wasn't attached. She'd never get any sleep this night.

She closed Grant's chamber door and was heading back to bed when she heard someone breathing behind her closed bed curtains. Her heart skipping beats, she grabbed hold of the curtains and yanked them aside.

One of the Irish wolfhounds was sleeping in her bed!

Chapter 10

AFTER HE'D WARNED HER WHAT A CAD ARCHIBALD was, Colleen must have scheduled a date with him anyway—and Grant didn't like it. But he couldn't help smiling about the noisy pipes when he curled up beside the white eyelet bed in the White Room. He had worried that one of his men had tried to spook her into wanting to sleep somewhere else, even though he'd made it perfectly clear he wanted none of that.

He was glad the groaning of the bathroom pipes was the only cause for concern. Then he frowned. As to the other matter, he was not happy about that at all. Somehow he had to make her see Archibald for what he truly was.

He had slept for maybe half an hour, maybe less, when his cook stood in the doorway of the guest room and said, "My laird, are you in here?"

Grant growled. Not in an angry way, but tired. What now?

He shifted, threw on his pants, and moved beyond the bed. "To what do I owe this intrusion, Maynard?"

The gray-eyed wolf ran his hands through his gray hair. "You know I don't like anyone messing in my kitchen after it's closed. And it's the rule that when it's closed, it's closed."

In truth, Grant had forbidden most everyone to be in the kitchen after hours. Only last year, he'd had to take a man to task for selling foodstuffs to humans at a profit, figuring the owner of the castle would never know and could afford it. The man had been banished from the castle, the pack, and the clan. When they discovered he'd been pilfering the food when the cooks and their assistants were gone for the day, Grant had made the rule that no one but his brothers, Darby, the kitchen staff, and himself, of course, could go to the kitchen without asking permission. And all accounts had to be strictly supervised.

Grant hated doing it, but he couldn't afford to have a thief among them again, so he couldn't ignore the situation tonight, giving the impression it was unimportant to him.

He stalked with Maynard to the kitchen and asked, "So who broke the rules?"

"That lass, my laird."

"Wait," Grant said, stopping Maynard with a hand on his shoulder. "The culprit breaking the rules is Lady Colleen Playfair?"

"Aye, and I knew you would be the only one to give her the order not to."

Grant shook his head. "The lass owns the castle and pays for the food. If she wants to have a midnight snack anytime day or night, she's welcome to it."

"But you said…"

"Aye, but when it comes to the lass, we have to agree with whatever she wants until she is gone." Grant would have to let everyone in the pack know that rule now. He thought it was understood.

They continued to walk to the kitchen when Maynard whispered, "I think she's touched in the head."

"What makes you think that?"

"She got one of the really good steaks out that you like, and she's making mincemeat out of it on the cutting board."

"What?" Grant had told himself she could do anything she liked. But to do that to a good steak?

"Aye. Dicing it up into itty-bitty bits. I tell you she's a wee bit mad."

When they reached the kitchen, Grant was surprised to see Colleen wearing only the long T-shirt, minus her jeans and no shoes on her feet. Not that he'd bothered with a shirt or shoes, either.

Just as Maynard had said, the lass was cutting the bloody steak into tiny pieces. What was she doing?

She gasped as she saw Grant and the cook enter the kitchen.

"Are you hungry, lass?" Grant asked, not imagining how she could eat the steak after the way she'd butchered it.

"No," she said, waving her knife at him. "Did you tell your cook it's all right for me to be in here?"

"Aye, that I did. But I wondered if I might help in any way." Most of all, he wanted to know just what she intended to do with the meat. Make a stew? In the middle of the night?

"No. I'm fine. Thanks. Well…do you have a plastic bag I can put this in?" she asked, looking as tired as he felt, yet her expression was all cheerfulness, as if she did strange things like this in the middle of the night all the time.

He'd caught her father drinking at all hours of the night, but he'd never expected anything like this of his daughter. What in the world was she up to?

—⁓—

The next morning, Grant slept much later than he ever did. No one bothered him, thankfully. He was certain Maynard had told all the clan who were interested in hearing that the lass was touched in the head.

Grant had been dying to learn what Colleen was up to last night, but she hadn't enlightened him, and he wasn't about to ask. Maynard had looked at him as if it was his duty to learn what the lass had been doing. Now, he had to share the bathroom with four other men, or…since the women were not here for now, he'd use Neda's bathroom to shower. He wanted to find out when Colleen was going out with Archibald. And where they intended to go. Though beyond that, he wasn't sure what he could do.

Dressed, he headed for Neda's chamber and was in the middle of a nice, hot shower when he heard movement in the room.

He closed his eyes and continued to soap his chest.

"Who is in there?" Colleen asked.

"Me," Grant said, figuring that would suffice for an answer. She had to know his voice by now.

"Oh."

"Were you looking for me?"

"No, I just wanted to see my grandmother's bedchamber. I thought no one would be here."

He continued to shower leisurely, sighing. He was tired from being up half the night. He wondered if she'd also slept in late. "Are you still there?"

"Yes," she said, and he thought he heard tears in her voice.

He frowned. "Is something the matter?"

"No. I...I didn't know my grandmother cared anything about me. My father..." She didn't finish speaking.

"Your father told you she didn't want to see you? That she was angry that he left and mated with an American, and any of his offspring would not be welcome here? She wanted you to stay in the White Room when you visited. No one was to ever use it but you. She asked for you on her deathbed." He wanted Colleen to know how much she had meant to her grandmother.

Colleen didn't say anything. Maybe she had left. He turned off the water and grabbed a towel. He hated to be the one to tell her the truth, but she had no one left to make it right.

"Your father lied to you." He walked out of the bathroom, expecting her to be standing there. She was gone. He took a settling breath. He wished now he'd gone against Neda's ruling and had fetched the lass home to see her before her grandmother died.

When Grant went to the great hall to see if the lass was there, he found his brothers instead. Enrick frowned at him. "You look a little worse for wear. Did you find out why the lass mutilated a steak in the middle of the night?"

"Where is she?" Grant asked, heading for the kitchen. He needed a mug of tea, and hell, the steak sounded good. In the first of the fridges, he found the package of diced-up steak. What in the world was she doing with it? "Where's Maynard?"

"Here I am. Do you want breakfast *now*?" Maynard asked, coming out of a walk-in cupboard. He acted as though he didn't know that Grant had been up half the night.

"Aye, if you wouldn't mind." But Grant didn't say it in a way that meant his cook had any choice in the matter.

His brothers smiled at Grant.

"Okay, so where is she?" Grant asked, folding his arms across his chest as he leaned his backside against a counter. And then he thought about the damnable date with Archibald.

"You wanted her gone," Enrick said. "Whatever you said worked."

Grant felt sick to his stomach. "What do you mean she's gone? You mean, just for a few hours. Right? Her bags are still here. Aren't they?"

"We didn't look. She didn't say anything to anyone. Just got in her car and drove off late this morning," Enrick said. "I didn't know if she'd already packed or what. She didn't have breakfast with us or anything. I don't know when she got up. Maybe as late as you? What happened last night?"

Grant glanced at Maynard.

"I told them about the steak, but I don't know about anything else," Maynard said, shrugging.

"Lachlan, check and see if her bags are still here," Grant said, not liking how shaken up he felt.

"Aye." Lachlan gave Enrick a look that said he wasn't sure what was going on.

Grant had wanted her to leave, but not like this. Not if she was upset about her father's deceitfulness and the fact that she missed seeing her grandmother before she died. That scenario was a little too harsh for the lass to deal with on her own, without someone to help ease her through it. And certainly not if she had taken off to be with Archibald and he was there to soothe her.

"Enrick, learn which direction she headed," Grant said.

Enrick shook his head. "Ian and his brothers warned us that you would have more trouble than you bargained for." He hurried out of the kitchen.

Grant scowled at Maynard, who quickly went back to preparing Grant's breakfast.

***

Colleen didn't know where to go, but she had to get away from the castle. Away from everyone who must have known about her father and grandmother when she hadn't had a clue. She felt awful that her grandmother had wanted so much to get in touch with her and hadn't been able to.

All the pictures, the album full of them, and the most recent photo of Colleen framed on her grandmother's wall proved her grandmother hadn't forsaken her. Thinking of the way her grandmother had preserved the little girl's room for the granddaughter she'd never meet added to Colleen's distress. She had to get away.

She brushed away more tears running down her cheeks. She didn't want anyone to see how much this affected her. Did they think she had anything to do with not reaching out to her grandmother? That she had shunned her like her father had?

They must have thought she was unkind and unfeeling.

She drove forever it seemed, passing isolated farms, seeing a few shaggy Highland cows in fenced-in pastures and black-faced sheep nibbling on shorn green grass on the sides of hills. When she arrived at a village, she slowed down and saw gray stone homes, two bed

and breakfasts, an inn, and Kelton's Pub. She was not a
drinker, not like her father had been. But she'd driven
for miles, didn't know where she was, and needed to get
a bite to eat and something to drink. She'd missed breakfast, and she hadn't eaten much dinner the night before,
not with Grant scowling because she was making him
sleep in the White Room. She was hungry.

She parked and entered the rustic-looking pub with
its dark bar and wood paneling and dark tables. And
stopped dead in her tracks.

Archibald Borthwick was sitting and eating at one
of the tables with three men. They were laughing and
joking with him. She wished she could turn around and
head out before Archibald saw her, especially since
she'd turned down a meal with him that he'd wanted
to have at a different location—and now here she was
alone, looking to have a meal.

She didn't want to talk to him or anyone else right
now. Two of the men with him eyed her, and one spoke
to Archibald. He immediately turned to see her. How
had they known who she was?

Now she was stuck with dealing with him. She was
not a beta and would not tuck tail and run, no matter how
much she wanted to avoid having anything to do with
him right now.

Archibald practically fell out of his chair to greet
her. So different from the way Grant had met her at the
castle. Yet with Grant, she felt he was showing his true
feelings, whereas with Archibald, she was beginning
to suspect something wasn't quite right. Maybe she'd
always felt that way—which was why she'd continually
given him excuses and not gone out with him. She was

stuck sitting with him now, though, as he showed her to another table away from his buddies.

She offered him a small, insincere smile. Not because he deserved it, but because she was still feeling sad about her grandmother and didn't feel the least bit cheerful.

"Are you all right, lass? You're a long way from Farraige Castle."

"Yeah. I just wanted to take a drive and learn more about what's in the area."

He looked skeptically at her, probably because she was alone and a *long* way from her castle. She'd said she was too tired to go out with him, but now she could go out by herself?

"Did Grant upset you?" Archibald said, sounding angered.

She couldn't tell if his ire was genuine or a show. "No," she said, shaking her head.

Archibald still studied her, looking concerned, then waved to a waitress to bring a menu. "Are you going back tonight?"

"No, not tonight." She needed a break from the castle and Grant and his clan. She hadn't realized what a strain it would be to act cheery all the time around Grant when he was trying his darnedest to make her want to leave.

Archibald smiled at her. Yeah, he thought he could ply his charm now that she was away from Grant and his protection. She wondered if he would turn her world upside down like Grant could with one smoldering, sexy kiss. If all Highland wolves were capable of such a thing.

"I'm going to check into a B and B and explore more of the countryside tomorrow." And get a good night's

sleep without having to deal with a monster dog in her
bed and rumbling water pipes in Grant's chamber.

All smiles, Archibald scooted closer to the table.
"You're welcome to stay with me. And I'd be honored
to be your tour guide."

"Thanks for the offer, but no, I'm fine." She would
love to have someone drive her around and tell her the
history of the area. But not Archibald. She was certain
that the more she saw of him, the more he'd think he
had an in with her. And the more she thought his story
about the friend arriving at the airport might have been
just that—a story.

"Are you sure? You could save your money. You
know your dad and I were good friends."

And that's what made her more than suspicious. That
it wasn't just a chance meeting between her and him,
but that he'd also befriended her father. Here she came
along, and he was trying to charm her next.

"So you and my father were good friends?" she asked.

Archibald must not have known how much that
would put her off. Because of her dad's drinking, she
and he had never gotten along well. And now that she
knew about his lying to her about her grandmother—
not to mention that he'd said Grant and his kin were
human—she liked her dad even less. If he'd still been
alive, she would have told him straight to his face what
she thought of him.

Part of the problem was that he had been very much
an alpha like she was, so they'd butted heads over the
years. Sarah Playfair, her mother, had been a beta en-
abler. But what could she have done? Wolves stayed
together forever.

She realized then that Archibald was talking about her father as if he was the greatest thing since the invention of mint chocolate chip ice cream. Apparently, he'd taken her dad fishing, hiking, and running as wolves—the last said in a "for her hearing only" way. So it did sound like he'd really been close to her dad. Better him than her.

She didn't care what Archibald had enjoyed doing with her dad. She was curious whether her father had ever talked to Archibald about her. Not that she cared what he'd say, but if Archibald had known about her, had he thought her unimportant in the scheme of things until her father died?

She ordered fish and chips and water, and realized Archibald hadn't noticed that she wasn't really listening to what he said. He just continued on, as if he would get on her good side for being such a good friend of her father's. That would be the day.

"Did my father talk about me?" she asked, feigning interest.

A shadow of concern appeared in Archibald's expression, but then he quickly smiled and said, "Aye, he said you were a bonny lass."

Either her father had lied, although she doubted he'd make the effort, or Archibald had. "So he told you how much I loved horses, then?"

She had never been near horses. But she wanted to catch him in his lies.

"Aye, I recall he mentioned something of your love of horses," Archibald said, looking a little uneasy.

She loved making him squirm. She'd had to deal so much with her father's deceitfulness that she couldn't abide it in others. And didn't need to.

"Did he tell you how proud he was when I earned my degree in mathematics?"

"Oh, aye. He said he wished he had your head for numbers and wished you'd visit while he was here so he could determine the discrepancies in the accounts at Farraige Castle."

She frowned. Her father had hated that she was earning a degree in mathematics, hated that the genes that had made her ancestors so brilliant in the field had skipped him. Was Archibald making up the rest? Or had her father wanted to prove something was wrong with the accounts just to antagonize Grant?

Her phone rang in her purse, startling her. By the time she answered it, the phone had stopped ringing.

Looking at the caller ID, she was a little surprised to see it had been Grant. Hadn't he wanted her gone? He should be happy and leave her well enough alone.

She called him back, noticing that Archibald was watching her intently. She suspected he wouldn't be happy that Grant was checking up on her, or that she would immediately call him back.

"Hello, Grant. It's me, Colleen," she said in her most businesslike tone.

"Where the hell are you?"

As usual, he was abrupt, to the point, and not pretending in the least that he was interested in her.

She smiled at his brusque tone. Why in the world did it appeal so much to her?

Chapter 11

GRANT COULDN'T BELIEVE HOW DAMNED POSSESSIVE he felt about Colleen. Maybe it was guilt over being the one to tell her about her grandmother. He hadn't handled the matter carefully enough.

The only good news was that the lass hadn't packed her bags and left with them.

Both Lachlan and Enrick looked on, waiting to hear what Grant had learned about the lass as he tried to come up with something gentler to say to her over the phone, despite his anger and concern about her leaving without a word to him or anyone else.

When Colleen didn't tell him where she was, he thought he might have upset her even more with his gruff, blunt tone. He couldn't help it. He'd been frantic to learn where she had gone once he realized she wasn't in the area. And he'd called several times, unable to reach her. Now that he had her on the phone, he wanted to know where the bloody hell she was.

But with Colleen, he had to temper his approach a bit, he realized.

"Sorry, lass. I've had men searching for you all over the place, fearing you'd had a wreck."

"Oh," she said coolly. "I'm at Kelton's Pub."

"Kelton's Pub?" He cursed under his breath. How had she managed to drive that far? "Are you lost? Forget it. I'm coming to get you."

"No. I'm fine," she said, sounding determined to do this her way.

She had every right to, he knew, yet he didn't want to worry about her even if he had nothing to concern himself with.

"How did she get there?" Enrick asked.

"Stay in the area," Grant said to Colleen, ignoring his brother. He could only deal with one conversation at a time. "I'll meet you at the pub in two hours."

"Forget it, Grant. I'll get a room at a local bed and breakfast."

He ground his teeth. He didn't like the scenario, but as long as she was fine, he really had no say in what she did or didn't do. Maybe she'd feel better when she returned home.

"Are you sure you don't want to stay with me?" Archibald asked Colleen in the background.

As soon as Grant heard Archibald speaking with her, he saw red.

The bastard was there? With Colleen? At the same pub? It was a date? What the hell was the deal with a bed and breakfast? *Damnation*.

Or maybe it hadn't been a date and she had gotten in touch with Archibald so that she could air her gripes about Grant and his clan. Or cry on his shoulder about her grandmother.

If she needed to talk to anyone, it would be Grant. He knew her grandmother. Not that bastard.

"I'm coming. Don't leave," Grant said to her, his voice a pack leader's command. Not that he had any business ordering her around, but he wasn't going to let Archibald have his way in this. He hung up on her before she could tell him no again and headed for his car.

"Do you want me to come with you?" Enrick asked, brow furrowed.

"I want you to take care of things here. Lachlan, you come with me. Archibald's with her at Kelton's Pub."

"The same place he used to take her father," Enrick said. "Bloody hell. That bastard will stop at nothing to win her over."

"My thoughts exactly." Grant just hoped she wasn't drinking to take away the sting of what she'd learned about her grandmother. He could see the man trying to take advantage of her vulnerability.

And he could see Archibald hugging her, consoling her, trying to kiss her. That had Grant growling again.

He and Lachlan climbed into his car and took off. Grant took several deep, calming breaths in an attempt to curb his temper. He was ready to pummel Archibald, because he was certain the man played to Colleen's sympathies. She needed someone like Grant to talk to her, someone who would be honest with her and not weave a fairy tale to win her over.

"What are we going to do?" Lachlan asked. "She's a grown woman and American, and doesn't have to listen to anything you have to say. She's not one of our clan members, not of our pack. She can do whatever she wants."

"I'll bring the lass home. I want you to drive her car back to the castle. She doesn't know the roads and most likely isn't used to driving on the correct side of the road, so it would be better if she didn't drive at night. Tomorrow, I want her rental car returned to the airport.

She shouldn't be paying for the cost of it when she can use my car anytime she wants."

Lachlan chuckled.

"What?" Grant said, annoyed.

"If you don't want her here, why are you making her depend on you for transportation? When have you ever let anyone borrow your car willingly?" Before Grant could comment, his brother added, "Oh, I see. You don't intend to let her drive it whenever she is of a mind to leave. Or you'll insist you or one of us goes with her. Which brings me back to my original question. Why do you now want the lass confined to the castle? Or is it that you think that will make her feel restricted, and she'll want to leave?"

"I would think the answer obvious. If she stays, and it appears she is, we don't want her roaming the country-side when Archibald has set his sights on her."

"So he invited her to stay the night with him," Lachlan said.

"Aye. At least, she had the good sense to say no. But if he pressures her…"

"Like if she starts drinking at the pub…"

Grant glanced at his brother.

Lachlan shrugged. "He can be persuasive, like he was with her father."

"Who was prone to drinking." Grant rubbed his chin. "The lass couldn't hold her liquor the other night. I don't believe she's anything like her father."

"It doesn't mean she won't drink to make herself feel better if we've upset her."

"Which is another reason we have to rescue the lass," Grant said.

Lachlan chuckled again. "I don't know, but somehow

it seems the scenario has turned upside down, from your wanting her gone to wanting her back. Didn't Ian warn us about this? What exactly did happen between the two of you that upset her?"

The issue with her grandmother. But he didn't want to discuss it with his brother.

"Enrick said one of our dogs got loose from the kennel last night. He suspected he entered through the wolf door in the kitchen. Although he wondered if Colleen had encouraged Hercules to come to her room. He smelled beef on the dog's breath," Lachlan said when Grant didn't answer his other question.

Grant frowned. "Besides encouraging the dog to want to stay with her, nothing bad happened, I take it, or I would have heard of it."

"You were preoccupied with the lass's whereabouts. But no, he is fine."

"Where was he?"

"Sleeping beside the lady's chamber door as if he was guarding it or wanted in. I had a real time convincing him to come with me."

Had the lass taken steak treats to bed with her? Grant shook his head.

"So you didn't say before, but how were the sleeping arrangements last night?" Lachlan asked.

Grant had no intention of telling his brother about the noisy pipes scaring the lass. "Just fine."

"Which is why you slept so late this morning when you never sleep until noon. The lass looked exhausted, dark circles under her eyes, and I suspect she didn't get a whole lot of sleep either. What were the two of you doing last night?"

"Sleeping," Grant said in a much too aggressive manner. His brother would know the truth of the matter—Grant only slept that late if he had been up half the night or he was ill.

He *would* have been sleeping if the lass and then Maynard hadn't woken him.

"Tell me the truth. Do you think she'll return to Farraige Castle with us? Or do you think she'll stay the night in the village?" Lachlan asked.

The truth was, as much as Grant wanted to return her to the castle, he had no idea what he would do if she wouldn't go along with the idea. Especially if she took Archibald up on his offer and agreed to stay with *him*.

~~~

Colleen wasn't sure what to do. Archibald was still trying to convince her to go with him, even more so now that Grant was on his way.

She finished a lovely meal and sipped on her water, still trying to decide. She did like the idea that she could follow Grant home and not worry about losing her way in the dark. She also had the notion that he might be changing his tune about her residing at the castle. But maybe—just maybe—he would even be better behaved if she stayed the night here. She certainly didn't want him or his people to believe that he could growl and snarl and dictate what she would or would not do. And that she'd go along with it. Even if he asked very nicely and she agreed to return with him, the situation would appear as though he was in charge and she would meekly acquiesce.

That decided it. She was staying. She reached for her purse to settle her bill, but Archibald quickly paid for it.

"You didn't have to," she said, "but thanks so much."

"I was more than happy to treat you to a meal. Now about your accommodations…" he said.

"I'll be more comfortable at a place of my own."

"Which is why you are here and not at your own castle," Archibald said, his tone challenging, irritated, perhaps a hint of his true nature coming through? She must have looked a little wary as he quickly added, "But all much appreciated as I had your lovely company."

"Thanks." She smiled a fake smile. "Yes, well, I have to go to ensure I can find a place that has a room before it gets too late." The pickings looked slim: small village, one small inn, and just a couple of B and Bs. She hoped that someplace was available, or she wouldn't have any choice *but* to return to the castle.

She rose from her seat and said, "Thanks again for dinner. It was nice seeing you."

"Do you want me to come with you? In case you don't find an available room?" Archibald asked, hurrying to rise from his chair.

"No, it's okay. I'll be fine." She left him then, before he got ideas that she should kiss him good night because he had bought her a meal.

"Call me," he called after her, "if you have any trouble."

"Okay," she said, not intending to, and she got out the door and away from him as quickly as she could. She'd assumed since she'd driven for a couple of hours before she stopped, that Grant would take just as long.

Or maybe not, because she had driven slower, unsure about the roads or where she was going. She glanced at a clock tower. And couldn't believe it. She'd spent a whole hour and half at the pub? Grant could be here in half an hour or sooner!

She had to hurry.

When she reached the first home turned into a B and B, she found it had no vacancy and had been booked through the end of the month. Disheartened, she feared she'd find the same at the other B and B. Maybe she'd have better luck at the inn.

The next place was another two-story gray stone home converted into a B and B with a pretty yard surrounded by a low, gray stone wall. When she walked inside, a dark-haired lady smiled. "Are you Mrs. Jones?"

"Um, no. I don't have a reservation. I wondered if I could get a room for the night."

"She has a *whole* castle to sleep in," Grant said, stalking into the lobby, his voice dark and threatening.

Colleen whipped around and gaped at him. "How did you know I was here?"

"Small village. I saw your car parked out front." He towered over her, scowling, and then turned his attention to the owner of the B and B. "You didn't have a room, did you?"

Colleen wanted to laugh. How could he make a question sound so much like an order that the B and B owner had better *not* have a room?

"No, of course not," the brunette said, frowning.

Colleen swore that if the woman did have accommodations for her, she would have quickly changed her mind once she caught sight of Grant and his growly composure.

"I haven't seen you in forever, Grant MacQuarrie," the woman said, her whole persona changing, becoming coyer.

Colleen wondered if he were to ask her if she had a room available for *him*, would she offer one right up? Her own, most likely. And Colleen had no idea why she was even thinking such thoughts. But worse, she wondered if the Highlander had stood on top of a hill in the glen and kissed the B and B owner like he had kissed Colleen.

"I've been busy managing the lass's castle," he said, casting another look in Colleen's direction, an attempt at being very businesslike, similar to how she would think a manager of said castle would behave, and not like some growly wolf-pack leader. "Colleen Playfair, meet Lily Cameron. Lily, Colleen is the new owner of Farraige Castle."

The woman gaped a little at Colleen, probably wondering why she would need to sleep at a B and B when she had the run of the castle. Which, because of Grant's iron rule, Colleen didn't. But she would keep working on it until she left for America.

"But you reserved—" the woman said.

Grant cut her a glare, and the woman quickly clamped her mouth shut.

Colleen wondered what *that* was all about.

"Are you ready for me to drive you home?" Grant said to Colleen. Only this time he tried to put on the charm.

She hated how much it worked. She knew he wasn't being sincere in the least, just like she now suspected that Archibald wasn't, either. Yet when Grant's eyes locked on hers, damn if she didn't feel all tingly and warm, and as much as she hated her traitorous body for it, her face flushed.

Men did not affect her in such a way. Not normally.

Despite his wearing pants and a shirt and boots, she still
saw him in the other way—kilted, half-naked, unshaved,
and sexier than any man she'd ever met up close. Not to
mention that she'd seen him wholly naked a number of
times. He was just too hot for her own good.

"All right. I'll follow you." She hated to concede de-
feat, but she didn't know why he'd say he would drive
her home. They had their own cars.

"If you're ever in the village," the woman said, and
Colleen turned to see that Lily had directed the comment
at Grant, "drop by and see me." She smiled brilliantly.

Colleen should have just walked out the door, showing no interest at all, but she couldn't help herself. She
wanted to know how Grant would handle the situation.
She suspected they had been lovers or had a one-night
stand or something. Which was perfectly acceptable for
a wolf who was not mated, but she hated that it still
bothered her.

"You know I will," Grant said, but from the tone of
his voice, Colleen knew he meant just the opposite.

She thought Lily tried to hide her disappointment
behind a fake smile. "You do that." The inference was
that she wasn't holding her breath.

Grant motioned to the doorway, then hurried to open
the door for Colleen.

"Just so you know, Grant MacQuarrie," Colleen said
as they headed outside and he shut the door, "I'm only
following you home because no rooms were available
here tonight. You're not—" She paused when she saw
Lachlan leaning against her rental car, arms folded. She
looked at Grant.

"Lachlan will drive your car. We need to talk."

She realized then how much he'd outmaneuvered her. And how things had flip-flopped between them. She wasn't sure how she felt about it. She respected Grant for being clever enough to come up with the plan at a moment's notice, and she gave him credit for his determination. And she kind of liked the fact that he wanted her home.

"Fine," she said, only because she didn't want to drive at night on unfamiliar roads, and truly, she was tired after the sleepless night she'd had. Not to mention the fight she'd had with the dog in her bed. He had taken up a goodly sum of the mattress, and she hadn't been about to share it with him.

She had the nagging suspicion that someone had sneaked him into her room while she had visited Grant in the White Room. How else would the dog have gotten in there? True, she had left the door to Grant's chamber slightly ajar, but she'd seen no sign of the dogs before she'd retired for the evening so she suspected they were kept in a kennel at night.

Fully expecting Grant to chastise her for driving off across Scotland without his permission—that would be the day—she was surprised on the drive back to Farraige Castle when he said instead, "Did you take some steak bits to bed with you?"

"What?"

"Enrick said Hercules slept outside your chamber last night."

So he thought she had enticed the dog to come to her room with meat treats.

She gave him an annoyed look. "Better there than in my bed," she said, letting him know someone had been up to tricks last night.

He glanced at her. "In your bed?"

"Yes. After we said good night, I discovered Hercules smack-dab in the center of the mattress. Despite the bed being big, the dog is huge. Believe me, moving him was no easy task."

"That's why Enrick smelled a hint of beef on him."

"What? Did you think I enticed the hound to my room and posted him as a guard dog?"

Grant smiled.

"Well, I didn't. Who let him out of the kennel and into my room?"

Grant's smile faded.

Apparently, he hadn't assumed anyone had done so on purpose.

"I'm sure someone neglected to lock him in the kennel last night," Grant said, though he didn't sound at all sure of it. "So you enticed him out of bed with the bits of meat?"

"Have you ever tried to coax a sleeping Irish wolfhound off *your* bed? He wouldn't even raise his head off *my* pillow to look at me. When coaxing and pleading with him didn't work—as an alpha wolf, you should never have to stoop that low to a dog—I pulled at his collar, pushed him, and called to him again. He wouldn't budge. He reminds me of a Highlander I know, come to think of it."

Grant again smiled.

"Earlier in the day, I'd found some bits of meat left over from the meal to train the dogs with. But last night, I had to go all the way down to the kitchen to get the beef. It was all I could find that wasn't frozen, and I wasn't defrosting something else and spending my whole night in the kitchen because I had a monster dog in my bed. Then I had to deal with your cook. Then with you. And then I had to carry the treats all the way back to the chamber. When the dog smelled the beef, he stirred and sat up, and I had his attention."

"I'll make sure he's kenneled tonight and doesn't bother you, lass."

"Who was responsible?"

"A lad. I will talk to him."

Okay, so she knew it was Grant's pack and she had no say in it, but her bed and her sleep were affected last night. She had every intention of visiting the kennels when the hounds were put up for the night and learning the truth for herself.

"Concerning another matter," Grant said, his voice sounding authoritative, and she stiffened a little, ready to fight the next battle. "I'll have one of the men take your car back to the rental place, and you can use mine any time you like. Or one of us will drive you where you'd like to go."

She snapped her gaping mouth shut.

"There's no sense in you paying all that rent when you can use one of the cars at the keep," he continued.

She stared at him. What happened to wanting her out of the castle?

When she didn't respond, he said, "All you have to do is ask."

"This doesn't all have to do with Archibald, does it?" She highly suspected it did.

"Not *all* to do with him. Why waste money on a rental when there's no need?"

She'd planned on buying a used car to drive while

she stayed here for the year. But now he was conceding that she was staying here for all that time? She couldn't believe it. Changing tactics? Or did he genuinely not mind that she was here to stay for the year?

"You weren't really worried I had a car wreck, were you?" she asked, still surprised that Grant had come to fetch her. He had no way of knowing she'd been with Archibald at the pub before the man had spoken.

"Aye." But Grant didn't say anything more than that.

"*Why* were you worried?" She couldn't believe he had changed his mind about her staying.

"You were upset when you left. I worried that in your frame of mind…" He took a deep breath. "I'm sorry you learned about how your grandmother doted on you in the way that you did. Your father shouldn't have stood between the two of you. I believe you would have gotten on famously."

The notion saddened her all over again. She hated her father for having taken that away from her.

"Thank you. I…wish that I had not listened to him." Then not wanting to dwell on the past, she had to broach the subject no manager wanted to hear about. "First thing in the morning, I want to see the financial records for my properties."

She didn't believe her father had found anything wrong with the books. Archibald was probably just trying to cause trouble between her and Grant.

"As you wish," Grant said, and she thought he sounded just a tad concerned.

Chapter 12

"SHE WANTS TO SEE THE FINANCIAL SPREADSHEETS," Grant told Enrick in the study when the lass retired to her chamber.

"You look worried," Enrick said.

"Aye. The matter with the thieving cook was dealt with satisfactorily, to our way of thinking. But what if the lass feels we were derelict in our duties for allowing the theft to go on so long?"

"You will convince her we had no knowledge of it and did everything to rectify the situation when we did learn of it. You seem bothered by something else tonight. And Lachlan said you're sending two men to return the lass's rental car. Have you had a change of heart about her staying here?" Enrick asked.

"She can't rent the car for a year."

Enrick smiled. "You do think she'll stay for the entire time."

"We'll have to see what tomorrow brings," Grant said vaguely.

"And what else?" Enrick asked.

"Someone might have sent Hercules to her chamber."

"That's why he was sleeping outside her room?" Enrick asked.

"In her bed."

Enrick frowned. "How did she get him out of her... the beef."

"Aye."

Enrick shook his head. "I'll make inquiries to see if anyone knows how the dog ended up there."

———٨٨٨———

Colleen knew she couldn't do anything sneakily around the castle unless it was the middle of the night and everyone was asleep. Even then, the cook had caught her in the kitchen last night. She would use the rest of the meat to train the dogs. She was not going to have them jumping all over her in the future, if she could help it.

Now, she wanted to see who was taking the dogs to the kennels and putting them to bed. As soon as she reached for the handle to the front door of the keep, a man's voice said, "Kind of chilly for a walk out there tonight."

Lachlan. She turned and smiled at him. "I'll be fine."

"Mind if I join you?"

She paused. "Because you want to or need to?"

His mouth curved up. "Because I want to, of course."

She knew she wouldn't be able to speak to the lad in charge of the dogs without someone else learning of it. "All right."

He opened the door for her, and then they walked outside. She heard the dogs barking to the left of the bailey and assumed the kennels were behind the stables. She headed in that direction.

"Are you checking out the horses?"

"Dogs."

"Ah," Lachlan said.

"How many dogs do you have?"

"Three—two males and a female. They're from one of Ian MacNeill's litters. I must say you handle them nicely."

So he had been watching surreptitiously. Had Grant also? She'd seen the men who were supposed to be working on the seawall stop to observe her. All had worn smiles. "I'm surprised no one has ever tried to train them."

Lachlan didn't say anything. She glanced at him. He smiled.

"You've tried?" she asked, not believing they'd had so little success. She thought the dogs were quite easily trained.

"Aye. They mind Grant best, but they ignore the rest of us, no matter how alpha we are."

She said, "If you ever want me to show you how, just ask."

"I do. Anytime we both have free time."

"It's a deal."

When they reached the kennels, she heard a boy talking to them, "Now, no more leaving the kennels on your own after I've put you to bed, mind you."

Had the lad seen her coming and was putting on a show for her?

"Laird Grant already gave me a talking-to, and I don't need him scolding me any further." The teen was waving his finger at Hercules, the dog thumping his tail on the ground as he sat in his run looking out the barred door. The boy was about fifteen, she thought, with curly red hair and a slight build.

Colleen cleared her throat and the lad jumped back, stumbling and falling. She realized then that he hadn't known they were coming. He must have been speaking so intently to the dogs that he hadn't heard their approaching footfalls.

"I am Colleen Playfair, and you are?"

"The kennel boy, my lady," the lad replied.

"Your name?"

"Frederick, my lady."

"Well, Frederick, are all the dogs tucked in?"

"Oh, aye, my lady. They shouldn't give you any trouble tonight." Frederick glanced at Lachlan.

Lachlan nodded.

"Do you know how Hercules got into the keep last night?" she asked, watching the teen's reactions.

"Through the wolf door. Had to be. No other way. But how he managed to get out of the kennel, that's another story," Frederick said, jamming his hands in his pockets.

"Are you certain you locked him up tight?"

"We don't lock them up, my lady. I mean, as you can see, their runs have latches on them. None of them has ever found a way to unlatch them."

"Someone must have let Hercules out," she said, suspecting that was the case unless the boy really had neglected to lock him up.

Frederick paled and looked at Lachlan as if he would defend his honor.

"She's not saying you let the dog out," Lachlan said in a reassuring way.

"No. Lachlan's right. I just wondered how he got into my bed, if you're certain he was in here last night and the latch was secure."

The boy's eyes widened.

Lachlan frowned. "Aye, how the devil *did* he get into your chamber? Sleeping outside the door is one thing, but I had not considered someone had opened your door and let him in."

Lachlan sounded so angry she was surprised. She didn't want to tell him she had left Grant's door ajar when she went to speak to him about the scary noises in his chamber. On the other hand, she didn't want Lachlan to think someone had entered her room when she was sleeping.

"Grant's chamber door was ajar. Mine was open to his chamber," she said.

Lachlan looked skeptical. "I now have the duty to see that the kennels are secure every night just because of what happened last evening."

He didn't sound perturbed about it, for which she was glad. She wanted to tell him it wasn't necessary, but she was certain Grant had given the order, and she didn't want to interfere with his pack business.

"Good to meet you, Frederick. I would love to show you how to train them after I deal with another matter," she said, thinking she needed to get started on the financial reports.

"Oh, aye, I'd love that. They can be a handful at times. I'd like to be able to show them who's boss."

She smiled at that, knowing just the feeling. Except in her case, it didn't have anything to do with dogs, but rather one brawny Highlander. "Then tomorrow, when I'm through with this other business, I'll come and see you."

The boy beamed and she was glad he didn't seem to be at fault for the dog being let loose. Yet she didn't entirely trust him. He could have been nervous because he felt responsible for the dogs and one got loose, but what if he was anxious because he *had* left the dog in Grant's chamber? She wanted to show him in her own way that there were no hard feelings.

She and Lachlan returned to the keep, but as soon as they did, Grant headed straight for her. He didn't look happy. Now what?

"She wanted to see the dogs in the kennel," Lachlan said, as if defending her for talking to the boy.

"Can we speak in private?" Grant asked her, more of a command than a question.

She folded her arms. "No. Say what you have on your mind."

Grant looked at Lachlan, who grinned and said good night to Colleen, then quickly left the foyer. So Grant got his way anyway.

"I told you I'd speak with the lad," Grant said.

"Yes, you did. I wished to speak with him, too."

"He didn't let the dog out of the kennel," Grant said gruffly, his stern gaze challenging her to disagree with him.

"Maybe not." But she'd still investigate further on her own to determine the truth of the matter. Just because she was curious.

"He lost his mother a year ago. The dogs have helped him to come to grips with his loss."

Stunned, Colleen didn't say anything.

"He's made mistakes handling the dogs in the past. Nothing that would have harmed them, but they were just a little beyond his control. He begged me to let him continue to be their keeper, though I have a man who actually is the one who serves that purpose. But we're letting the lad be in charge as much as possible to aid him in his grief."

Colleen nodded. "I offered to help him with training the dogs." She felt terrible about the boy, but she wasn't upset with him. She only wanted to know how the dog could have gotten out. "I fully intend to work with him tomorrow after we go over the finances." Then she walked off without waiting for Grant to say a word.

And she thought she'd come out on top this time. Why was it that everything seemed to be a battle between the two of them?

Footsteps approached from behind and she looked over her shoulder to see Grant following her, his gaze steady on hers. "Did you need to talk to me about something further?" she asked.

His lips parted—his so-kissable manly lips—as if he wanted to say something more to her, but then he just stared at her as if he wasn't sure what to say or do.

"About the…" He paused.

The brawny, sword-wielding, defiant Highlander was tongue-tied? Because of her?

"Yes?"

"About the kiss…"

She waited, though the silence between them was killing her. Was he going to tell her it was a mistake? "Yes?"

He shook his head. "Have a good night."

But he didn't turn and walk away. He was still staring at her, and she did what she should never have done. For a second time, she drew close, took hold of his shoulders, and gave him a kiss, only this time on the…cheek.

His mouth curved up wickedly, his eyes showing the same heated expression, right before he slipped his arms around her and pulled her tight against his body—his already aroused body—and kissed her. Hot, hard, in charge, possessive, filled with want and need and so much more. Then he broke free before she was ready to let go of him or the sensation of his sexy, masculine lips against her mouth. He bowed his head, then turned and left her standing there. Bewildered. A little shaken. A lot hot.

She just stared after his retreating backside and wondered if that was a sign that she'd lost the battle to keep her distance, or he had. What exactly had just happened between them? Again.

Thoroughly rattled, she couldn't go to bed now without thinking of him—his lips pressed against hers, or his arousal pressing against her belly. Still wondering why Grant had kissed her, she retired to her chamber.

Just like when she'd left her rural home to stay in a city and had to get used to the city noises—sirens, car traffic, dogs barking—she knew she'd eventually get used to the noise in the pipes as they gurgled and groaned and creaked. At least tonight she knew she wouldn't have a furry, long-legged bed companion. No one would pull that stunt again. Not with Grant and his brothers aware of it.

So what would be next? That led her to half wishing the wolf of a Highlander would join her in bed this time. She knew she wouldn't want to coax *him* out of her bed.

She groaned at the thought. She was supposed to be the owner and, as such, *not* making any attempts to seduce her manager. Wouldn't that be considered sexual harassment on the job?

Grant was grabbing a whisky in the study when his brothers walked in and joined him. "I thought you were going to bed, Lachlan," Grant said.

"Enrick caught me and asked if I wanted to have a drink before I retired for the night. I assumed he meant we were having a talk with you."

Grant nodded.

"So," Enrick said, "has anyone been assigned to watch the lass's room tonight?"

"For what purpose?" Grant asked, then finished off his whisky.

Enrick poured himself and Lachlan some. "To ensure the lass's sleep isn't bothered."

"There should be no need for that." Grant poured himself another drink. "Once we were made aware that the dog had not been locked up as he should have been, we knew someone had to have led him to her room. The word should have spread to let everyone know the lass is staying and no one should give her any trouble."

"I'm surprised the lass didn't shriek in distress when Hercules jumped in bed with her," Enrick said. "Lachlan said she had left the chamber door ajar."

"It doesn't matter what the circumstances were," Grant said, not about to mention that she had come to see him in the White Room, and that must have been when the dog was let into her room, "as long as no one does anything else to attempt to unsettle the lass."

The brothers smiled.

Enrick said, "So you truly have had a change of heart concerning her."

"She may not be as much like her father as we first worried. But time will tell," Grant said.

"How was your sleep last night?" Enrick asked.

Grant gave him a look to not go there. "Are the men nearly finished with painting the rooms next to mine?"

"The one, aye," Lachlan said. "The other should be finished tomorrow. Paint fumes will linger a bit longer."

"Tell them I want a rush on it."

"You're moving in there?" Enrick asked.

"Why not see if the lass would agree to move into the newly painted chambers?" Lachlan asked.

"Just the thought I had." Grant felt as though he'd been dethroned once he lost the right to sleep in his own chamber.

Worse, he hated how anxious he felt about her checking over the books tomorrow.

As to the kiss? He had wanted to apologize to her for kissing her on the hilltop. But when she had kissed him on the cheek in such a benign way? *Bloody hell.* He couldn't let her think that that was acceptable, either.

What had he been thinking? How much he wanted to kiss her again and see if it was just as hot as the first time. And it was, which led him to want a longer kiss, and a hell of a lot more. Putting on the brakes had been harder than he ever had imagined it could be.

And that was the first sign he was truly losing the battle against the lass—in all manner of ways.

Chapter 13

EARLY THE NEXT MORNING, COLLEEN WAS EAGER TO peruse the estate's finances, and she seemed to be trying to keep their relationship more businesslike. She was trying to keep from looking at Grant—like a woman who was afraid to show any interest in a man. Not lowering her eyes in a come-hither way, but more indicating that she couldn't deal with this right now. She was cheery, both during breakfast and after as she'd followed him to the office, so she hadn't seemed upset about the kissing, but she was attempting to avoid the issue.

And he should have, too. So why did he keep trying to catch her eye, wanting something more? A word that something else was going on between them? That this wasn't some imagined and passing fancy?

Trying to get his mind on the subject at hand, Grant looked down at Colleen seated at the desk, appearing totally enraptured with the graphs. He knew her ancestors were brilliant mathematicians, but that didn't mean the gene would always be carried down from generation to generation. Her father had taken issue with a number of expenses—just to give Grant a hard time—but in the end he couldn't find fault with the way Grant had managed the properties.

Since that time, they'd had the theft in the kitchen.

So when he pulled up the information on his computer, he was surprised to see Colleen set up statistical graphs—one of her ancestors had invented them, sure, but—

She very studiously created them for a vast number of fiscal years, for everything from food supplies to maintenance on the buildings. He watched her, fascinated at how quickly she set them up, as if she did this on a regular basis.

"Like graphs, eh?" he asked, stating the obvious.

She smiled. "My favorite kind of math. Pictorial, great for seeing trends, much easier on the eyes than looking at tons of numbers."

"Hmm," he said. He had to admit she was right.

She continued to work on it while he watched, half trying to sense what she felt as she looked over the charts, while hoping the accounts would meet her expectations.

She finally looked back at him as he watched over her shoulder. "You don't have to stay here. It'll probably take me a couple of days to make up all the charts and go over them. Maybe longer."

"Aye, then, lass. If you need anything else, just call me."

"I will. Thanks, Grant."

He hesitated to leave. He realized just how unlike her father she was. Not bombastic, take charge—even if she did kick him out of his bedchamber—not cold and calculating. He wondered how she'd act when she found the discrepancies in the foodstuffs, though. His stomach clenched a little at the notion.

He left then, knowing he had a busy day ahead of him, seeing to his people's needs, ensuring everything ran smoothly, and yet, all he could think of was what Colleen might say about the finances.

Later that afternoon, everyone gathered for the meal, except Colleen. Maybe the time had slipped away from her.

Grant said to Darby, "Will you fetch the lass? Let her know the meal is served."

Darby let out his breath. "Aye, I will. Do you want me to spy on her when I do it? See how she's feeling concerning the finances?"

Grant shook his head. "We'll know soon enough."

"She's not much like her father," Enrick said. "I mean about the charts and graphs. He just took exception to the numbers when he didn't like them, even though there was nothing wrong with them."

"Aye."

Everyone waited to eat until Grant gave the word.

Sitting on the other side of Enrick, Lachlan said, "Did she seem upset about anything when she was looking over the graphs?"

"Nay. She was mainly just charting the figures way back as far as she could go."

"What will that tell her? The world has changed so much since the early days when the castle was first built," Enrick said. "Not even her father cared about that. He only wanted to see the financial income and expenses for the two years before he inherited the properties."

"Aye. She seemed enthralled with developing the charts, seeing the history. We have nothing to worry about." Grant hoped.

Darby entered the great hall without the lass, but Grant assumed she was coming. Darby shook his head.

"Eat," Grant said to his people. They had work to get back to.

Darby joined him and leaned over to whisper, "She isn't in your study."

Grant frowned. "What?"

"Aye. She had turned off the monitor, and she's still got the files up, but she wasn't there."

"The bathroom?"

"I checked. Nay."

Where the hell was she? Maybe…taking a nap? "Did you check the lady's chamber?"

"Aye. She was not there, either."

If she had forgotten about the time, he hated for her to miss the meal, but on the other hand, he didn't want anyone else to have to miss theirs to search for her when there was no real need.

He pulled out his cell phone and called her. No answer.

His first thought was the seawall and her misadventure there. Then her running off to the village more than two hours away. Now what? He had to remind himself that she could do what she liked with her time. She was not a member of his pack.

Then he realized his men had returned her rental car, and she hadn't asked for the keys to his car. She had to be on the property.

"Okay, thanks, Darby. Enjoy your meal."

Enrick buttered a slice of bread. "So where do you think she is?"

Hell if Grant knew. "I have no idea."

But he was determined to find out right after the meal, hating that he wanted to skip lunch to search for her right this very minute. Even so, he ate his chicken, baked potato, and broccoli faster than he'd ever done. He told everyone to finish their meals, not wanting them to think that since he was leaving the table, they also had to. As was usually the case.

"Do you want me to help you locate her?" Enrick asked, spearing another broccoli floret.

"I'll come, too," Lachlan offered, setting his fork on his plate.

Grant glanced at their meals. Both were only halfway finished with their food. "Nay, I'll find her. It shouldn't be that hard."

That's what he thought. He first went to the gardens, thinking maybe she'd stretched her legs out there, taking a break from the financial reports. Then he checked by the seawall, thinking she might be watching the waves break over the jagged rocks below, having forgotten all about the meal.

But she wasn't in either location. That had him worried. Where was she?

—␣␣—

Colleen loved dogs. She'd felt bad that she was still so wrapped up in the financial reports that she hadn't seen Frederick yet. She headed out there to see if she could give him a couple of tips before she returned to her work.

She loved analyzing charts and seeing trends, even as far back as in the beginning, and could get wrapped up in them for hours. Some of the records that far back were spotty, but she was amused to see that one of her early ancestors, a countess, had a cat. Unusual for those times when cats just roamed freely to catch mice and rats and weren't considered pets. But there was a detailed description of all the expenses the cat had incurred, including the cost of taking the cat on trips. Fascinating.

Some could only see the dollars and cents behind the math. She liked to see the human or, in their case, the *lupus garou* side of the expenditures and income.

She soon reached the kennels, which were fashioned in the same manner as the castle—gray stone with miniature towers gracing each corner. She entered and called out, "Frederick?"

No one was about. She hadn't seen anyone anywhere, in fact. *The meal*. She hadn't meant to get so sidetracked that she'd forgotten about the meal. She was used to eating when she was hungry, not with a pack and on a schedule. She sighed, not wanting to make a big scene by entering the great hall so late.

One of the dogs barked from a fenced-in yard, and she smiled as she headed for the dogs' yard. If she got hungry later, she could just raid the kitchen, now with Maynard's approval. She would just pay better attention to the time when it came to dinner.

She stalked toward their gate, noting that since the first feast—served with medieval flair—the wolfhounds had not been in attendance at the meals.

They woofed and jumped at the fence. "Down, boys, girl."

She thought briefly of taking them to lunch, as if they had been forgotten for the last couple of meals and she was doing her duty by bringing them to join the pack.

Before she opened the gate, her phone rang and she glanced at the caller ID. She closed her eyes briefly. Archibald. She answered it. He was persistent, if nothing else.

"Hi," she said.

"Are you at the kennels?" he asked, a smile in his voice.

If he liked dogs, he couldn't be all bad.

"Yes. Just came out to see them."

"Did you want to get together tonight?"

"No, sorry. Next week sometime?" How many times did she have to tell him she wanted a week at least to get settled in? She wasn't in the mood to date him or anyone else. Then she ran her fingers over her lips where Grant had kissed her last night. And she smiled, then shook her head. He wasn't dating her, either.

"You're killing me, you know?" Archibald said cheerily, not annoyed with her. Which was a good thing or she'd hang up on him.

The dogs were barking and going crazy, wanting to love her. "I've got to go, but we can talk later."

"I'll call you later tonight."

"Tomorrow." She really meant it when she said next week. She guessed she wasn't used to alpha males wanting their way in things. She was so used to her former mates and her cousins being betas that she hadn't realized how hard it was to say no to an alpha and mean no.

"Call you tomorrow."

She pocketed her phone, opened the gate, and shut it behind her. She smiled at the dogs as they excitedly greeted her, backsides wagging along with their tails, their huge heads poking at her, tongues licking, teeth nipping. Okay, so she knew she should be all business, no playing around and make them mind from the beginning, but... She leaned down and gave them each a hug, laughing as they caught strands of her hair and nibbled on them, bumping her, each of them trying to wrest her attention away from the other dogs.

"Did you forget about the meal, lass?" a gruff voice said from the direction of the gate, and she whipped around to see Grant studying her.

"I did. But I'm not all that hungry. I'd forgotten to drop by and show Frederick how to train the dogs, so I came by to give him a few tricks."

"He's at the meal." Grant wore the most elusive smile as he watched the dogs tackle her. "Tell me, is this the way you go about training them? If so, I've been doing a good job of it."

She chuckled. "Oh sure. We're just warming up." She thought he looked a little worried. "Is something the matter?"

He shook his head. But she already knew him well enough to know something was bothering him.

She ventured, "I hope you hadn't worried about me missing the meal."

"We did," he said, coming into the pen. The dogs hurried to greet him, too.

"I'm sorry. I'm not used to eating on a schedule."

"Darby will fetch you in the future."

"He doesn't have—"

"The owner of the castle should eat with the staff," Grant said very seriously, almost sternly, as if she had to abide by the "rules" now that she was here.

She wanted to remind him the staff was *his*, and she didn't belong to his pack. That she was the owner of the castle, but as far as his people went, she hadn't any say in what they did or didn't do—his words. So she didn't need to be anywhere that she didn't want to be. But she bit her tongue.

"Everyone expected to see you at the meal," he said,

watching her while petting two of the dogs. Hercules returned to her side to get more attention.

Then she suspected what had been the matter. *Grant* had expected her to be there, sharing a meal, conversing with him. Did he feel stood up? Tickled at the notion, if that's what this was all about, she stifled a smile. "I'll try to be there next time."

"About the kiss last night…"

She started laughing.

He smiled. "You seem to be avoiding me."

"I think it's better to just stick to business."

"You know there's more going on between us, lass." At least he looked hopeful that there was.

Before she could say anything, footsteps on a cobblestone path headed their way, and they looked to see who was coming but couldn't see whoever it was for the trees.

"Everyone has finished eating. Would you like Maynard to fix you a plate?" Grant asked in a placating way, and she was glad he was off the subject of kissing. Though she suspected that was all because of someone approaching the pen.

"No, really, I'm fine." She didn't want the cook to have to make up a special lunch for her just because she couldn't get to the meal on time.

Frederick came through the trees and smiled to see Grant and her with the dogs. "Have you come to teach me how to handle them?" he asked her, sounding enthusiastic.

"I sure have. Then I have to get back to looking over the ledgers." She thought Grant would leave, but instead, he stayed—to get a lesson or two himself, perhaps. Or maybe he just couldn't believe she could wield a magic wand and make the dogs behave. She pulled out her pen and clicked it. All three dogs ran over to her and sat down on their rumps, tails wagging, eyes focused on hers. She smiled.

"Where are the treats you use to bribe them?" Grant asked, sounding amazed that she didn't offer the dogs anything for their obedience.

"I don't always give them treats. Petting them, hugging them, praising them all work, too—they adore being loved. I used treats to first get them to pay attention. But now, I can alternate with playing with them or other ways to show how much I enjoy being with them."

"Is that just a pen you have in your hand?" Frederick asked, sounding amazed.

"Yes. Just an ordinary pen. Though this one is rather a nice writing pen. But if you'd like, you can have it. Anytime you want to get the dogs' attention, click it, and they'll come running. Eventually, you can just give hand signals and they'll respond to that."

Frederick glanced at Grant as if he wasn't sure if he should do this. Before Grant could tell him he could, Colleen said, "Let's let your laird show us how easy it is."

She swore that Grant paled to a degree. She hadn't meant to put him on the spot—well, maybe a little—but she knew he could do it.

She gave him the pen and he cast her a look that said he would get her back. She grinned.

He clicked the pen, and the dogs looked at him but continued to stay beside her. "Maybe you'll need the treats at first," she said, smiling.

Grant shook his head and folded his arms.

"I'll get them," Frederick offered.

"Right crisper drawer in the fridge, the one closest to the oven," Colleen said.

"Right." He raced off.

"You're good with dogs and kids," Grant said, sounding as though he admired her for it.

And she appreciated that. "Thanks. They naturally sort of gravitate toward me," she said, scratching Hercules's ear.

"Will this really work with them—clicking a pen without giving treats?" he asked, still not sure she knew what she was talking about, as if she had some magical gift with the dogs.

"Sure, and once they're better trained, you won't need the pen, either." Colleen studied Grant's furrowed brow as she petted the dogs. "Are you sure there's nothing you're worried about?"

Chapter 14

COLLEEN HOPED SHE WOULD FIND THE INCONSISTENCIES in the accounts this afternoon and get it out in the open, because she was certain now that something was wrong with them—just from the way everyone was behaving around her.

After training the dogs and having fun showing both Grant and the lad how to do it, Colleen returned to work on the charts and graphs. She was certain from the way Grant had stood over her when she was trying to convert all the data into charts earlier that he was worried about some financial mishap. And then Darby had hovered over her on another occasion, as if he was trying to sense how she was feeling—smelling the air, taking in her scent.

Maynard announced himself, startling her. "A tray, my lady."

She couldn't believe the cook had brought up a tray with a sandwich and chips and hot tea. "Thank you. That was really considerate of you. But you really needn't have. It was my fault I didn't show up for the meal." Though she had to admit she was hungry now.

"Laird MacQuarrie believed you would wilt away if you didn't have something to eat," Maynard said.

She studied him, his gray eyes meeting her gaze. She smiled. She suspected Grant hadn't told Maynard to let her know that. "Well, thanks to you and Laird MacQuarrie."

Maynard didn't leave and she said, "Is there something else? This will be fine for me."

He glanced at the charts on the monitor. "How's it looking?"

Why was he asking? Had Grant put him up to it? She couldn't imagine the cook would have any interest in the financial matters.

"I haven't analyzed the figures yet. It could take days." She was beginning to think something really was wrong with the books. She would have to look more carefully at the figures since she hadn't found any problem yet.

"Aye. Um, his lairdship would like to meet you for a walk in the gardens at five."

She raised a brow.

"He thought you might need a break."

She didn't believe it. "He thought I might forget the time for the meal. Right?"

Maynard grinned. "Aye, that he did, lass. There's no fooling you."

"Thanks, Maynard."

"Aye…well…I'll leave you alone now." But he didn't.

"Bye," she said, and he finally seemed to take the cue. He quickly dipped his head, then left the study.

She was still wondering why Grant had been so concerned she'd missed the meal. Afraid she'd run off? She didn't have her car any longer.

Maybe he was trying to get on her good side in case she found a problem in the accounts.

—∿∿—

Some hours later, someone darkened the doorway, and Colleen turned to see Grant standing in it. "A walk in the garden, lass?"

She realized then it was well after the time she was supposed to meet him. She smiled a little. "Now you know what my obsession is."

"Charts and graphs. You're nothing like your father," Grant said as he escorted her outside to walk in the rose gardens.

It was mild out, a little cooler than earlier in the day when she had worked with the dogs.

"Thank heavens for that," she said.

He looked a little surprised. "I take it you and your father didn't get along well."

"You're right. He had…a drinking problem. He was not a happy drunk when he had too much liquor. But then…" She frowned at Grant, suddenly realizing her father must have been a holy terror to live with here. "Did you know?"

"Aye."

"Oh, I'm so sorry. Was he really awful when he stayed here?"

"Nothing we couldn't handle."

She wondered just how Grant and his kin had handled him. She never had been able to. She observed him for a moment, his dark eyes studying her in return. "You thought I'd be just like him."

"The thought had crossed our minds."

"Well, I'm nothing like him."

"Aye, we learned that quickly enough." He didn't say anything more for a while, then let out his breath in a way that said he wasn't sure how to broach the next topic. "I wanted to ask you a question about another matter having to do with the sleeping arrangements."

His chamber. She almost laughed. She suspected they'd have this discussion every day for a year if she didn't let him back into his own room. When he didn't say anything, she said, "Yes?"

"The adjoining chambers next to mine have a bathroom en suite."

"The rooms that are freshly painted?"

"Aye. Maybe you would prefer staying there and you'd have the same arrangement you have now, except both rooms would be yours to do with as you wish."

She pondered that. By all rights, the lady's chamber was hers. She liked the colors and the way it was decorated. By giving up the chamber, she was signaling that Grant had won the battle. Then again, did it really matter?

Yes. Having him sleep elsewhere signified she owned the castle. Psychologically, she felt moving to the other chambers would make her a guest again. An unwelcome guest, because no one had invited her here.

Was she putting too much significance on things? As long as she was well aware of the position she held, she didn't need a room, throne, crown, or any other symbolism to prove she owned the castle, as much as Grant seemed to need his room to prove he was in charge of his pack.

She swore Grant attempted not to show any hint of emotion—as if she'd say no if he looked too hopeful. "Okay, but I like the lady's chamber's decor and—"

"You can stay in that room if you'd still like," Grant quickly said, as if he still wanted to share the bathroom with her.

"No. I'll take the other adjoining chambers if you'll

have the furniture from the lady's chamber moved to the one next door that has the bathroom attached."

Before she was prepared for his reaction, he gave her a curt nod and looked like it killed him not to shout out with profound exuberance. He glanced around and saw a gardener nearby watching them, which made her think Grant had it mind to kiss her for giving his room back to him but couldn't with one of his people watching. Instead he said, "I'll have it taken care of at once."

Then without another word, he stalked off for the keep. And that signaled the end of their walk together.

Wishing he'd kissed her, just to thank her, though not wanting any of his people to see and get the notion there was more going on than just profound thankfulness, she sighed and continued strolling along the garden path. She enjoyed the chilly sea breeze, hearing the waves crashing down below, and headed to the seawall. She had another half hour or so before the meal was served, and she intended to walk for a while longer.

She hadn't gone to the seawall and looked at the path she'd taken since she'd been dumb enough and drunk enough to traverse it. Curious if it was truly dangerous or if Grant had made more of a fuss than was warranted, she reached the wall and peered over. She noted movement below. Her heart nearly stopped.

Two wolf cubs, maybe around ten years old or so, were close to the breakers striking the rocks below. She yelled at them to return to this side of the seawall immediately, at the same time climbing over it herself to reach them.

"Stop! Come back here at once!" she shouted, not having time to get help in case either of the wolf cubs lost their footing and ended up in the rough sea.

One of them glanced back at her, his eyes widening.

Giving herself a near heart attack, she slipped on the treacherous, moss-covered rocks, trying to reach the wolves. They were much too close to the breakers. One rogue wave could sweep them off their feet, drag them under, and dash them against the rocks.

"Come back here, now!" she shouted, not having time to strip and shift. She wasn't sure what she could do, whether she was in her wolf coat or not, if the wolves fell into the frothing surf. She wondered then if anyone had ever survived such a mistake.

The one wolf began to head back up the slippery path, tail tucked between his legs. With horror, Colleen saw an enormous wave rising up before the other wolf could move out of its path.

Colleen dove for the wolf and grabbed him, just as the wave hit them. The force of the water knocked them both off their feet and sucked them into the sea.

As soon as Grant got the call that someone was in trouble at the cliffs, he took off at a dead run and exited the keep. Several of his clansmen hurried with him to reach the seawall.

Troy, eleven years old and always getting into mischief of one sort or another, howled from beyond the seawall. It was a mourning howl—warning the sea had taken one of his friends.

Cursing, Grant dashed through the garden and saw

Darby sprinting toward him. "The lass and Ollie are in the sea, my laird."

"The lass?" Grant shouted, not slowing down. "What lass?"

"Lady Colleen, my laird," Darby said, keeping pace beside him.

"Why in God's name were they beyond the seawall?" As if Grant and his brothers and so many others hadn't done the same thing when they were younger while exploring the danger over the years.

"It appears the two youngsters were playing beyond the wall. The lady saw them. She yelled for them to return, but they didn't, or at least in Ollie's case, he didn't have time. It was too late. By the time I reached the wall, the lady had grabbed for Ollie, the wave struck, and they were pulled out."

"She…Colleen, was she in human form?"

"Aye."

"Bloody hell."

"What are you going to do?"

Grant vaulted over the stone wall. "Rescue them."

"Somehow I knew you'd say that," Darby said, scrambling to get over it and join him.

Lachlan leaped over the wall in his wolf form right behind them.

"We could all drown over this," Grant warned as he took the path too quickly and slipped and slid on the rocks.

"Aye," Darby said.

Enrick hurried to join them, carrying ropes. Two other men followed.

Colleen choked and coughed as she held on to Ollie

in the choppy water. The waves drew them out, then threatened to toss them back against the rocks.

The water was freezing, though Ollie would be fine in his wolf coat. Colleen would be chilled to the bone and unable to function before long.

Grant quickly tied one of the ropes around his waist, and while the other men held on to the rope, he let a wave take him out. Colleen attempted to swim away from the rocks with Ollie, but the cold was taking a toll on her strength.

Grant swam out to her and grabbed hold of her while she kept a tight grip on Ollie. Grant held her snugly, trying to warm her frigid body with his own, the chill driving deep.

"Pull!" he shouted to the men on the rocks, though he knew he needn't have. The men were already hauling him in as fast as they could, fighting against the strong tug of the currents and his and Colleen's weights. Luckily, Ollie didn't weigh all that much.

When the next wave swept them into the rocks, men grabbed Colleen, while Lachlan seized Ollie by the scruff of his neck and hauled him quickly away from the breakers.

Darby gave Grant a hand.

Colleen coughed and spat up water as Enrick tugged her higher up the rocks.

"Good job, men," Grant said, his teeth chattering from the cold as he made his way up the path after Enrick, thanking God that they'd all reacted quickly enough to save them. "How are Colleen and Ollie?"

Maynard took Ollie from Lachlan and hefted him over the wall. Lachlan leaped over it and shook a spray of water off his fur everywhere.

"Ollie looks fine," Maynard said.

Troy jumped over the wall and poked his nose at Ollie. He nuzzled his face against Troy's.

They hadn't had anyone die on the cliffs in years, so Grant felt he'd been remiss in not reminding the younger members of the pack just how dangerous the rocks could be. Not that such warnings had kept him and his brothers from exploring beyond the seawall.

"Notify their parents," Grant said, following his brother and Colleen into the keep. He had to get into dry clothes himself.

"I'll start a fire in her chamber and in yours. She can have a hot shower to warm her up," Enrick said.

"Aye." Grant would use the room she would move to since it wasn't furnished yet and take his own hot shower. He couldn't believe she'd risked her own neck to save one of his pack members and nearly gotten herself drowned.

"You shouldn't have gone after him, lass," Grant said. He was glad Ollie would be all right, but instead of one drowned child, they could very well have had a drowned woman, too. And more, while trying to rescue them.

Colleen didn't say anything. Too cold, maybe. Too traumatized, possibly.

When they reached his chamber, he grabbed a towel from his bathroom and a dry change of clothes, but shivering, she reached her cold hand out and touched his arm, then said, "Stay here. I'll go next door. I'm moving there anyway."

"Nay, lass," he said, and suddenly he didn't want her to go anywhere. She deserved the room of honor. "The furniture needs to be returned to the other chambers.

You take a hot shower, get into something dry and warm—and rest. I'll check on you in a while."

She nodded and Enrick finished starting the fires for her, then left to start one in the guest chamber for Grant. "I think I lost a good ten years off my life," Enrick said as Grant joined him in the chamber.

Grant heated the water for his shower. "Aye, you and me both. Ask Maynard to get some hot tea and something hot to eat for the lass, will you? I want her to rest after her ordeal. The great hall is too drafty for her to eat in tonight after the chill she's taken."

"Aye, which means she's giving up her room and moving in here?" Enrick asked.

Grant shook his head. "Nay. I am. The lass said she was happy with the room she's in. She stays. I'll move here. That's the least I can do after she nearly drowned herself trying to save one of our kin."

Enrick smiled. "You know, I don't think she would have had to do so for you to change your mind."

"I had every intention of moving her here," Grant said, not wanting his brother to think he was so soft.

Three men knocked on the door. "You said you wished us to move furniture, my laird?"

"Aye, return the furnishings that were here before the painting was done. I have changed my mind about moving the furniture from the lady's chamber," Grant said, still shivering from his dunk in the cold North Sea.

"I'll have Maynard bring you some hot tea, too," Enrick said, smirking, then left Grant to his shower.

Grant had barely dressed when Maynard arrived with a tray in hand, Darby accompanying him, which surprised him even more.

"What's going on?" he asked.

"The lass is taking her meal in her room," Maynard quickly said.

That part Grant understood. Why they had brought *his* meal up here was what he didn't comprehend.

"We thought you might want to be close by in case she is suffering from the ordeal, my laird," Darby said, looking stiff and uncomfortable.

"Is she feeling bad?" Grant asked, shoving his shoes on, concerned about her health.

"If you were a wee lassie half-drowned in the icy water and banged up against the rocks, wouldn't you be?" Darby asked.

Grant conceded his valet was right. "Aye, of course, I'll see to her."

"To eat with her, maybe?" Maynard asked, looking hopeful.

Grant studied them for a moment. "Set the tray on my table. I'll see if she wishes the company first." He couldn't assume she would.

"But you'll stay close at hand if she needs you, aye, my laird?" Darby asked.

"What is this all about?" Grant asked, suspecting his men were up to something more than concern for the lass.

"You should mate her," Darby whispered, as if Colleen might be able to hear him through all the stone walls dividing the rooms.

"What brought this all on?" Grant asked, surprised as hell. Though he suspected his people thought his mating would ensure they never had to worry about the owner of the property deciding to get rid of the pack.

"She saved Ollie," Darby said, as if that said it all.

Maynard nodded emphatically.

"Aye, but that doesn't mean the lass is interested in staying here or mating with me." Or that he wished to mate her. He'd considered it briefly, but the ramifications of this being for a lifetime, since they lived very long lives, and concern that she'd get homesick and want to return to America...

"She hasn't been mated in a really long time," Darby said, as if that should make all the difference in the world.

Grant frowned at him, then folded his arms. "Have you been checking into her background?"

Darby stiffened further. "We had to be certain she would suit."

"You mean, suit me?" Grant was amused, though he couldn't let on.

"Aye, of course, my laird. Not me," Darby said, sounding indignant.

Maynard tried to stifle a chuckle.

Grant attempted to keep a straight face, barely managing. "Well...would she?"

"Would she what?" Darby asked, looking puzzled.

"Suit? Me?"

"Well, she has not been mated in a very long time."

Grant almost laughed. "Was that the only remarkable thing you learned about the lass?" He wasn't about to tell Darby that he had also done some checking up on her once she came into the inheritance. So he knew she'd been mated twice. But was not currently mated. No offspring, and they had seemed to be happy matings. Could she have no children of her own?

"She had two mates," Darby whispered. "Both died

of legitimate causes, no foul play, and she had nothing to do with their deaths."

"You're worried about me." Grant was surprised, amused, and pleased.

"Aye, always, my laird," Darby said. "But I believe you will be safe with her."

"Thank you. I will check on the lass, then." Grant waited for them to leave. He wasn't going to speak with her while Darby and Maynard breathed down his neck.

"Do…you need any help in…well…" Darby glanced at Maynard, who motioned for him to get on with it. "With… courting the lass? We could ensure you had picnic lunches, meals set out in the gardens at a table for two…"

"It's supposed to storm the rest of the week."

"Aye, well, later. Whenever the weather is good. Or we could—"

"Nay, I'm not courting the lass. She is the owner of the castle, nothing more."

"She saved Ollie," Darby reminded him.

"Aye, she was a brave lass to do so, but as I said, it doesn't mean she wishes to join our pack or be mated to me. Off with the both of you now so I can ask if she wishes to dine with me tonight."

"Aye, of course," Darby said, ushering Maynard out of the chamber.

Grant wondered if his brothers knew anything about this as he stepped into the hall and knocked on Colleen's door, half expecting her to say she was too tired to eat with him or anyone else.

Yet he was hoping she might consider dining with him. He thought he might enjoy courting her—but without his people pushing him to do so.

Chapter 15

STILL CHILLED TO THE BONE, COLLEEN SAT BY THE FIRE in her emerald velvet robe, Norse-decorated sheepskin boots, and nothing else, intending to slip into bed afterward. She sipped her hot tea and was about to spoon up some of the fish stew Maynard had so thoughtfully brought up to her when a knock on the door sounded.

"Yes?" she called out. She was exhausted and glad to eat up here and not in front of Grant's clan tonight. Thankfully, she was okay, except for still being chilled and weary.

"It's me, Grant."

A little more than surprised, though she suspected he wanted to ensure she was uninjured, she said, "You can come in."

He opened the door and stood there, taking her in with a sweep of his gaze. "Are you all right?" He was frowning and looked concerned.

"Tired, cold still, but getting warmer. How about you? And Ollie?"

"No need to worry about me. Ollie's fine. Grounded. And so is his friend Troy. But otherwise he is safe and sound, thanks to you. Would you mind too much if I joined you for dinner?"

"Here?" she asked. She wasn't properly dressed to eat with Grant in the bedchamber or anywhere else tonight. And why wouldn't he be eating with his pack?

"Aye, if you don't mind."

She hesitated. He would never guess she was naked under the robe. "I'd like that very much. Come, join me." She thought he meant to share her meal right then and there.

But he said, "I'll be right back."

Before she could consider removing her robe and throwing on some jeans and a sweater, he returned with a tray of food, and she realized Maynard must have also left Grant's meal in his room and Grant wanted company.

"You didn't plan to eat with your people tonight?"

"I wanted to be close by in case you needed anything," he said, sitting down at the table with her. He sounded genuinely apprehensive.

His concern touched her. "I really am fine."

The square oak table in her room seemed even smaller when trying to accommodate Grant's long legs. His knees brushed hers when he sat down and felt wickedly seductive. She was shocked at the touch, but more so when his mouth curved up marginally.

"I want to thank you for rescuing Ollie," he said.

"He needed help. I was the closest one who could reach him," Colleen said matter-of-factly. She would have done it for anyone.

She took a deep breath and exhaled, wanting to discuss another matter. "I've been pondering over some of what you told me earlier about your father's drowning. Do you think my dad was responsible for Robert MacQuarrie's death? And your mother's?" Colleen asked, needing to know the truth.

"I believe Theodore Playfair had the most to gain from my father's death. Or he thought he did. He resented that Neda doted on my brothers and me. And he fought with her over wanting to manage the estates."

"His drinking, I'm sure, contributed to the way my grandmother felt. I imagine that the news didn't go over well with my father," Colleen said, dipping a spoon into the stew.

"Aye. You are right on both accounts. I don't know about my mother. Maybe Theodore felt if Eleanor was gone, my father would be so distraught that he couldn't continue to manage the properties. My father was in bad shape for quite a while. My mother would never have been on the cliffs during a storm or at any other time.

"She had three toddlers to care for. She adored us and was very happy. My father was terribly depressed when she died. The whole clan pulled together to watch out for him. If he had died on the cliffs closer to the time my mother drowned, we might have assumed he did so out of grief. But years later? Nay."

Colleen agreed with Grant's assumption. She watched as he buttered his bread and waited until he'd finished eating the slice to pose another question. "I hate to ask, but was my father around when your dad was so depressed?"

Grant scooped up some of his stew. "Nay. Many believed Theodore was responsible for my mother's death. No one could prove it. But he was not welcome. When my father didn't take his own life shortly after my mother died, Theodore left for America and mated with your mother.

"Theodore returned every so often to ensure his mother left the property to him and didn't give it to my father, I'm certain. Great animosity existed between the two men.

And he hated me and my brothers. When my brothers and I were away at university, my father drowned on a blustery, cold winter's night, just like my mother had many years earlier. Again, no witnesses. It seemed too easy to dismiss as mere coincidence." Grant finished off his meal.

"It wasn't the anniversary of your mother's death or anything?" Colleen guessed, fingering her buttered slice of bread.

"Nay. My father had been talking to me about my brothers and me coming home for the holidays. He was so proud of us. When my father died, I couldn't believe it. Neda called me home, and I took over management of the pack and the estates. And Theodore was still there. He was outraged, so certain that upon my father's death, he would manage the estates. Neda explained to him that my father had trained me and the pack was mine to lead once my father died.

"If Theodore could have gotten away with it, I'm certain he would have killed me for it. Even so, I had my doubts that he could have killed either of my parents—not on his own. He stormed out of the castle and returned to Maryland. He didn't come back until he inherited the castle."

She took a deep breath, hating that her father could have been involved in anything of the sort. "I'm sure he hated that on top of everything, you were a young man."

"Aye."

But Grant hadn't believed he had acted alone. Who else then? "You said Archibald was like his father and grandfather. Uilleam Borthwick murdered yours to try and take over the management of the castle. How was Archibald's father like that?"

"Haldane Borthwick had been visiting Theodore both when my mother died and then years later when my father drowned. Purely by chance? I think not."

She considered the ramifications, surprised Archibald had been associated with her father for so long. She had thought it was only more recent, upon her father's inheriting the castle. A more devious reason for the friendship might exist.

"I'm surprised my grandmother would have allowed Haldane Borthwick to visit if she had any notion he might be as dangerous as Uilleam had been."

Grant finished his hot mug of tea and set it down on the tray. "Neda was away both times. I'm sure they planned it that way. The first time, she was visiting a dying aunt. She was grief-stricken to learn our mother had died and immediately took us under her wing. My father was heartbroken. From what older members of the pack told us later, they thought he'd forsake all food and join his mate. The only thing that brought him out of his anguish was the daily reminder that he had triplet sons who needed his guidance and love, and our pack members did everything to ensure he remained focused on the job until he could work through his grief."

"I'm so sorry about your parents, Grant."

"I thank you, lass. Your grandmother was like a mother to us. My father never took another mate. We dearly loved Neda."

Colleen was certain that had she ever met her grandmother, she would have, too. "My father wasn't here when Neda died, was he?" Colleen asked, fearing the worst.

"Nay. Once I took over and worried that Theodore

and Haldane had caused my father's death, whenever your father returned for a visit, I had guards posted to watch him day and night. Not that he ever knew it. But we were concerned for Neda's safety."

To her way of thinking, Grant and his brothers would have been as much at risk. "What about you and your brothers' welfare?"

"We really weren't concerned about our own safety, but later we learned our pack members watched out for us. They were really proud of having been so sneaky that we didn't even know it." He smiled.

She smiled back and thought how wonderful it was to have an extended family that watched the boys' backs. "I can imagine it wasn't easy trying to keep track of all three of you without one of you having a clue. So what of Haldane? Is he still alive?"

"Another wolf killed him years later. No one knew who killed him for certain, but we suspected one of my father's friends resented Haldane, believing he had murdered Robert and gotten away with it, and so sought revenge."

She pondered that, wondering if that man was still in the pack. "Is the wolf who you suspected of killing him still alive?"

"Aye."

She waited expectantly. When Grant looked at the fire, she suspected he didn't want to give away the identity of the man. "Who?" she asked softly.

"We believe it was Darby." Grant's unfathomable gaze swung back to her, and she felt as though he was watching her reaction, ready to defend the man's honor.

"Your faithful valet," she said, seeing the man in a new light—but only in a good way.

"Aye. I think he only applied for the position eons ago to be my bodyguard, just in case."

She sighed. "I think he was afraid I was going to have him fired. He didn't like that I was in your chamber," Colleen said, recalling her confrontation with him— mainly because she had only been wearing a towel, and she thought his brusqueness had been an effort to hide his embarrassment.

Grant chuckled. "Aye. I think that's the most worried I've seen him in a long time. He said he'd ask Ian if he'd take him into his pack, but truth is, Darby and Ian's ghostly cousin, Flynn, don't see eye to eye."

"Flynn's a ghost."

"Aye."

She shook her head. She did not believe in ghosts. "What about Archibald? You said he is like his father and grandfather. How?"

"He wanted to manage the property just like they did. At first, we believed he was trying to work a deal with your father when he visited. Maybe help to get rid of Neda, which was one of the reasons we guarded her at all times. If she had died, Theodore would have owned the castle, and since he had no knowledge of how to run the estates, he might have installed Archibald as the manager.

"Not that he would have known how to take care of the estates. And my pack would have given him a difficult time of it. Maybe Archibald was blackmailing your father. Maybe he knew just what Theodore and his father had done with regard to my father's death. The two of them were drinking buddies. Not that Archibald drinks overly much, but he was always picking your father up and taking him to pubs."

She nodded. "So they weren't just fishing buddies. When my father took over, why *didn't* he install Archibald?"

"Theodore was deep in his cups more often than not. Some of that was Archibald's fault because he took your father to the same pub where you were to plot."

No wonder Grant had been upset to hear she had been there with Archibald. If only she'd known.

"A couple of my men followed them and listened in on their conversations. Archibald told Theodore what he'd do and Theodore agreed, all while drinking. But thankfully it was all talk and nothing more. Then he returned to Maryland. We thought that was the end of your father's interference here."

She smiled a little ruefully. "Until *I* showed up. My father's daughter. A week after he returned home, my father drove himself off a bridge and drowned," Colleen said. She sighed deeply, remembering the call from the police and wondering why it hadn't happened earlier the way he drank and drove.

"He'd been caught driving over the limit on several occasions, and his license had been revoked. He shouldn't have been driving, but that didn't make any difference to him." She shook her head. "If he drowned your father, it seems fitting justice that he died that way, too. I was just glad he hadn't taken anyone else's life with him."

"I'm sorry, Colleen. This has to be hard to learn all at once."

Yeah, it was. Not because she had cared about her father, but because she cared about Grant's. "My father had never been a loving dad. The more I learn about him, the less I realize I knew him. I believe the only thing he really loved was his bottle." She finished her tea and set the cup aside.

"I have to agree with you there," Grant said stonily.

"Have you ever questioned Archibald about your parents' deaths?" Not that she thought the man would give up the secrets, but Grant might have noticed a change of scent or posture or mannerisms, something that would indicate Archibald knew something.

"Aye, I have. If he knows what truly happened, he won't tell me."

Thinking out loud, she said, "So Archibald thinks to gain the properties through me, then."

"I suspect he was keeping an eye on your father, and when he learned Theodore had died and you inherited, he was waiting for you to follow in your father's footsteps. Then he conveniently met you at the airport."

She stiffened a little, her gaze holding his. He might as well know the truth. "I assumed he was you at first, and that he had come to pick me up and take me to the castle." She smiled a little. That might teach Grant to allow his enemy to come for her instead. "But then I texted Julia and said I'd arrived, and she told me what you had planned for me. She sent a picture of you and Ian, so I'd know who to look for when I arrived at the castle."

"Bloody hell, lass," Grant said with regret. He reached for her hand and squeezed it with a much too tender touch, when she was trying to keep a more businesslike posture, especially because of the way she was dressed. "I'm sorry for not being the one to pick you up. To show you Scottish hospitality like I should have from the very beginning." Then he frowned. "You couldn't have thought he was me."

She chuckled. "Or one of your men. When I said such, his face fell, but I still assumed his meeting me there was just by chance. Does he have a pack?"

She realized she'd never really talked to anyone about her father like she had with Grant. Her cousins had been terrified of him; her mother covered for him.

"Nay. Five men stick with Archibald. He and his father and grandfather never had a following. So if he mated with you and took over the properties, he'd be the owner and tell me what to do."

She shook her head, not even considering the possibility. "And make life miserable for you."

"Aye."

"But you and your pack could leave," she said, just speaking in general. Not that they would have to.

"And go where, lass? This is our home. This is what we know how to do well."

Grant looked as though they would fight and die before they'd leave their home. Colleen thought about that as she stared into the golden flames and realized this really *was* their home. Not just a place they managed. But theirs. And had always been.

Between the fire, the stew, and tea, and Grant's knees brushing against hers, she was getting hot. But she wasn't backing away from him as much as she knew she should, while she wickedly enjoyed the intimacy of their touch. Wishing in a naughty way that they could do more.

"It will never happen," she said emphatically.

"I don't want you to leave," Grant said, his voice somber, his eyes dark.

He sounded so sincere that she was really taken aback. He really must have had a change of heart.

She smiled a little. "I have nearly a year before I do. Maybe in that time you'll change your mind."

"Nay. I should have gone to America and brought you home to Farraige Castle so you could have been with your grandmother," he said, again so serious, as if they'd finally made a connection—a tentative friendship.

"You should have," she heartily agreed. "I wish I'd known her."

"Then I wouldn't have wasted all that time not getting to know you."

She raised a brow. Was he serious? "And you wouldn't have tried to scare me off when I first arrived," she teased.

"I never expected you to stand there recording us, or that my brothers would join you as if they were your bodyguards. I should have known I'd already lost the battle."

She smiled. "You had. As soon as Julia gave me a heads-up, you had lost. Well, except when it came to the whisky, but that was my fault. I should have known better."

He shook his head. "I'm sorry about not welcoming you like I should have," he said again, his voice full of regret.

"Truly, I don't believe we'd be here like this today if you hadn't. I might have thought you were terribly dull."

He chuckled.

"I would love to run in the glen over the hills as wolves sometime."

"Aye."

She wanted him to know from the bottom of her heart that she would never have replaced Grant or his pack. She reached over to pat his hand. "Archibald would never have run the estates."

Grant rose from his chair and took her hand gently and pulled her from her seat. "You can't know how I felt when I saw you and Ollie in the sea."

She swore Grant's eyes misted with tears. And she hugged him to say she was sorry for his losses, and to thank him for saving her and Ollie.

For a long time, he held her close, rubbing one hand down her back, his other lying gently on her hip. His head rested on the top of hers, her cheek pressed against his chest. He smelled of his shower, of spices, and more—an interested male wolf.

"I nearly had a heart attack seeing the two of you in the water like that."

Then she realized how deeply affected he had to have been, with the memories of his mother and father drowning off those same cliffs, and his inability to save them. "You were so brave to jump in after us."

"I acted on instinct," he said.

"Just like I did," she said, sighing against his chest, listening to his heart racing, smelling his hot wolf interest.

He cupped her face and lifted it so he could gaze into her eyes. "Next time…"

She heard the scold in his tone of voice. "Let's not let there be a next time." And this time, she initiated the kiss—but not on his cheek.

The pipes grumbled in the bathroom, and she cast Grant an elusive smile before they got back to kissing— the hot, heavy, and needy kind.

Grant rubbed his body affectionately against hers, tantalizing her, making her body heat and tighten and moisten just for him.

Tongues came into play, and with the fire and their

kissing, she was burning up. She didn't figure it would go any further than some really hot kissing, but the next thing she knew, he was stroking his hand down her back, and she had her arms about his neck while she gyrated against him. She hadn't meant to, not the way she was dressed, but it just seemed like a natural thing to do with him.

All she could think about was him in a kilt, and then him without, and how his very hard body was making her feel hot and desirable. She couldn't help but want to rub up against him in a wolf's courtship kind of way. Did he know how much his touch affected her?

Yes. He could smell her turned-on scent just like she recognized his. So it had been just as much of a turn-on for him.

What was it about the alpha Highland wolf that made her lose her business sense and want to take this in a different direction?

"Lass," Grant groaned against her ear as his body moved against hers.

She loved the way he sounded like he was dying to have her. He cupped her velvet-covered breasts, caressing her mouth with his, their breath coming quickly.

He slipped his hand inside her robe to touch her breast and froze.

"I didn't expect company," she said and sucked on his tongue, not about to apologize or be embarrassed. Even if she was.

He reached for her tie and smiled such a wolfishly wicked grin that she quickly stayed his hands. "Not too far."

"Agreed," he said, his voice rough with need.

As wolves, mating was for a lifetime. If they were careful, fooling around was the only alternative for sexy wolf loving without the forever commitment. Not that wolves took even this kind of sexual play this far unless they believed they might have something to build on.

Then he untied her robe and parted it. She heard his intake of breath before he murmured, "Beautiful."

"You probably say that to all the women you rescue from the sea," she said.

"Since you are the only woman I've ever rescued from the sea, aye," he said, smiling.

He leaned down and took a nipple in his mouth as his hand stroked the other, making her wrap her leg around his calf and rub. She would leave her scent on him, like a wolf claiming him, even if this wasn't forever.

Her fingers slipped under his shirt, and for the first time, she was able to lightly scratch his back, running her fingers up and down his skin, adoring every bit of him.

Every part of him was sexy. His mouth was made for kissing, she decided as she combed her fingers through his hair and kissed him back, feathering, nipping, licking, pressuring. Before she knew it, she was on his bed—the laird's bed—their pulses racing to the moon, the heat flaring between them.

She hadn't been with a man like this in a very long time, and their passionate touches were wilder and more intimate then she had ever experienced.

He stroked his hand down her belly.

Her body pulsed with excitement as he nibbled her ear, his hand drawing lower, through her curls, and then between her legs. She barely breathed as she anticipated his fingers stroking her, slipping inside her, plunging deep.

She wished they could make love all the way.

She couldn't resist touching him any more than he could her, but this time, Grant was fully dressed. Did he feel they were safer that way?

Burning with unquenchable need, she sucked in her breath as his fingers stroked her, just as she'd imagined they would, his gaze steady on hers, watching her reaction, adjusting to the way his touch made her feel.

She wanted to jerk his shirt off and yank down his pants, but he was stroking her into submission. As much as she couldn't believe she would submit to an alpha male, she couldn't think or feel beyond the pleasure of his…touch.

And then she had the sensation of being lifted heavenward as he renewed his kisses on her mouth. They were insistent, bold, and hungry, until she couldn't halt the wondrous feeling carrying her away. She cried out, loving the way he'd made her come, the intimacy, and passion unlike anything she'd experienced before.

She pulled at his pants again and tugged at his shirt but he kissed her softly on the mouth and then the forehead, saying it was over in a maddeningly frustrating way. She wanted to pleasure him as he had her.

He let out his breath on a sexually unfulfilled sigh. "I'll let you get your rest now."

He closed her robe. He wanted more. He wanted her touch. She knew it. Why was he holding back? Because he didn't want her to get the idea that he wanted her in a more permanent way?

In disbelief, she stared at him. She didn't want to rest. She wanted to feel every naked bit of him. She'd seen him that way enough times, and every time she'd wanted to touch and stroke all those glorious muscles.

"What's wrong?" she asked, unable to hide feeling a little bit rejected. She knew that he was right. That this was the best thing to do. But she felt it was like offering a secret to a friend and the friend not offering one in return. She felt vulnerable, exposed.

He took her hand and kissed it as if he was trying to appease her.

She didn't want to be appeased. She pulled her hand free.

"You should rest." His voice was husky with unfulfilled need. "I'll…see you in the morning."

That was it?

"Are…" She frowned, then folded her arms. "Don't tell me you're afraid of me."

He smiled, and the look was pure alpha wolf—the hot, sexy male variety who was not afraid of anything. Least of all her.

"How did you guess?" Then he was off the bed and heading for the door.

Wait. He was going to leave her on his bed after what he did to her?

He didn't say good night, and she didn't either. They looked at each other with considering gazes, a million thoughts running through her mind, and then he shut the door on his way out.

She was so frustrated, she could scream. She threw his pillow at the door. Then feeling half-aggravated and half-satiated, she curled up on his mattress, smelling the sexy alpha wolf and wishing they could have snuggled together in the big bed for the rest of the night.

And knowing just why he chose to leave her alone. Neither of them wanted a mating. So why was she wishing otherwise?

She heard the shower going in the bathroom adjoining hers, and she wondered if Grant was taking care of his own unfulfilled sexual frustrations. If she'd wanted a mating, she told herself, she'd have joined him in the shower and let her feelings be known.

She stared at the bed canopy for what seemed like forever. She definitely couldn't sleep in his bed sober and smell his scent all over the sheets all night long. Grumbling, she left his bed and returned to the lady's chamber. She retrieved her phone from her purse and called Julia. What she needed was someone to talk to. Someone who knew her. Someone who could tell her that she had to get her mind on track.

"I want to get together with you tomorrow. Would that be all right?"

"Absolutely. We'll have our girls' day out party. Can you stay overnight?"

"Yes!"

"Good, but here's what I want you to do. Don't let anyone catch you at it," Julia said with a conspiratorial challenge to her tone of voice as she explained what she wanted Colleen to do.

That's just what Colleen needed to hear. They were going to have fun.

Here Grant thought being rough and gruff with her would have chased her away. Sharing one-sided intimacies had done the trick better than anything else he could have done to make her want to leave and never come back.

"Is everything all right?" Julia suddenly asked.

"I'll talk with you tomorrow." No, everything wasn't all right.

Chapter 16

GRANT DIDN'T WANT COLLEEN TO FEEL HE WAS LEAD-
ing her on, coming on too strong, or creating a problem
for them both with the direction they were headed. But
damn if he didn't want more. All of it. Her, the mating, the whole savory, sweet pastry that was Colleen—a
feast he couldn't get enough of.

She had been just too enticing sitting in her robe and
slipper boots, her knees brushing against his. He had
tried to stick with the conversation, one that had been
well overdue.

When she told him that she had thought he had come
for her at the airport when it had been Archibald, he
wanted to show her just how much he regretted not coming for her instead.

Grant had pulled back, wanting to see her reaction.
Still wondering about the kisses they'd shared in the
glen and later in the keep. She hadn't pulled away either,
and he kept thinking about kissing her again. Just…kiss-
ing her. One thing led to another, and before he could
stop himself, he was stroking her to completion.

He told himself it couldn't be helped. How was he
to know that when he slipped his hand inside her robe,
he would connect with flesh, feeling no barrier between
them, no nightshirt covering her breasts or anything else
beneath the robe?

She had a drugging effect on him. That was the only

way he could explain his reaction to her—because he'd had no intention of taking it that far with her. Ever.

Even a cold shower had done nothing to alleviate his need for her. He couldn't stop thinking of the wounded expression she wore when he ended the intimacy between them, but if he'd stripped, he would have wanted to take it all the way. Neither of them was ready for that kind of long-term commitment.

So why was he becoming aroused all over again, just thinking of her naked body lying on his bed and her responsiveness to his touch? And why did he want to join her in his bed in the worst way?

A small bag in hand the next morning, Colleen hurried to find Lachlan and ask for the keys to Grant's car. She had gotten up really early, hoping Grant was still asleep so she wouldn't run into him.

She wasn't sure what was going on with Grant's clansmen, but many had made a special effort to go out of their way to say good morning to her while performing their various duties. As if they'd known Grant had nearly made love to her last night, and they thought maybe she would be his mate soon. Like that would ever happen.

Grant better not have thought that pleasuring her was like a payment for her having saved Ollie. And that was all there was to it.

Frederick was the only one who hadn't seemed pleased to see her. He had immediately disappeared when she caught sight of him, before she could even wish him a good morning.

Darby had asked if she'd needed anything. Maynard had wanted to fix her a special breakfast. But all she had wanted to do was leave. She couldn't deal with Grant this morning. Not after the way he'd left her last night as if he'd made a horrible mistake. She couldn't imagine sitting next to him at a meal, thinking about the way his hands had been all over her, his mouth on her breasts, her tongue in his mouth. She groaned.

She was torn between regretting the intimacy between them and wanting a hell of a lot more.

Which was just why she needed to see Julia and get her head on straight.

Two men offered to take her bag to the car while Lachlan watched, looking damned concerned. Enrick had hurried to speak with someone, but neither of Grant's brothers went to see him, so she assumed they knew he had no problem with her leaving.

And nobody asked where she was going, which was just as well. Because truthfully, it was no one's business—specifically, none of Grant MacQuarrie's.

Grant woke to the sound of someone knocking on the guest-room door, and he was instantly wide awake. Colleen had awakened a need in him he hadn't felt in a very long time. Something deeper than wanting just sexual fulfillment.

He'd never considered the possibility that he might care for the lass. Not after the way her father had behaved toward him and his clan. He hadn't thought she would risk her own neck for one of his people, or love the castle and the lands surrounding it like he did. He'd never thought she would have despised her father as much as he did.

Someone knocked again. "Aye," he called out and pulled on a pair of trousers.

Lachlan opened the door and said, "I thought you'd want to know that the lass took your car out for a spin."

"What?" Grant said, his voice verging on a growl. He couldn't even imagine such a thing. He'd expected her to still be asleep in his bed, like he'd been in the guest bedroom. Or maybe looking again at the finances if she'd decided to get up early.

"It's all right," Lachlan said. "Enrick sent two men to follow her. They're reporting back to him as soon as they know where she's going. You did say she could drive your car anytime she wanted to if she wished to go somewhere."

Grant frowned at him. "One of you gave her the spare keys to my car without asking me?"

Sounding exasperated, Lachlan said, "You told her she could use your car, Grant. If you hadn't really meant it, you should have let us in on the secret."

Grant knew his brother was right, but he wasn't about to admit it. He threw on a shirt. "Who went after her?"

"Maynard—"

"Our cook?" Any number of men who seemed better suited to the task should have gone in his place.

"It's his day off."

"Who went with him?" Grant shoved his feet in his shoes.

"Darby volunteered. Well, actually, several did, but Darby and Maynard were so adamant about going that Enrick chose them."

"When did they leave?" Grant stalked out of the chamber.

"Twenty minutes ago."

Grant glowered at his brother. "Why didn't you tell me that she'd left *twenty minutes ago*?"

"We were trying to get someone to follow her pronto before we lost sight of her."

Grant let out his breath in exasperation.

"They'll watch her, Grant. She'll be all right."

"Give me the keys to your car," Grant growled, thrusting his hand out.

Lachlan's brows rose in surprise. "You want to go, too? Isn't that kind of overkill?"

"Last night we talked about her father possibly being responsible for our father's death. That Archibald might have known something about it," Grant said in a rush, feeling panicked when he rarely felt that way. But he didn't want her anywhere near the bastard.

"Bloody hell. You think she's gone to talk to Archibald? I'm going with you."

Enrick stalked toward them as they reached the foyer of the keep. "Darby called and said the lass is still driving."

"Has she gone in the direction of the village where Kelton's Pub is located?" Grant asked.

"It's a long way to the village. She might take any exit way before that and—" Enrick said.

"We're going. You take care of the place while we're gone," Grant said.

Enrick looked a little surprised, then he smiled.

"What?" Grant asked, annoyed, stalking out of the keep.

"I didn't expect you to chase the lass down *personally*. Again."

"If she's seeing Archibald and he causes her any trouble, she needs protection. If his buddies are with him, Darby and Maynard won't be any match for them."

Enrick swore under his breath. "She is still seeing that bastard?"

"Maybe. Maybe not. I don't want to risk it." Grant climbed into his car, Lachlan slipping into the passenger's side.

"I thought you and the lass were getting along last night—"

"She knows Archibald may have inside knowledge about our father's death."

"She can't mean to question him," Enrick said, his eyes wide. Now he realized the concern Grant had for the lass.

"We don't know, Enrick. But what if she did? I'll keep in touch." Grant and Lachlan drove out through the gate and down the road to the one the lass and the others took.

He couldn't believe that Colleen would do this. Or that his people wouldn't have stopped her before she left. Or that he felt sick to his stomach that she could be in a world of danger.

"He wouldn't harm her," Lachlan said as Grant drove way over the speed he normally did. "He needs her if he's thinking of getting hold of her properties. He can't force himself on her."

Grant gave him a cutting look.

"Okay, he could try. But he knows it wouldn't work. He's got to encourage her to agree or we'd kill him. Every last one of us would. Saving Ollie was all it took to pull the pack together to get behind her.

She's no longer an outsider, Grant. Our people have accepted her."

He knew they would. He wondered just what had been said at the meal while he had pleasured the lass last night.

Lachlan pulled a sheet of paper out of his pocket and said to Grant, "Darby initiated this. Every adult man and woman in our clan agreed to sign this. The women did so electronically. Everyone else signed on the paper. And one teen also affixed his signature."

"Let me guess. Frederick, our new dog obedience trainer."

Lachlan smiled. "Aye. So if Archibald has any designs on the lass, she has our whole pack at her back. We're only waiting for one thing."

"What's that?"

"For you to tell the clan you and she are mated." Lachlan gave him another smile. "Ian warned you where this would lead, you know."

Yeah, he had, and despite Grant trying to tell himself it wouldn't work, he was already trying to figure out a way to convince the lass it would.

——∿∿——

Colleen wasn't sure how long it would take her to reach Argent Castle. Thankfully, Lachlan hadn't seemed to mind—too much—that she was taking Grant's car to make the trip. No one had attempted to stop her, change her mind, or escort her there.

After last night and the incredible way Grant had made her feel, she had to know what Julia thought of the situation. Colleen wondered if she had anything to discuss at all—if Grant was pulling back and not interested in anything further to do with her beyond strictly managing the property. Still, Julia was an American wolf and had mated a Highland wolf. She had some insight into their thinking.

She half expected Grant to avoid her today. And she was feeling the same way.

Julia called, and Colleen fumbled to get the phone. "You got the items, right?" Julia asked.

"I did."

"Good, we'll have fun playing some games during our ladies' day out. We'll have an all-girl themed party, but I'm including a few guy games. Not that the guys are actually included. Just some of their unmentionables. You didn't get caught, did you?"

Colleen said, "No, and boy, am I glad for that. I can't imagine what Enrick or Grant would have said, had they caught me in their underwear drawers."

"They know you're going to be here, right?"

"Nope. No one asked and I didn't offer." Wasn't that the way it was supposed to be? The owner didn't have to explain her every move to those who managed and worked her estates. She didn't think they really cared. And she was fine with that. She wasn't used to anyone watching every move she made. She needed some space. Especially right about now.

"Hmm," Julia said, "all right, but I'm certain Grant will be upset that you left without saying…"

"Uh, no. He's not in charge of me."

Silence.

"Julia?"

Julia let out her breath. "All right. But I suspect if

he didn't know you were leaving and where you were going...Well, maybe I'm wrong. We're more than thrilled about your visit. We've made all kinds of plans for when you arrive, and the ladies are all in a tither. We'll do a sleepover, movies, pizza, ice cream, ride horses. You name it, we'll do it."

"That sounds like fun." Though Colleen had never ridden a horse before. "I didn't mention to anyone that I was going away overnight." Not when she was in such a rush to leave before having to see Grant, but she hadn't thought about keeping his car overnight. "I guess I will need to let Grant know I'm going to have his car for longer than anticipated." She was glad she'd have that much of a reprieve.

"No worries. Ian can give him a call." Julia sounded much relieved that Grant would be told where Colleen was going.

"Thanks," Colleen said, not really wanting to talk to him after what happened between them last night.

Not until she had time to think over what they were doing without his indomitable presence. She wasn't used to dealing with an alpha male like him. She really had to get her emotions under control and quit thinking about him in terms of...well, anything to do with his hot, sexy, kilted or naked body. She had to think of him as if he were her manager wearing a business suit and tie.

"Got to go and watch my driving," Colleen said, still uncomfortable driving on the narrow roads and in the wrong lane.

"All right, see you in a bit."

Colleen glanced in her rearview mirror and swore the car behind her had been following her for the last hour.

Having no place to pull over where there was safety in numbers, she continued to drive to Argent Castle.

Suddenly, the car slowed down and some maniac raced around it and sped toward her. She slowed way down also, pulling over as far as she could on the practically one-lane road. He passed, honked at her, and slowed in front of her, flashing his brakes.

"What the..." She couldn't see the driver through the tinted windows. But he had to be drunk or some kind of nutcase. Her stomach clenched with annoyance.

Then she noticed that the car behind her had sped up to block her in. Panicked, she stopped the car suddenly, and the driver almost rear-ended her. Before she could get out of the car, a furious-looking Grant climbed out of the vehicle in front of her and headed for her.

Oh...my...God. Someone must have told him she had taken his car, and *he* had not approved it. Just great! She was buying a used car, pronto.

The men in the other car just stayed there and waited.

She opened the car door and frowned at him. "What do you think you're doing?" she asked, irritated with his high-handed ways.

"You're not seeing him," he said, reaching his car and towering over her—a hot-under-the-collar Highland warrior, and not one ounce of him looked like it could fit into a suit and a tie.

"What are you talking about?"

He hesitated, looking puzzled. "Where were you going?"

"You know, you could have asked me that to begin with in a nice way. A phone call would have sufficed," she snapped, so irritated that he would chase her down like this and act as though she was the bad guy.

"Reception isn't always the greatest out here," he said, trying to talk his way out of this.

She wasn't buying it. "Where did you *think* I was going?"

He shoved his hands in his pockets.

"*Grant?*"

"To see Archibald."

"*What?*" She couldn't help how angry she sounded.

"To ask him if he knew about my father's death."

"Oh." She thought Grant was worried that she'd intended to take up with the man, as in dating and mating, after she had told him she had no intention of letting Archibald get his hands on the estates. She took a deep, calming breath. "I'm on my way to see Julia. And I won't be home until tomorrow, later sometime. I don't know when."

He motioned to the car behind him and both men got out. Maynard and Darby? What was going on?

"Darby, you and Maynard can return home. I'll take it from here," Grant said.

Lachlan got out of the passenger side of the car in front of her and waved.

"Go on home, Lachlan. I've got this covered," Grant said.

"Wait, you're going to walk home?" she asked Grant.

The men looked like they didn't want to witness *this* conversation, yet they hung around as if they thought they might still need to give Grant a ride back to Farraige Castle.

"Move over, lass. I will drive you to Argent Castle."

"We're having an all-night girls' party, and all day, too, if you must know."

"Good, I need to speak with Ian and his brothers. That will work perfectly for me."

In disbelief, she moved over to the passenger's side. She didn't believe he'd had any intention of speaking with Ian or his brothers until she made plans to visit them.

"This is what you meant by letting me borrow the car anytime I wanted?" she asked, scowling at him.

Grant smiled.

She shook her head. "You couldn't just call Ian?"

"Bad reception sometimes."

She didn't believe it for an instant. Well, maybe sometimes, but not this time. "You really didn't think I was getting together with Archibald for any other reason, did you?" She had to know beyond a doubt that he didn't think she was interested in the man.

"No, lass. It's as I said. I was concerned you might think to ask him about your father's contribution to my father's death. I didn't want you getting involved in that. So what brought on this sudden urge to see Julia? I thought you were spending the day studying the financial graphs."

She was sure her whole body blushed. She didn't want to reveal that her leaving had all to do with one wickedly sexy wolf who had seduced her last night, abandoned her, and was now trying to take charge of her today. And how she didn't know how to deal with him when her emotions got in the way.

Grant's phone rang and he answered it. "Ian, yes, I got word the lass intended to keep my car for longer than we thought. Which is fine. I'm coming with her, so make another place at the table, will you?"

She heard Ian laughing. Grant glanced at her. "Aye, I'm keeping her out of trouble on the way there. What's the deal with this wild all-day and all-night party Julia's holding? Is it something we've got to be concerned about?" he asked Ian.

Colleen smiled. "Yes, if you're a man." That earned her a smile. "Ask Ian if Julia's had any of these parties since she's been there."

He asked Ian, listened, and then he said, "Okay, so you don't know what this is all about, either? Well, between your pack and me, we should be able to manage them all right."

Colleen chuckled. "Not on your life."

"See you in a while, Ian." Grant ended the call and said to Colleen, "So what do you do for ladies' night out?

She smiled. "Whatever we feel inspired to do. Haven't the women in your pack done such a thing?" She wasn't about to tell him she'd stolen a pair of his boxers and Enrick's also, and if she'd known he would actually be there, too, she wasn't sure she would have snatched them. Well, yeah, she would have. She had no idea what Julia intended to do with them. She sure hoped Grant wouldn't learn of it prematurely. Or afterward, either.

"Not that I know of," Grant said.

"That should be changed." And she intended to while she was here. "Where *are* the women in your pack?"

"On holiday."

"Did you think having only braw men at Farraige Castle would scare me off?"

"Nay, lass. I was afraid the women would attempt to befriend you and agree to anything you wished to do. But it didn't work out as well as I'd planned." He gave her a small smile.

"Oh?"

"I'm afraid you won my men over, and me. And even without the woman being there, you won them over as well." He sighed. "So...you're not going to tell me about this ladies' day and night out?"

"Just think of it like a guys' day out, sword fighting and then feasting afterward, without the sword fighting."

"Without the sword fighting it would lose all its appeal," he said and smiled at her, and that wolfish smile made her heart leap.

She wondered how she'd managed to get away from him, only to be stuck with him once again, and her feelings for him were twisted into knots even worse now.

Her cell phone rang and Grant glanced at her. She hoped it was just one of her cousins, but she suspected it was Archibald since he said he'd call her today. She fished out her phone. It was. And she really didn't want to talk to him right now.

"Hello?"

"Hi, it's me, Archibald. I said I'd call and I wondered if you'd like for me to take you out for supper tonight."

"I'll be at my friend's place tonight and tomorrow."

Pause.

"You have friends here?" Archibald asked, sounding surprised.

"Yes. Julia MacNeill of Argent Castle."

Another long silence. Did he not know Ian MacNeill, or was he on the outs with them, too?

"Okay, well, if I don't get a chance to see you before you return home, I'll call you tomorrow night."

"Do you want me to tell him to get lost?" Grant asked loud enough that she was certain that Archibald had heard him with his wolf hearing.

"If Grant gives you any trouble at all, I'll take him to task," Archibald said in a very nice way.

But she didn't think he would deal with Grant in a nice way if she asked Archibald to help her out.

"Did you know anything about Grant's parents' deaths?" she asked.

"I knew it. He's been filling your head with stories of how the Borthwicks did terrible things. But John MacQuarrie was a lying bastard who stabbed my grandfather, Uilleam, in the back. I know that the MacQuarries have always claimed they had managed the estates for the Playfairs from the beginning. But it's all a lie. Uilleam was their first manager—but John did everything in his power to turn Gideon and Neda Playfair against him. Ask Grant about that. I'm sorry that you've had to hear all the lies. I had hoped we could talk so you could learn the truth. I'll call you tomorrow and we can talk."

He ended the call and she looked at Grant. "Why would he say that Uilleam was the first manager of Farraige Castle?"

"Trying to get you to believe we've lied about everything? Spreading the seeds of doubt? You are already worried we've told you a lie, lass. Isn't that so?"

<center>~~~</center>

When they arrived at Argent Castle, Grant was still disconcerted about Archibald's claims and didn't believe them, but what bothered him was that Colleen seemed to think he might be telling the truth.

Ian greeted them with a gaggle of women. Julia, Ian's mate, was all decked out in a pirate-wench costume. Grant raised his brows to see the redhead with her curls tied back with a black-and-white bandana, and wearing a low-cut white blouse with voluminous sleeves and a gold corset that emphasized her breasts. A long, full skirt and boots finished the look.

Shelley, Duncan's mate was similarly dressed, except all in blue and silver. Grant recalled that the lass had caught Duncan's eye because of all the silver she wore, and other reasons, of course. As Ian's youngest brother, he had made a fine catch. Werewolves were not fond of silver. The ancient tale that silver bullets could kill still pervaded their beliefs, so Grant knew she had to be a spitfire.

The real pirate of the bunch, or at least where her relations were concerned, was Cearnach's mate, Elaine. Cearnach was second in charge of the MacNeill pack. Her uncles had stolen Cearnach's sword when he was a strapping lad, and now she wore it fastened at her side.

Grant was surprised to see Ian's mother and aunt arrive in full costume as they greeted Colleen as well. Their costumes were not as busty as the younger women's were, but they were all decked out in long skirts, fancy three-corner hats topped with outrageous feathers, and Ian's mother had a *sgian dubh*, the knife sheathed at her waist. Grant recognized the handle as one Cearnach had hand-carved.

Even Heather, Ian's unmated cousin, was in attendance. She wore a Scottish version of a pirate's costume in plaid.

"Looks like we should be armed as well, or the lasses are sure to steal anything that is not bolted down," Grant said, wanting to enjoy the goings-on and not waste another minute thinking about Archibald and his attempt to upset Colleen.

She looked like she had forgotten the conversation completely and was enjoying being with the other women already.

Colleen offered him a glorious smile, and he smiled at her in return. The ladies all chuckled, then Julia took Colleen's hand and Shelley grasped her other, and they hurried her back into the keep.

"I don't have a costume," she said.

"We'll fix you right up," Heather said.

In a normal situation, Grant would not have cared anything about what the women were up to and would have been pleased to visit with Ian and his brothers. But he was dying to know what the lasses had in mind. As much fun as they looked like they could have, he wanted to join them. He would be the sword-wielding Highland pirate, and the wenches would be his to command. Especially Colleen, as he suspected she would fight him every step of the way, and he loved a challenge.

Ian slapped his back. "Come. We will see them later."

"Colleen said they would be busy all day and through the night and tomorrow as well," Grant said.

"Aye, but you wouldn't let that stop you from raiding their party sometime later when they're least expecting it, would you?" Ian asked.

"I like the way you think, Ian," Grant said and joined the brothers in the great hall. He half expected the women to be in there. "Where are they?" he asked when he saw that it was empty.

Cearnach motioned toward the kitchen. "In the garden room outside. They've closed all the blinds and it's their pirates' hideaway."

"They've never done this before?" Grant asked, wondering what he was in for if Colleen decided to do this with the women at his castle.

"Nay. First time. Apparently Colleen and Julia did this regularly with their girlfriends back home. Do you remember Calla? The wedding and party planner?"

"Aye. She saved Cearnach from drowning when he was a lad. And he saved her from a bad marriage."

"Well, she's planned most of the activities. So no telling what they'll be up to," Ian said. "Let's retire to the living room and have something to drink and plan our own adventures."

Grant noted the evil look of pleasure on his friend's countenance. His brothers shared the same expression. Guthrie, Ian's brother, quickly joined them in the direction of the study. "I overheard the lasses say they were going on a boxer raid."

"As opposed to a panty raid?" Cearnach asked. "What do they propose to do with our shorts?"

"They won't bother with mine," Guthrie said, sounding relieved.

"Not mine, either. Too far for them to go to fetch a pair," Grant said, just as thankful.

"That leaves us," Ian said to Cearnach and Duncan. "But, Guthrie, I wouldn't be so sure about your clothes."

The men all laughed and tried to come up with ideas for catching the women when they attempted to steal from them.

"You didn't install a spy among the women?" Grant asked. "That would have been my plan."

"They have been making preparations for this since the day the lass arrived," Ian said. "Remember how I told you my mother wanted my brothers' help and wouldn't let them come with me to spar with you? I believe they had intended to have it a little later, but when Colleen stated she wanted to see Julia today, they moved the date up."

"Aye."

"She had them helping with this project. They've been decorating for days," Ian said.

Guthrie folded his arms. "Calla knows how to spend more money than any other woman I know."

"She's a party planner. That's her job," Ian said. "Now, to this other matter, Grant, how are you and the lass getting on? I take it she's nothing like her father, and you might manage living with her for a year."

"I believe I might have been a wee bit hasty," Grant had to admit.

They heard loud music beating outside.

They all looked in the direction of the gardens and laughed. Grant knew Ian and his family had every intention of crashing the ladies' pirate party with tricks of their own. He was glad he'd caught up to her on the road and come along for the ride.

Chapter 17

COLLEEN HAD NEEDED THIS—TO RECONNECT WITH Julia after all this time and to make new friends here with Julia's new relatives. She couldn't believe that Julia had actually married, as had Shelley and Elaine, when their wolf kind normally just mated and it was a done deal for life.

Ian had a title, Julia had explained. To pass down to their offspring.

Colleen wore a white peasant's blouse, a beautifully embroidered red corset, and a navy blue full-length skirt as the music blared and a fire pit glowed with red-orange flames. They danced on the stone floor that had been cleared of the sofas and dining table, having the time of their lives.

Though Colleen had wanted to speak with her friend privately, she figured she'd find the time since she was going to be here all night.

"Did you see the looks on their faces?" Calla asked, taking Colleen's hand and swinging her around on the floor.

If Colleen ever had to marry, and that was something she'd never considered before, she wanted Calla to plan it for her.

"Oh, aye," Lady Mae—Ian's mother—said, all smiles. "I don't think I have ever seen my sons want to learn more about what we were up to than I did today. They are dying of curiosity."

"So when do we decorate our flagpole?" Elaine asked.

She was the only one of the women actually descended from pirates, though she insisted that her uncles were privateers, therefore they were commissioned to do the job. But still, the rest of her family were out-and-out pirates, and that fascinated Colleen.

"Let's do it now," Julia said. "Before we really start celebrating and forget to! You did bring a pair of Grant's and Enrick's, didn't you, Colleen?"

"Yes. Luckily, Grant was staying in a guest chamber so I was able to search for the perfect pair." Colleen held up a pair of blue plaid boxers. She was glad the guys didn't know about this and weren't planning to get back at the women. "Thankfully, Grant had already taken some with him to the other room or he would have wondered why I was rummaging through his underwear. Enrick had already left his room this morning before I grabbed a pair of his."

The ladies laughed.

"Good. We suspected Grant would follow you here sometime today. We didn't want him to feel left out." Julia waved a pair of red, white, and blue striped briefs she'd gotten for Ian. "I claimed him for America even if he remains in Scotland."

"Does he wear them?" Colleen asked.

"Oh, yes. He's great at trying to please me."

Colleen loved him already.

Shelley twirled a pair of black, active mesh boxers. "Duncan likes black."

"On you," Elaine teased. She stretched out a pair of boxers—white, semitransparent. "Love these on Cearnach."

Colleen hadn't expected Ian's mother to have snatched anyone's underwear. She was widowed. But she shook out a pair of longhorn-steer-decorated boxers. "Shelley's Uncle Ethan's."

Grinning, everyone clapped.

Calla showed off a pair of black briefs for Guthrie. "I didn't want him to feel left out. I figured he'd have boxers with dollar signs all over them."

"They would have cost too much," Julia teased. "He's in charge of the purse strings, Colleen. Even for this affair, he was fussing. It's coming out of my book sales, so I told him to think of it as a promotional party. He grumbled that I wouldn't be selling my books to any of you but giving them away free."

Colleen laughed. She slipped her hand in her bag and pulled out another pair of briefs, this pair red. "Hot, eh, Heather? I don't know how I'm going to explain how I was in Enrick's underwear drawer when I return to Farraige Castle."

"Thanks, Colleen," Heather said, beaming.

Colleen wanted to ask if Heather had an interest in Enrick. She must or Julia wouldn't have asked her to grab a pair of *his* briefs.

Everyone turned to Aunt Agnes. She smiled brightly and spread her hands. "Not me. No love interest and I certainly don't want to snag any man's trunks just to say I did it."

Julia dug in a bag and pulled out a pair of hot chili pepper boxers. She tossed them to her aunt and said, "Shelley's Uncle Jasper will do."

Aunt Agnes caught the boxers and frowned. "I don't want him thinking I stole his boxers," she said with a sniff, holding them far away from her as if she might catch something while she stared at the flaming-hot chili peppers imprinted on them.

"Are we ready to hang them on the pole, ladies?" Julia asked, heading for the door.

"Aye, aye, captain!" the women all shouted.

Colleen laughed. She had missed these parties with Julia and her girlfriends, but this wasn't anything like she'd experienced.

They headed outside into the cool mist and stood before the flagpole as Julia pronounced the pirates' claim to the men's underwear and then proceeded to attach them to the pole as if they were flags blowing in the chilly breeze.

"We need to starch them so they stiffen," Heather said.

The ladies all laughed and Heather blushed. "You have dirty minds."

They all laughed again.

"What's next?" Elaine asked.

"Pizzas!" Calla said. "They should be arriving any moment."

"Everyone armed and ready?" Julia asked, just for the authenticity.

"Aye," everyone said.

Colleen suspected Julia intended to put this in a story someday. Julia had even given Colleen a sword, though she thought it was one of the lads' practice swords, as dull and lightweight as it was.

They headed into the castle, armed and ready to confront anyone who thought to give them trouble, and saw the men with the boxes of pizza, looking as though the treasure was theirs and they weren't eager to give it up. The whole lot of them wore smug smiles.

Ian gave Julia a challenging look. "We paid for the booty. You want it, you'll have to fight for it or win it."

Ian and his brothers, Grant, and two older men who must have been Shelley's uncles Ethan and Jasper smiled back at the ladies, not appearing interested in handing over the food.

"Don't think to spoil our party," Julia said with a threat in her voice, though Colleen knew it was all playacting.

"We plan to make it more to your liking. Either you order your own pizza, in which case we might confiscate it as well when the *ship* comes in, or you include us in your game," Ian said.

"You don't mess with pirates unless you are willing to pay the price," Elaine said, brandishing her sword—in reality, Cearnach's sword of his youth.

The women agreed. The men laughed.

But they appeared to be at a standoff.

"All right, our pizza's getting cold. So what do you suggest?" Julia said.

"A three-legged race. Men against the women," Uncle Ethan said.

"You're taller and could outdistance us," Ian's mother said.

"A sword fight," Duncan said.

Both the men and the women looked at him like he was crazy.

"Bobbing for apples," Colleen said. She was the champion apple bobber in her county. And Julia was just as good at it. Surely some of the other ladies would do as well. Hopefully, Ian and the rest of the men wouldn't.

"A seaworthy challenge," Julia declared.

The men got a big plastic tub, filled it with water and

apples outside on the stone patio, and the game was on. Julia went first, as alpha pack leader at Argent Castle. She pulled two apples out before Ian told her she had enough. She grabbed two of the boxes of pizza.

Ian went next, and no matter how hard he tried, he could not grasp a bobbing apple with his teeth. His shirt and face wet, he finally conceded.

"You will not put this in a book of yours," he warned Julia. Her smile said that's just what she'd do.

Colleen was next as owner of Farraige Castle and grabbed three apples before Grant said, "Enough. Show-off."

Everyone laughed. Grant did not look happy about trying this new venture, and he did as poorly as Ian. No one else was able to fish out any apples, though everyone laughed hard enough about it.

Uncle Ethan eyed the apples that Julia and Colleen had managed to snag and said, "They had the longest stems of any of them."

"No, they didn't, Uncle Ethan," Shelley said. Using her hands, she pulled out two from the water and showed the stems on those.

The ladies grabbed their boxes of pizzas and in sashaying, pirate lady fashion, they headed outside with their booty.

"Brilliant idea," Julia said. "I never even considered that."

"I remember how we played that at fall festivals and how good we were. Glad we trounced them," Colleen said, having so much fun that she never wanted this to end.

When they crossed through the garden and reached the gazebo, they stared at their pirate's flagpole. All the men's underwear were gone, and in their place hung colorful silk and lace bras.

"When...who...?" Elaine said.

They sniffed at them.

"Seems all of them at one time or another grabbed our things," Colleen said. "When we were so busy watching the next player, one of the men must have slipped out to grab a bra and attach it to the pole."

The ladies laughed and hurried to take down their bras.

Chapter 18

COLLEEN HAD THOUGHT THIS WAS STRICTLY GOING TO be a ladies' night adventure. Not anything involving the men. She couldn't believe how the men were playing with them. It was too much fun.

Sitting on the soft moss-green couches that fit together like a meandering stream around the glowing fire pit, the ladies ate slices of pizza and sipped merlot.

They shared stories of how they met their mates. Julia's mother-in-law talked about how impossible Uncle Ethan was, though Colleen noted the way Lady Mae talked about him in an annoyed, but endearing way, and Heather described who her dream man would be. Colleen wasn't certain if she was talking about Enrick or not. Aunt Agnes was mum. And Calla talked about how Guthrie MacNeill was the most irritating man who held the purse strings for the clan.

Colleen thought Calla sounded like she had the hots for him.

Julia began telling how she and Colleen had met on the run as wolves and became best friends. "I was about ten years old, off exploring without any pack members, and had caught Colleen's scent. I was curious who she was. Then I encountered a mother bear and her cubs. My fault, really. I smelled signs of them but didn't heed the warning. I was too interested in learning who the strange she-wolf was crossing our territory.

"She could have been all wolf and not *lupus garou*, for all I knew. But I was always on the lookout for a wolf cub my age. Then I got curious about the bears. Nearly a fatal mistake on my part," Julia said. "Colleen came to my rescue when she heard me snarling and growling and barking in a startled 'I'm going to get myself killed' way."

Colleen shook her head. "You and me both."

"What did you do?" Heather asked, wide-eyed.

"All that we could do. We kept going in different directions. With two of us, the mother bear was afraid we might attack her cubs. We finally were able to outrun her and spent a couple of hours trying to find each other again," Colleen said.

"Yeah, best friends forever after that," Julia said.

Colleen set her wineglass on the coffee table. "I couldn't believe it when you told me you'd come out here to work on a movie, perfect for providing details for your next book, and ended up mating with the pack leader!"

Julia smiled. "Yeah, but I couldn't believe how you picked up your first mate, either."

Elaine tilted the wine bottle and said, "We're out. We need more for our storytelling."

"I'll get us a couple more bottles. I know this story," Colleen said.

"Are you sure?" Julia asked. "It's always a fun story."

"When you tell it," Colleen said, smiling.

"I could go with you," Heather said.

"No, no, that's fine. I'll be really quick." Colleen didn't want to stop Julia's spiel, but she really didn't want to hear it again, either. She uncurled herself from the couch.

"Her first beta mate had tried hard to approach her at a barn-dance social. The guys had been pushing him all night to cross the floor to ask her to dance. She waited and finally, giving up on him, crossed the floor instead and asked *him* to dance."

The ladies chuckled.

Smiling, Colleen opened the door to the garden room. Yeah, he was cute and she never regretted taking him for her first mate.

Julia continued with the story, "No one had expected her to become interested in a beta like him. But he was the sweetest guy, and she loved him for it. She nearly gave him a heart attack when she asked him to dance, though."

Colleen closed the door and headed down the stone path toward the keep. Grant was so different. If he was intrigued with her at that same dance, he would have made his interest known at once, probably elbowing everyone out of the way if they approached her and glowering at anybody who even considered such a move. She wasn't sure if she could have handled a wolf like him way back then. Now? She wasn't certain anybody else would ever measure up to the way she felt about him.

She walked quietly down the moss-covered path, listening to the wind whipping through the trees, her skirt flying, and wondered if she could have an all-girls' party at Farraige Castle—not in quite the same manner, but as a way to get to know the MacQuarrie women better when they returned home.

She watched for any movement outside, figuring her concern was silly. No one would be observing the garden room. The men laughed inside, probably imbibing too much whisky and having their own fun. She slipped inside, not sure why she felt so apprehensive, but her skin crawled with unease, as if any moment something would come out of the dark and give her a heart seizure.

Just as she attempted to tell herself how silly that was, something in the dark touched her arm, and she swallowed a scream. A small light shown from a hallway, and between that and her preternatural wolf sight, she could see her way in the kitchen, but no one was here. She did *not* believe in ghosts, even if a ghostly cousin of Ian's purportedly hassled the lasses in his clan.

She should have allowed Heather to come with her, but she thought that only one person going would be quieter than if more of them went. She could see the men wanting to take the game a little further.

She found the door to the cellar and opened it, then headed down the wooden steps. They creaked with every step she took, sounding as though she was setting off an alarm bell signaling "intruder alert."

When she reached the stone floor, she hurried to the racks in the far back corner where Heather had picked out the other bottles of merlot.

She was about to grab two bottles when she heard someone coming down the steps. A man's heavy tromping. He wasn't making any effort to hide that he was coming. He could smell that she had just been here, too. Did he think she was still down here? Or maybe he suspected she'd come and gone, and he had missed her. He was probably only here to grab more wine for their own party upstairs.

He approached the wine racks where she stood, and she barely breathed. Carefully, she unsheathed her sword with a soft swish loud enough for any wolf to hear. She hadn't expected that unsheathing her sword would be so noticeable.

A man chuckled.

Grant. She sighed with relief. Yet her skin still prickled with awareness. Whether he was playing the game or not, she still felt a wolf's wariness, a natural tendency to be on guard. On the other hand, they were alone in the dark, and that had her thinking of kissing and other possibilities, which she swore she was going to ignore this very minute!

"What a delightful scent I smell," he said, drawing closer, his stride shorter now, his voice seductive, playful, and *very* interested.

She would not let him get her all excited again, not let him melt her with his touches and then leave again.

"I hear your breathing, lassie, and your heart beating out of bounds. The lass isn't stealing the laird's wine, is she?"

She couldn't help it. She smiled. He *was* playing the game still. "Don't come any nearer, Grant," she ordered, unable to see him yet for all the racks of bottled Chablis, merlot, Riesling, and pinot grigio. Her darn heart was beating even faster now, her blood pounding. The anticipation of his stalking her was killing her.

He laughed, his voice dark and sexy. "You are not in charge of *this* castle. You are a pirate. What should I do with a pirate who is stealing the laird's wine, eh? When he is my best friend?"

She smiled, though she wasn't ready to face Grant, even in play like this. She thought she heard an eagerness, a wolf's determination, and something more that drove him toward her.

"I believe I've found the lassie I want to keep for my own."

Her jaw dropped. He couldn't be serious. He had to be teasing. Playing the game.

He came around the corner and his dark gaze met hers, then lowered to take in her corset. "I like this style on you. You should play dress-up more often."

She looked down at the kilt he wore and the fur-covered bag in front of his crotch—the sporran—which made her want to lift it and see if she could get a rise out of him. "Where did you get the kilt?" She loved seeing him in it and couldn't think of a better way for him to perform his part.

His eyes darkened even further with intrigue as he moved in closer.

"I have a spare one and set of clothes in the trunk of my car at all times. Since you lasses wished to be pirate wenches, the men and I donned our kilts to entertain you in the right manner."

"You...you are still playing the game."

"Aye, until you ladies are through."

Okay, so that's what she thought. He didn't *really* mean he wanted to keep her for his own. She could play the game.

"Don't come any closer," she said, waving the sword at him. She suspected he wasn't going to let that deter him.

"I like your determination, playfulness, and resource-fulness. Next time we bob for apples, I want you on my team." He moved in closer.

She backed up, bumping into sacks of grain and barely catching herself before she fell on top of them.

"Did you come down here for some wine?" she asked, trying to get him back on task, which shouldn't include stalking after her.

"Nay, lass. I had first lookout." He drew closer.

"First...lookout?"

"Aye, you see, each of us has vowed to capture any pirate wench who approaches the keep. You were the first. I claim you." He pressed into her space, forcing her to move her sword ineffectually to the side.

She laughed. "You are too funny, Grant, though I have to say I love your sense of humor."

"I'm serious," he said, his voice rough with need, his hands on her shoulders, caressing, endearing. He wasn't playing now. No teasing light in his eyes. He was all business, his eyes dark with desire. "You can't tease me by looking like you do, stealing my trunks in a way that's tantamount to saying you have claimed me, lass, displaying them for the whole of Ian's pack to see, and then say it is all pretend. You are not pretend. You are real. The way your heart beats when I am near, and mine beats just as rapidly, the way your scent changes, telling me you want me like I want you—this is real."

She smiled up at him, unsure what to say. She was normally not tongue-tied. But around Grant like this, with his close proximity, the way his musky male wolf scent tantalized her, the way he looked at her as if she was sex in a risqué costume, her emotions swept her away. Yes, she'd been mated twice before, and those had been agreeable matings, but she hadn't felt the same for them as she did for Grant. A raging torrent of emotions—of lust and longing and sexual arousal—unbalanced her, making her feel as though she needed a safety line. And someone to tell her if this kind of a relationship was healthy and would work out for a very long *lupus garou*'s lifetime.

Yet could she walk out on him today, give up on him and the castle, and turn over her inheritance to her cousins? Could she stay here a whole year and a day, and be just the owner of the castle, while he served as her manager? And get over the physical attraction to him that had her wanting so much more?

She knew she couldn't. She'd thought about what Archibald had said, but she didn't believe him. Grant's grandfather and parents had been murdered. His people had worried that Grant and his brothers were next. Archibald had to have lied to attempt to cause dissention between her and Grant.

Her heart was beating like a she-wolf who was caught, tested, and forced to tell the truth. Yet she couldn't say it. What if she was wrong about Grant and her being right for each other?

Or what if she was still fantasizing about *them*, and he was just playing with her—as part of the game?

"Why did you really leave this morning and come here?" he asked, his tone of voice gentle, coaxing, but he wouldn't let her go, wouldn't step back out of her space. He was forcing her to hear his own rapid heartbeat, the smell of his arousal, and the feel of his heated body.

"To see Julia." That was true. She had to see her and bounce her thoughts off her friend as they had always done. How could Julia have mated Ian without talking it through with Colleen first? Yet she hadn't wanted to talk to Julia with the other ladies present, and she hadn't believed Grant would end up here, too.

"About?" Grant asked, his hands cupping her face, his thumbs caressing her cheeks, his gaze locked on hers, alpha to alpha.

You. Colleen took a deep breath. No, not about him. But about… "Us."

"You and me?" he asked, his eyes misty with sexual craving.

"Yes, if you must know."

He grinned. "Aye, lass. That was all I wanted to know."

He leaned down to kiss her, but she stopped him, her hands on his shoulders. "That's it? What if I was going to tell her that…well, that…"

"You were going to tell her that we have a need for each other that we can't quench. A wolf's need. You know how it is for our kind. We find the right one, and that's it for us," he said, serious as could be, still eyeing her with determination. He wasn't going to back down.

"But…"

"Your other two mates were betas."

She frowned up at him. He had been checking up on her?

"Aye, you adored them. You were saddened to see them go. You pined for years after each of them died. But what you had with them was not the same as what we have between us."

"That's what's wrong," she said, her hands slipping to his back, her eyes averting to his gloriously muscled chest.

"Nay, not wrong." He lifted her chin and kissed her forehead. "You do not have the luxury of brushing me aside and saying that because I wasn't like your other mates, I'm wrong for you. They were good for you when you needed them. But now you need…"

"You?" She couldn't help sounding a trifle annoyed. He was so arrogant and, God, so appealing. He was right. He seemed to be just what she needed in her life, but she didn't want him saying so. She was used to being in charge and deciding what she needed, no one else.

Even in the case of her prior mates, she had been the one to tell them she thought they should be together, not the other way around.

She took in another deep breath of him and considered his expression. He might be smiling at her in an interested way, all serious, but it was the way his heart was beating just as fast, the feel of his arousal pressed now against her, the way she wanted this more than she thought she should that made her hesitant.

"Aye, you need me. But not any more than I need you, lass," he said, kissing one cheek with reverence, and then the other.

"You left me last night," she accused. What if he pleasured her here, just like she wanted him to, then hurried off again, abandoning her, only this time among the bottles of wine?

"Aye, lass." He sighed and rested his forehead against hers. "I'm not good at this—this courtship phase with a wolf. I know what I want, and I'm fairly certain of what you want."

"A mating?" she asked. She had to know. For certain.

"Aye, a mating."

Did she want this? To be a pack leader, and not just in charge of a couple of beta cousins? Did she want to live here with Grant and his family and his clan?

"This isn't a way for you to return to your chamber, is it?"

He chuckled. "You are a canny lass. But I don't intend for you to sleep in the lady's chamber, *ever*. You have a year to decide, but I will be working on convincing you the whole time that you wish to be mated to me."

She opened her mouth to speak. If he put it that way, she would never last. She slipped her arms around his neck. "Try me."

Someone pounded on the cellar door.

Colleen's heart skipped a beat. "You locked the door?" she asked, hoping he had.

"Aye, how could I capture you if your pirate mateys showed up and came to your aid?" He brushed a kiss against her forehead.

"Colleen, are you in there?" Heather called out.

"Why is the door locked?" Julia asked.

"We are negotiating terms of surrender," Grant hollered back. "I'm not releasing my captive maiden until we get this right."

Colleen laughed at him. She could just imagine what the ladies would think of that. Was he playing? Or for real?

The ladies were silent for several heartbeats. Then Julia said, "Is this why you wanted to talk with me, Colleen?"

"Yes!" And leave it to Grant to keep her from doing so.

"Then I approve. Get on with the surrender terms. Tell Grant you accept his surrender in full. Don't let him get anything by you." Julia paused. "Can we get a bottle or two of wine first?"

Colleen loved Julia.

"You will have to wait," Grant said, then winked at Colleen. "We are busy."

"All right, just this time!" Julia said, then squeaked. "Run! Ian… Run, Heather! Get the troops!"

Colleen laughed. "I should be with my pirate cohorts, aiding them against the kilted lot of you."

"You, lass, are out of the game. Except for the one you and I are playing now."

She caressed his bare arms. "Does that mean you love me?"

"Ever since the day you recorded every bit of me sparring with Ian MacNeill."

"I got your best side, too."

"You got my arse!"

"Yes." She laughed. "As I said, your best side."

He reached around and cupped her buttocks. "Yours is not so bad, either. But do you love me?"

"From the time I saw you so valiantly fighting Ian, to when you slept as a wolf on the floor of the White Room and then rescued me and Ollie from the sea, I knew you were truly special. You are a good pack leader and clan chief, and I adore you."

"And love me."

She smiled wickedly and reached down to caress his kilt-covered buttocks. "Yeah, I do. It wasn't hard to do. But I worried…"

"That I wasn't like the other wolves in your life. You will *not* find that to be a problem."

"Oh, I think I might," she said.

And then he leaned down to kiss her, his mouth hungry on hers, but this time she wanted to hold him where he wouldn't let her touch him the last time. She reached

down, her hand slipping over the soft fake fur on his
sporran, and felt his erection stir beneath it and his kilt.

Her touch had him groaning against her lips, right
before he thrust his tongue into her mouth and leaned
his erection against her hand.

His hands caressed her breasts and he smiled. "No
bra, lassie."

He'd know, as he'd retrieved it from Ian and Julia's
chamber and attached it to the pirate's pole. He pulled
her blouse down and exposed her nipples, the corset
pushing her breasts up for his pleasure.

She lifted his kilt so she could cup him, and his eyes
darkened with intrigue as she felt his cock, hard and
pulsing and heavy in her grasp.

He groaned her name as she stroked him, right before he suckled one of her breasts, his mouth warm and
wet, his tongue lathing her nipple. She moaned at the
exquisite sensations he stirred deep inside her. She was
becoming wet for him, and he knew it. Smelled her
readiness, just as she smelled his.

She wanted to tell him how much he turned her on
when he wore his kilt, but she suspected he already
knew that or he wouldn't have changed. She pulled it up
so she could touch his tautly muscled buttocks, while his
focus remained on her breasts, his tongue licking one,
his thumb stroking the other. In the cool, damp cellar,
she was burning up with his heated breath and touch.

She ran her hands over his ass, squeezing it, arching against his erection. He didn't remove her clothes
like she thought he would, but eased her onto the sacks
of grain, fumbled then with her long pirate skirts, and
yanked them up.

Omigod, this was so…medieval. She loved it. She didn't attempt to remove his kilt. Just lifted it and saw his masculine need for her swelling to the occasion.

She never thought she would mate her next wolf like this—in a Highland castle's wine cellar with a hot alpha wolf wearing a kilt and nothing else, while she wore a medieval wench's gown and nothing underneath.

Then again, somehow it seemed appropriate to mate with a Highland alpha wolf just like this.

His large hand moved between her legs and urged her to spread them for him. He stroked and caressed her all-too-willing nub that ached for his touch. He kissed her mouth that was every bit as possessive and insistent. She licked and nipped his lips and tongue until he began to bring her to climax, and then her fingers dug into his sexy rump, her body arching to his strokes.

"Surrender," he whispered to her.

She smiled, wanting his surrender first, and yet not. She needed this, to reach the peak, to explode into a million sparks of wonder, and before she could think another thought, she did. Shattered with the utmost intense pleasure.

Grant had decided this the moment Lachlan had handed him the signed petition from his pack. The feelings he had for her had been building since the minute he'd met her, despite him trying to deny it was so, and he'd known those feelings would end in this.

Maybe not exactly here, like this. But he knew with the way he felt about her, and the way she felt about him, they couldn't have waited much longer. He couldn't have been any happier to take the she-wolf in Ian's cellar dressed as they were, knowing just how turned-on he made her when he wore his kilt.

He was proud to wear it, never thinking that it would turn his potential mate on, but damn, if she didn't do the same to him, no matter what she wore or didn't wear. He couldn't stop thinking about her wearing that velvet robe and nothing else while she regally ate dinner with him.

He eased into her, savoring the feel of her wet sheath surrounding his cock, opening for him, caressing him, as her hands stroked his skin everywhere—back, arms, arse—making him hotter.

And then he was in all the way to the hilt and pulling out again, treasuring not only the sex, but that all this felt right—the mating, the joining, the change in pack leadership.

He would treasure his faux captive she-wolf forever.

He thrust more deeply into her as she took his tongue hostage and sucked. He loved when she did that. He ramped up his speed, kissing her back like there was no tomorrow, still reeling from the fact she'd said yes, and then he came in one euphoric, explosive moment.

Yet he continued to move against her, feeling sure she was about to come, until she exclaimed, "*Oh...my... God.*" And slumped against the sacks of grain, her orgasm clenching around his cock.

Now what were they going to do?

Chapter 19

GRANT HAD MOVED SO THAT HE WASN'T RESTING ON top of Colleen on the grain sacks, looking down at her, one elbow propping him up, the other hand caressing her hair. He seemed to be lost in thought after making such wondrous love to her.

Colleen had loved her past mates. She truly had. But being with Grant was a world apart from anything she'd ever experienced. She loved battling with him to be on top, instead of being with a beta wolf, where she had always been the initiator. She loved how passionate he was and how much he got into the role she and her friends were playing, in a good-natured, hot and sexy wolf way. She would cherish their first mating forever.

He looked down at her with such an intensely proud and loving expression that she smiled up at him.

"We have a problem," he said, kissing her cheek, her brow, her lips.

"What is that?" She suspected he meant about telling the others that they'd mated, though she supposed they'd assume as much.

He played with a tie on her corset. "If we were at Farraige Castle, we wouldn't leave our bed for a week."

She laughed. Now that was the difference between the alpha and the beta. Her previous mates would have waited for her to say so.

"But here, we have a real dilemma." He was smiling

so broadly that she couldn't wait to hear what he would say. "I've captured my pirate she-wolf."

"Who says I haven't held you hostage down here?"

He laughed. "Oh, aye, you have. And still do."

She blushed as she felt his cock stirring inside her. "Insatiable."

"Aye. But I don't want to share my conquest with anyone else…at the moment."

She sighed. "As much as I hate to admit it, I feel the same way." She loved the intimacy between them and wasn't ready to give it up. But they really did have to rejoin the party. Or…maybe not right away. She licked his chin. "I do believe we're still in negotiations."

And with that, they began to negotiate all over again.

———

When Colleen and Grant left the cellar, she had two bottles of wine in hand, ready to return to the outdoor garden room, but Grant escorted her out there, not wanting any of the other men to take her hostage if they were still playing the game.

"Seems like since you are my enemy, I should not allow you to escort me," she said, snuggling close to him in the chilly wind.

"I'm protecting my investment." Then he kissed her, waiting for her to enter the garden room and having a devil of a time not regretting that she was sleeping with the women tonight instead of him. The thought of waking next to her in the morning was what he truly craved.

"'Night, lass. But remember, if I catch you beyond the garden room…"

"You have such a one-track mind, Highlander. Did you know?"

"Aye." He smiled.

The door opened and Julia said, "Good, you brought more wine. Should we take him hostage?"

Colleen smiled and Grant grinned, then turned on his heel and returned to the keep before they truly decided to do so.

He found Ian and the others sitting about the fire talking about battles they'd fought over the years when they spied Grant joining them.

"So tell us," Ian said, "how did the terms of the agreement come out?"

"The lass knew she couldn't get a better deal."

The men all laughed. It seemed strange yet right to be here with his lifelong friends when he mated Colleen, just as she was with her best friend, Julia. And he suspected Ian's extended family would be her friends as well.

He rather liked this ladies' day and night out, as long as he was included.

Hoots and hollers and a few feminine howls sounded beyond the wall to the keep in the direction of the gardens.

"Sounds to me that the terms of the lass's surrender worked out well for the rest of the lassies," Ian said, giving Grant a salute with his whisky.

"Aye, only next time they have one of these parties, I want my brothers to be here, too. They have missed out and that won't do. What is planned for tomorrow?"

"You do realize that this is supposed to be for the women only, right, Grant?" Ian asked.

"Aye, so as I said, what will they be doing tomorrow?"

They heard a bark outside. But it wasn't one of Ian's Irish wolfhounds. It was the bark of a wolf.

The men started stripping out of the kilts. Forget what tomorrow would bring. Tonight, they would chase the she-wolves in their own wolf coats.

––––

Colleen thought the idea of running as wolves would be fun. Though she believed they'd slip out without the men knowing. But one of the she-wolves barked. *Julia*. Was she giving her mate a heads-up so he knew what they were doing beyond the castle walls? Probably. Colleen would do the same with Grant.

The other time Colleen had been a wolf in the Highlands, she'd been drunk and maneuvering cliffs. This time she had a nice buzz from the wine and was running with a she-wolf pack in an ancient forest. How cool was that?

They weren't running in the cool misty woods in a follow-the-leader pattern, but spread out, exploring the sights and scents and sounds, like wolves would.

They hadn't gone very far when she heard growling, two female wolves to the left of her somewhere in the forest. Before she could turn and investigate, Julia raced past her. Colleen dove after her in wolf rescue mode.

Five male wolves approached. Colleen didn't know any of the men in their wolf form and they were down-wind of her. But the females growled in a highly dangerous way, not in play. The other she-wolves quickly joined them as a united front.

The females bared their teeth in warning, snapping and snarling, while Julia raised her snout and howled.

Colleen knew she was calling in male reinforcements. Definitely not good.

The males only took a moment to consider the situation, then turned tail and bolted. The females did not follow. A matter of minutes later, Grant and several male wolves appeared. They quickly assessed the females, ensuring they were uninjured, then Grant and Duncan—Colleen recognized him by scent—stayed with the females while the rest of the men took off after the fleeing wolves.

Who were those wolves? Julia and Ian had scent-marked this area of woods, so Colleen knew the encroaching wolves had to have known better. On the other hand, fewer females were born to a werewolf pack, and she wondered if their appearance had to do with attempting to find a mate among the she-wolves of Ian's clan.

Seemed a dangerous way to go about it. And she suspected it wasn't the case.

Grant nuzzled her face for a moment, then went back to standing guard with Duncan, who had greeted his mate, Shelley, in the same manner.

For a good twenty minutes, everyone continued to listen for any sounds other than the wind whipping through the trees. Then a wolf howled, and Julia howled back.

Ian was the one calling to say everyone was all right, and Julia let him know all was well here. They still waited for them in the woods until the other males returned and greeted the females. The jaunt through the woods was over for now.

After they ran through the back servants' entry gate,

Ian waited for Julia so she could let him know her plans. She was back to doing their all-girl thing and headed for the garden room.

They were going to watch *Prince of Persia* next. Forget a chick flick. The ladies wanted to watch a swashbuckling adventure with a touch of paranormal and romance. But before they watched the movie, in various forms of nightwear, warm robes, and slippers, the ladies all settled down on the sofas around the fire to discuss what had just happened in the woods.

Calla said, "Cearnach rescued me from a bad mating and marriage. The one wolf we faced out there still thinks he can get me to change my mind."

Elaine said, "Some of the others were my cousins. The lot of them. True pirates. The bad kind."

"And one other," Julia said. "I'm certain if Grant had known, he would have torn after him himself. Well, he'll be highly pissed as soon as Ian tells him who he was."

"Who was he?" Colleen asked.

"Archibald Borthwick. Friend of your father and no friend of Grant's."

―◊◊◊―

Grant knew about Calla's former fiancé and how Cearnach wanted to save her from a bad mating, and did. But he was surprised that the ex-fiancé continued to stalk her.

"We'll get them," Ian said. "This is the first we've seen of them since the big fight where several of Elaine's cousins were injured. But what I don't understand is why Archibald Borthwick was with them."

Grant's blood turned to ice. "Archibald?"

"Aye. He's as much a pirate as the rest of the men, only he attempts theft in a different way. Word has it he's got some notion he might still have a chance at running things at Farraige Castle," Ian said with a knowing glint in his eye. He knew that Grant wouldn't let the bastard get near Colleen in any way, shape, or form now that they were mated.

"Why the hell were they here?" Grant asked, though he realized that Colleen had told him where she would be for the night, so he knew she was here.

"I imagine they're after the same thing—Baird McKinley still wants Calla, and Archibald has some notion he has a chance with Colleen. Things didn't work out between Archibald and her father, but maybe he thinks mating her will even work better in his attempt to get his hands on Farraige Castle," Ian said.

"Like hell he will," Grant growled. He would kill the bastard if he thought to lay a hand on his mate.

"I doubt he knows you've mated her yet. I'd make it known in a grand wedding soon," Ian said.

Grant intended to do just that.

Guthrie said, "Just don't let Calla plan the wedding. It will cost the clan a fortune."

Ian smiled. "I have a task for you, Guthrie."

His brother frowned at him.

"Now, don't get all negative on me. Calla's been staying with friends—not even her own relatives—attempting to keep a low profile while Baird is still harassing her. I want her to stay here with us. She won't agree to it. Cearnach has been more of a friend to her than any of us, but even he couldn't persuade her. She insists Baird won't make her hide away. She has her party-planning jobs to do."

"Aye, I understand how she feels," Guthrie said warily. "What has this got to do with me?"

"Julia's asked if she would stay, but she's given her the same song and dance."

Now *Guthrie* was grinding his teeth. "You can't think *I'd* ask her to. What if she planned parties for every day that she stays here?"

"She hung your shorts on the pirate's pole. I never would have thought she'd do such a thing." Ian smiled. "I want you to ask her to stay."

"Ian…"

"That's all, Guthrie. Just ask her to stay with us for her own protection. You don't have to do any more than that."

"Aye," Guthrie said, "but what if she sees more in my asking her to stay than I mean for her to see?"

Ian chuckled. "You can do it. Just get her to agree."

"If Colleen decides she wants to use Calla's wedding planner services, the lass can stay with us until the wedding's done," Grant offered.

Guthrie sighed audibly.

"But she's staying with us after that, Guthrie," Ian said. "You will make it happen."

Grant bit back a smile. If he could deal with Colleen, who he'd thought would be the bane of his existence, and turn the situation into one that he could live with as one happy wolf for the rest of his life, maybe Guthrie's ordeal would turn out just as well.

He saw the way Guthrie scowled.

Maybe not.

Chapter 20

COLLEEN WASN'T READY TO TAKE THIS ANYWHERE yet. She'd mated with Grant, sure. But she had never had a wedding and had never expected to have one. It was all so sudden and…nothing she'd ever given any consideration to.

But the ladies were excited about the prospect, and everyone was asking her a million questions and offering a million suggestions. Before she even had a chance to answer all the questions.

"Be right back," Calla said. "I've got to get my laptop and I'll show you some wedding ideas."

"I'll go with you," Heather said, "in case the guys try to take you hostage or anything. You know how *that* turned out last time."

They looked at Colleen, and she felt herself blushing all over again. Here she was, supposed to be having an all-*ladies*' gathering, and she ends up mated to a very sexy he-wolf. That had to be some kind of record.

She wondered if Calla had hoped she would have better luck if she went alone. Maybe catch Guthrie's eye, after having stolen his underwear from his drawer and claimed him on the pirate's pole. Colleen had been so busy meeting everyone that she hadn't noticed if Guthrie returned the interest, even though Calla insisted she only grabbed Guthrie's underwear so he wouldn't feel left out.

"What does everyone's schedule look like?" Julia asked, beaming. "We have a wedding to attend."

———

Grant was still trying to figure out a way to coax Colleen away from her slumber party to sleep with him tonight. He shouldn't have been so possessive and needy, but she was his mate and he wanted her with him on their first night.

They heard the back door open and then Calla say, "Okay, Heather, I've got fabric samples and wedding books in my car. Who would have thought our first-ever ladies' night would turn into a wedding-planning event?"

Grant smiled, then left the men in the living room when Ian said, "Go, Guthrie. Ask her to stay with us afterward."

Guthrie muttered something under his breath about lassies and money and how the two soon parted company.

Grant smiled, then saw the lasses near the foyer. "Can I have a word with you, Calla?"

She smiled at him, albeit her expression was a bit wary. "Aye."

"Guthrie and I can help you with whatever you need to bring in," Grant said.

Calla glanced in Guthrie's direction and arched a brow. He folded his arms. "Aye."

"Thanks." She and Heather headed outside.

"If you would like," Grant said, catching up to her, "you can stay with us at Farraige Castle to make all the plans."

"I would like that," Calla said. "Makes it much easier to plan the event."

Grant glanced at Guthrie, who wasn't saying anything. Grant swore that if Guthrie had pockets in his kilt, he would have his hands shoved in them. Grant tilted his head to the side, silently appealing to him to ask Calla to stay at Argent Castle after the wedding was concluded.

Looking mutinous, Guthrie didn't say a word.

When they reached Calla's car, she handed Guthrie a heavy catalog of fabrics. "Since you are so braw and gallant, you can carry the heaviest of the items."

He grunted.

She smiled, then turned and fished out a couple of bags for Grant to carry, another book for Heather, and her laptop. Once she'd emptied her trunk, they walked back to the keep. Grant cast Guthrie another look, telling him there was no time like the present. Ask already.

Guthrie scowled back at him, then cleared his throat. Everyone looked at him expectantly.

Guthrie said, "Ian wants you to stay here after the wedding."

Grant rolled his eyes. That hadn't worked before, and he was certain it wouldn't work now.

"I've told him and Julia no," Calla said.

Grant had been right.

"It's not safe out there with Baird stalking you everywhere you go. You were lucky tonight that we came to your rescue, but…" Guthrie continued.

"Aye, and I thank you. I'm not going to hide away from place to place, not doing my job because Baird and his brothers and cousins are harassing me. I won't."

They walked in silence for some time. Grant really thought the lass would go along with it because he suspected she did have a fondness for Guthrie.

"Unless…" Calla said and paused dramatically.

Everyone looked over at Calla, waiting for the rest of what she had to say.

"Julia wants me to plan a Christmas party at Argent Castle."

Guthrie groaned out loud. Grant could just imagine Guthrie thinking about the expenditures for such a venture.

Calla smiled. "I'm not saying she will. She hasn't asked, but if she does, maybe while I'm planning the affair, I can stay here for a while."

"Christmas is too far away," Guthrie said.

Grant was surprised he said so as they made their way around the keep to the gardens out back.

"Okay, then here's the deal. If I stay, I have to be allowed to leave anytime I want," Calla said. "I know Ian, and he'll want to keep me confined within these walls until Baird no longer has an interest in harassing me."

Guthrie said nothing. Grant couldn't speak for Ian, or he would have said it was a deal.

"So the only way this will work to satisfy Ian's need to keep me safe and my need to do my job is if you will accompany me everywhere I go."

"I have a job to do," Guthrie said quickly.

Calla frowned at him. "Aye, as do I. My terms are nonnegotiable. I don't mean for *you* personally to have to escort me everywhere, but as in you—*your kinsmen*."

Looking vastly relieved, Guthrie nodded. "Ian can send out others to guard you, and that should be perfectly acceptable to him."

She pondered that and then said, "Agreed."

Grant breathed a sigh of relief. He wasn't even involved in the matter, but he did care about Calla's safety.

"But…" she said.

Grant wanted to shake his head. The terms were agreed upon. The lass couldn't already be changing her mind.

"That's only if Julia asks me to plan a Christmas party for her."

Guthrie didn't look happy about that. Would he tell Julia that? Encourage her to have a party when it went against every financial bone in his body?

Grant wondered which way it would go.

Calla changed the subject abruptly and said to Grant, "Since Archibald Borthwick was here tonight, it made me think about him and Colleen, and I thought you should know this. He wasn't at my wedding as friend of the groom but only because he was trying to learn when Colleen Playfair was coming to Scotland and forgot the time. I didn't think anything of it because I didn't know his connection to Colleen. I thought he was an old friend of the family."

"Hardly," Grant said, although Archibald might claim to have been a friend of Theodore Playfair.

"Baird had said, by rights, the castle should have been Archibald's."

So Archibald had told Baird this tale, too. "How did he figure that?" Grant asked as he opened the gate to the garden path that led to the garden room. They could hear the ladies all laughing and having a good time of it. He wanted to know what they were talking about that was so funny.

"You know how men are. They were drinking, boasting,

and making wild claims. I had no idea what they meant by it. I didn't even know if they were talking about Farraige Castle. I thought that Archibald was friends with Colleen, though. She said she'd never met the man before she came here. So that had me wondering what was going on."

"Aye. He's like a leech, looking for a free meal ticket. So did you gather anything from what Baird and Archibald said that might give you a reason why he thought he should own the castle?"

Calla sighed deeply. "His grandfather Uilleam Borthwick had been the manager—and that was one of the reasons. The other was that Uilleam had shown interest in Colleen's grandmother when her grandfather died. He had every intention of mating her."

"What?"

Neda had never once mentioned, nor had his own father, that Uilleam had not only managed the estate but intended to mate Neda. Grant didn't believe it.

"According to Archibald, his grandfather had been the manager. He said that Uilleam was successfully courting Neda Playfair at the time. And that it was only a matter of time before she would agree to a mating. But he said that John MacQuarrie, their scribe, lied to her, saying Uilleam was crooked. Uilleam was fired. Worse, your grandfather took over and managed the estates. Until Uilleam murdered him."

Grant couldn't believe it. Yet, if it was true, it made some sense. All these years he'd thought his family had managed the keep since it was built. Now he was learning that Archibald's grandfather had been taking care of the property from the beginning. But still, Archibald could be lying, trying to say that Grant's family had been the cause of all the trouble in the beginning.

"So if Uilleam had mated with her, he wouldn't have had to worry about cheating on the accounts because he would have controlled them," Grant said, "if this isn't one big lie."

"Aye. Agreed. If it's true, though… What if he did love Neda Playfair? Maybe it wasn't all about the money and properties. But once she turned on him, he was bitter and took his revenge out on your grandfather for telling on him and then getting his position."

Grant could see that. Not that he thought Uilleam loved Neda, but that he was so close to having everything—not just as the property manager, but as the owner while Neda was his mate.

"My grandfather must have had enough proof to sway her, or she wouldn't have believed Uilleam was cheating her."

"She might have also suspected something wasn't right. Women's instincts," Calla said.

And that was probably the reason why Archibald's father had tried so hard to get back all that the Borthwick line had lost because of the mistake his father had made.

—∽∽—

The fire was still going in the garden room, making the room cozy, and the women's sweet scents wafted in the air. It was in the wee hours of the morning that all the ladies had finally stopped talking. Colleen stared up at the roof made of skylights that showed off a gray, cloudy night, no sign of stars or the moon. The garden room had cool stone towers that mimicked the castle's at the four corners of the curtain wall. She was considering making such a place at Farraige Castle for her people to enjoy. She smiled at the notion that the pack was indeed hers, and that they were not just living on her property.

She heard a pebble hit one of the floor-to-ceiling glass windows and turned her head. Julia and Heather had shut the soft green shades over the windows to make the room more private earlier that day. So they couldn't see who was bothering them now.

Julia groaned. "They should know better than to disturb us," she grumbled under her breath.

Colleen smiled. Julia needed her nine hours of sleep to be able to deal with life the next day. Colleen watched as Julia opened the garden room door just a crack. "Grant," she said, feigning annoyance. "I should have known. This is an all-girls' slumber party, you know."

"Can I speak with Colleen for just a minute?" Grant asked, sounding as if he was attempting to appease her, but Colleen heard the hint of aggressiveness in his voice that said if Julia wasn't agreeable, he'd barge right in and have his way anyway.

Colleen loved him for it.

"To give her a good-night's kiss and that's it, right?" Julia asked, as if she was responsible for every member of her pirate crew, and she wanted to ensure the terms were agreeable.

"Aye," he said with a smile in his voice.

Colleen draped her blanket around her like a shawl and got off the couch to get her kiss. She wondered how many of the ladies were awake and ready to watch the show.

But when she passed Julia, who was already returning

to her made-up bed, Colleen didn't expect Grant's quick action. Still only wearing his kilt, he grabbed her up. She squealed, and he hurried back to the castle with her.

The door to the garden room shut, and she heard no one coming after her to rescue her. So much for her pirate comrades-in-arms.

"A kiss, you said," Colleen told Grant, wrapping her arms around his neck as he smiled down at her.

"Aye, a kiss."

"And nothing more. That is it."

"You will demand more of me, I'm sure. It won't be my fault that I don't return you to the garden room for the rest of the night."

"Does anyone else know that you came for me?"

He chuckled. "They would think me a beastly sort if I didn't rescue my bonny mate from the clutches of those wayward wenches."

"And have your way with me."

"Aye."

She laughed. She never thought having her first ladies' night out in Scotland could end like this.

He'd barely carried her to a guest chamber and set her down before he showered her with hard, lingering kisses, as if the hours they had been apart had been too much, his hands on her shoulders, holding her close.

And she adored him.

"You can't do this at every ladies' night party I have," she said, the blanket she'd covered herself with slipping off her shoulders.

"Hmm," was all he said as he quickly divested her of her red heart-patterned flannel pajama top and tossed it on the floor. Her matching pajama bottoms soon joined it.

He scooped her up and carried her to the bed, the navy curtains already pulled aside.

Red rose petals had been strewn all over the white sheets, and she smiled as he set her down on the soft, fragrant petals.

"Who did this?" she asked, not believing any of the men would have done such a thing.

"Calla and some of the other ladies snuck away and decorated the bed."

"You all were in collusion."

He smiled.

She couldn't believe the women had been so sneaky. And here she thought they'd just returned to the castle to brush their teeth and the like.

He stripped before she could offer to remove his kilt. And then he joined her on the mattress and closed the bed curtains.

His eyes were like pools of midnight, fathomless, desirous, drinking every bit of her in as he ran his hands over her skin. She'd seen him naked so many times already—marveling at his gorgeous form every time. She didn't feel shy about observing him like this. But it was his exploration of her naked body that made her want to pull up the covers.

He held himself so still, except for his fingers trailing down her breast, her waist, sweeping down her thigh. His touch, though gentle, ignited a flame deep inside her. She felt the all-too-familiar wet heat forming between her legs, the sign her body wanted him—was ready for him. Again.

As if he had finished taking his fill of her, he pushed her legs apart and separated her folds with his fingers, bringing her to life as he stroked her feminine nub, at the same time kissing her mouth. Slowly at first. And then matching her wildly passionate response. Their frantic heartbeats and rapid breathing were in sync. Their kisses verged on desperate as he rubbed his engorged cock against her hip.

She felt the flame roaring inside her, the need rising, and reached down and cupped him. He groaned out loud, and she smiled. But when she stroked his cock, his fingers stole into her wet sheath, and she wanted so much more. Him. Inside her. Now.

She was so close to coming. So very near the edge. She rolled her thumb over the top of his erection, and he groaned her name this time. He cupped her face, lined his body up with hers, and drove his cock between her legs. Deep, penetrating, hungry. Then he tongued her mouth as if he were the pirate pillaging her.

Primed, she came, shuddering with release.

Grant continued to drive into her, following her over the edge. She felt sexy and well loved, tired and satiated. She wanted to stay here with him the rest of the night, but she felt guilty, too, as he sank against her, just as blissfully sated.

She sighed. "Don't you think I should return to the garden room and stay with the other ladies, since that's the reason I'm here?" she said, curling up against Grant's hot body. He smelled delectable—of the woods, whisky, and all male wolf. She didn't make a move to leave him or the bed, despite what she'd said.

"Hmm," he said, closing his eyes and pulling the covers over them. His arms wrapped around her in mated bliss.

"I should," she insisted, her voice sleepy, and she closed her eyes. She luxuriated in the feel of him. The way his warm breath fanned the top of her head, the sound of his heartbeat settling down, his muscles hard and warm beneath her body, the smell of him—all earthy sex, male, spicy, and delicious.

"Hmm."

"You're ignoring me," she said softly.

"You try to leave the bed, lass," Grant said in a husky, satisfied voice, "and"—he kissed the top of her head—"you will not be successful."

Hearing the smile and a hint of a challenge in his voice, she chuckled. She loved her alpha mate. And loved that he did not want her to leave the bed. As tired as she was, he'd have to carry her anyway.

"Wait until you fall asleep," she said, smiling.

"Hmm," he said and tightened his hold on her.

When they awoke much later that day to a knocking on the door, Colleen shook her head. Though she had planned to slip away to prove to him that he wasn't in charge of her, she hadn't wanted to be anywhere but with Grant last night. Then again, waking him later to insist he make love to her probably had proved she would have her way—at least in that regard.

Grant let out a tired sigh when the person knocked again at the door.

"Anyone still alive in there?" Julia called out cheerfully.

Colleen smiled.

"Aye, negotiations were tough but somehow we

managed to work through them," Grant said, smiling down at Colleen.

She kissed his mouth, glad she hadn't gone anywhere this morning.

"Breakfast—*late breakfast*—is being served. Or would you rather take it in your chamber?" Julia asked.

"Downstairs," Colleen said, afraid they'd never leave the bed at this rate, especially if they had breakfast in bed.

Grant ran his hand over Colleen's breast, making the nipple rise to his touch. She softly groaned. "We'll be down in a few minutes," Grant said.

An hour and a half later—amusing Julia and everyone else—they finally made their appearance.

Chapter 21

AFTER PACKING UP AROUND MIDDAY, COLLEEN AND Grant returned to Farraige Castle. This time they also took Calla with them so that she could stay there until the wedding and reception were over. They hadn't believed Baird would run them off the road in an effort to get Calla back on the way to Farraige Castle, but taking extra precautions, Ian had some of his men follow them there.

Grant had every intention of making a really early night of it so he and Colleen could get some sleep as well as some private time. He couldn't help that every time he thought about her wearing that saucy pirate-wench costume, or without, he'd get hard and want her all over again.

Colleen was in the study trying to sort out all the stuff about the wedding with Calla when Enrick and Lachlan cornered Grant in his chamber. *His chamber*. He smiled. He never imagined he'd mate the lass and be able to return to his chamber because of that.

Enrick stood with his arms folded, the smile in his eyes saying he was highly amused. "You never mentioned that this was your plan to get your room back."

Grant chuckled.

"Or that you'd worked out a way to counter Archibald's moves," Lachlan said. "Fast work. We thought you'd ask our opinion about what steps you could take to woo the lady."

"As if I'd ever need your advice in that regard," Grant said cheerfully.

"We really didn't expect you to return as mated wolves and now have a wedding plan in progress," Enrick said. "We are both curious as the devil to know what happened between the two of you. Duncan called us and said you were staying because the lass was involved in some woman's party. But he wouldn't say what was going on. Just said you and she were negotiating terms in the wine cellar at the moment. We figured for certain the two of you were still at odds."

"Aye, but it appears you did well with the negotiations," Lachlan said.

"We should have followed you there," Enrick said. "Hearing all the laughter in the background, I'd say it sounded like the lot of you were having a grand time."

"I told Ian the next time the ladies gather for such a party, you'll have to come, too," Grant said.

"What about Archibald?" Enrick asked.

"I've sent men to carry the word to all the places we know Archibald frequents that Grant MacQuarrie is now mated to Colleen Playfair and that the wedding shall soon follow. That should put a stop to him trying to see her." Grant explained that the bastard had approached the woods surrounding Argent Castle in an attempt to see Colleen.

"Not good," Enrick said. "Though maybe now he'll give up."

"We can hope," Grant said, having every intention of ensuring Colleen's safety.

"Archibald is sure to want to strike back at you, so we'll need to take precautions," Lachlan said. "Now that you've mated Colleen, I take it you want me to cancel the reservations at the B and B in the village that you'd made for the lass."

Grant had forgotten all about mentioning the situation to his brothers. When Lily heard Colleen's name and started to tell her that she had a reservation there, he'd quickly let the B and B owner know that wasn't happening. "Canceled," Grant said. "Lily met Colleen. She knows the story."

"What about the lass borrowing your car?" Enrick asked. "We don't want to give your keys to her again if it means having a mad chase on the roads trying to hunt her down."

Grant rubbed his whiskered chin. "If she asks for my keys, let me know, pronto."

Smiling, Enrick shook his head.

"Oh, and these are yours." Grant pulled Enrick's underwear out of Colleen's bag and tossed them to him.

Enrick frowned and breathed in the scents on them. "I didn't want to mention that Colleen had been in my underwear drawer. I asked Lachlan if she'd been in his, but he said no. We discovered she'd been in yours. So we were just a little apprehensive about bringing it up— especially when we learned you'd mated her." He took another whiff of them. "But I smell Heather's scent on them, too. What's up?"

"Apparently, Heather had asked Julia if she would encourage Colleen to capture a pair of your trunks to add to the pirate's pole."

"Pirate's pole?"

"Aye. The lasses had several of ours dangling from the pole. Which we promptly replaced with their bras."

His brothers laughed. Lachlan said, "Don't leave us out of the next bash you're involved in. Sounds like too much fun."

Enrick said, "Heather claimed mine?" He sounded like he was still mulling that over.

"Aye. Want to tell us anything about that, Brother?" Grant asked, amused.

"Nothing to tell. This is news to me."

To Grant also.

"I would say you have all the luck," Lachlan said, "but Heather is nothing but trouble. So I'd say I had all the luck." Lachlan shoved his hands in his pockets and grinned.

Colleen was so inundated with choices, starting with the wedding gown—MacQuarrie plaid or an off-white affair since she'd been mated twice before, even though she'd never had a wedding ceremony. Calla told her she could wear anything her heart desired. Colleen had asked Grant, and he said the same—whatever she wanted. He would love her in it. He had been absolutely no help at all.

They had to discuss the color of flowers and the kind of food to serve at the reception. Then they had to consider the particulars of the bachelorette party, which meant a ladies' day and night all over again. Different theme, but Colleen thought that the pirate ladies' theme had appeal. Calla had suggested they do something else, though, just for the bachelorette party.

Colleen was curious what the bachelor party would consist of. Maybe she and the ladies could crash it.

Enrick had contacted all the women of their pack to return home early for the wedding. And to his surprise and Grant's, they had demanded that they get to extend their holiday by that many days. He had created a monster, and it served him right.

Enrick and Lachlan had escorted Calla to a birthday party she was hosting late that afternoon for a ten-year-old in another town, so they were serving as her bodyguards. They didn't mind watching over her, but both had vehemently opposed dressing like clowns. Even so, they did it out of a sense of obligation.

Happy to not have to consider anything wedding-related for the whole afternoon, Colleen immersed herself in the finances of the pack and found discrepancies centuries earlier and again last year. Neither was related because the time that had elapsed between them was more than several hundred years.

But still, she was curious about the first—mostly because Grant's grandfather had not been managing the estates as the MacQuarries had claimed. Archibald had been right, though prior to him mentioning it, she'd never heard of anyone else administering them. As she went through the old documents that had been scanned into the computer, she realized Uilleam Borthwick had been the administrator of the estates at their inception but continued for only a few weeks. Which was probably why future generations didn't know about it.

John MacQuarrie had been the scribe. Then Uilleam was no longer manager, and John had been elevated to administer the estates. She let out her breath. She had to tell Grant that she'd found proof for Archibald's allegations.

She imagined that when Robert and then Grant himself took over the estates, they would have been more concerned with the current and future state of affairs, not something that had occurred much earlier.

The more recent discrepancies had to do with the misappropriation of money for food and had steadily increased for four months until they abruptly stopped. So it wasn't a case of a major feast the pack had, which she hadn't any problem with. She pulled out her phone and called Grant, who said he was overseeing the patching up of the old chapel to use for the wedding.

"Aye, lass? Up to my armpits in mud, so anything you want to do about the wedding is fine with me."

"We wish to have you serve as our male stripper for the hen night, or as we Americans would call it, the bachelorette party," she teased.

Silence.

She smiled. Not often did she render him speechless. She sighed. "I was going over the accounts and found a couple of discrepancies."

"I'll be right there."

"No rush," she said, meaning it. She hadn't realized he was quite so busy, and she certainly didn't want to pull him away from the job. Unless he just wanted a break from working on the chapel.

"Nay, I'll be there. Just let me wash up a bit."

She sighed as he hung up on her. She hadn't wanted him to think it was anything that was current and had to be taken care of right this minute. But she wondered if Uilleam had doctored the accounts, Neda had caught him at it, and he was fired. What if John MacQuarrie had been the one to let the cat out of the bag? Then he got Uilleam's job and Uilleam sought revenge. Not just because he wanted to be manager, but because he *had been* the manager. And John had discovered the theft and told on him. And then *he* became the manager.

Not long after she and Grant ended the call, he arrived, no shirt, clean trousers, his skin freshly washed, his face a little flushed from rushing to get there.

She rose from the desk chair and gave him a hug. "Hmm, you smell like spices and the sea, and wolf, of course. You didn't have to hurry. I just found something I thought you might want to know if you didn't already."

"The discrepancies in the foodstuffs. Aye. I took care of it. The man who had been working the books had been in league with the head cook. Maynard now holds the head cook's position."

She chewed on her bottom lip and considered Grant, not saying a word. Was this what Archibald meant when he said discrepancies existed in the accounts? Why hadn't Grant told her?

"This is what you've been worried about? Maynard was concerned. Everyone has known about this but me?" she asked, annoyed.

Grant frowned. "The man was made to pay for the theft. The accounts were set right. As you can see, we had more money in the accounts for several months as the man paid the clan—well, you—back."

"Yes, but why didn't you tell me?"

"I took care of it."

"Yes, but…I understand that part, Grant. But you should have told me." She let out her breath. "Is there anything else?"

"Nay, I went through the accounts for a couple of

years back, but saw nothing else that would indicate he or anyone else had been pilfering money."

"Did you ever look at the historical figures?"

Grant considered her as if he wasn't sure what was going on in her head.

"Okay, no, then. Did you know that Uilleam was Farraige's first administrator?"

Grant's jaw hardened. "Aye, Calla said she had heard it was so. She told me when she was getting the wedding books from her car. But we didn't know if it was all a lie. You found evidence to corroborate the story?"

His voice was dark and growly, and Colleen realized the notion that his grandfather was the very first administrator had been an honor for his clan and his pack. She felt bad that anyone had to spoil that for him. But maybe it explained why Uilleam had killed Grant's grandfather.

She showed Grant the documents, explained what she thought had happened, then said, "Did Neda keep journals?"

"Aye," he said slowly. "They were stored when she died. We didn't think anything of it, but we didn't want your father to destroy them if he had a mind to."

"Understandable and good thinking. Can I see them?"

"Aye." Grant started to leave the study, and she followed him. "I can have them brought here to the study," he said.

"How about having them delivered to Neda's chamber? I want to spread them out there, organize them, see what I can see. I don't want to make a mess of the study, and no one is using her chamber right now."

"I'll help you." He called someone on his cell and

said, "Get a couple of men to grab Neda's boxes of journals and bring them to her chamber. Thanks."

Colleen looked up at him as they strode toward the women's corridor. "You were building a wall, nice manly work." She reached over and ran her hand over his muscled chest.

He gave her a wicked smile. "You're sure you still want to read Neda's journals?"

She laughed. "Yes. I have a one-track mind myself. I want to learn what Neda had to say about this."

"Calla said Archibald told Baird that Uilleam was courting Neda."

Colleen's jaw dropped. *"No. Really?"*

"Aye, that's what she said." Grant put his arm around Colleen's shoulders and continued down the hallway to Neda's chambers while Colleen considered that news.

"So he wasn't just the first manager of the estates. He was trying to woo Neda into mating him, and he would have been the owner, too."

"Sounds like that from what you've discovered and from what Calla learned."

"Which would be all the more reason for Uilleam to be so angered and kill John. Hopefully, she mentioned it in her journal," Colleen said.

"You really aren't angry about me not mentioning the discrepancies, are you?"

"Yes, I am. You should have told me when I first arrived. I should make you do a striptease for us at my bachelorette party."

"You think I would mind?"

Colleen felt her body warm. "Actually, *I* would. I mean, I love looking at that hot body of yours, but I don't want everyone else to get an eyeful."

He laughed.

"I suppose no one else would have kept journals. Your father, perhaps, who might have said what he felt had happened to your mother."

"Nay."

"Archibald told me that you were stealing from me. I wonder how he knew."

"I wasn't stealing from you, lass," Grant growled.

"I know. He made it sound like you were in charge so you had knowledge. Which you did, and you hadn't let me in on the truth. So how would he know?"

Grant didn't say anything until they arrived at Neda's chambers and found ten taped boxes sitting squarely on the floor beside her bed. Grant got out his knife and cut through the tape. "I wouldn't think the thief would tell Archibald or anyone else about what he'd done, for fear he'd never get a job again."

"Unless he bragged about it."

"Or Archibald…" Grant shook his head and began lifting journals out of the box.

"Or Archibald what?" Colleen began sorting the journals by decade.

"This is going to take forever," he said, cutting through the tape on another box. "Or Archibald knew the man had done it."

"As in he had been involved in the theft somehow? How long had the cook worked for you?"

Grant stopped what he was doing and stared at her. "Since your father took over."

She let out an annoyed sound. "So Archibald and my father were behind cheating himself out of money?"

"Nay. Your father wasn't sober enough to focus on

the accounts. He had issues with several things but nothing that was a problem. But he had found this great cook and wanted to install him as the main cook."

"Was he a great cook?"

"Aye. He was."

"But one of Archibald's men, maybe. So he may have thought all he had to do to discredit you was say that you were responsible for the theft, and Archibald's man would have made sure you were somehow seen as the villain."

"But your father left, then he died, and I discovered the theft and booted the cook out."

"And failed to mention it to me." She started organizing the second box of journals.

"You are still sore with me over it."

"Yes, because Archibald tried to discredit you as one of the bad guys." She sneezed. The books were full of dust. "This will take forever."

"I took care of it," he reiterated.

She glanced at him. "You thought I'd be like my father. High-handed. Unreasonable. Threaten to fire you?"

Grant paused. "Aye, lass. After dealing with Theodore, I didn't know what to expect from you."

"I'm nothing like my father."

"Which is one of the reasons I mated you."

She chuckled.

He cast her one of his hot, sexy, wolfish smiles.

He finished cutting open the rest of the boxes, and she started on the third one while he began separating the journals into piles. "Wait, I think these look like the very first. Calf skin leather. Very old. Earliest date."

"Okay," Colleen said, taking the precious journal in her hands and sitting on an embroidered rose-colored chair. "Why don't you see if you can find anything around the time of your mother's death? See if you can learn what Neda thought. Maybe the journal shortly after your father's death also."

The reading wasn't easy. Colleen didn't recognize some of the terms or the ancient way of spelling things or the old cursive handwriting. But then she came to the part about Uilleam and she said, "Ohmigod, Grant, he *was* courting her. She had lost her mate, who was Theodore's father, my grandfather, Gideon Playfair, and then she had hired Uilleam as her manager when her other manager died. Her husband had hired the first manager."

"So there was a manager even before Uilleam. How did the other manager die?"

"Accidental death. Fell off the cliffs while they were building the walls of the keep on the leeward side." She glanced up at Grant, her skin crawling over the similarity to the other deaths.

"Convenient," Grant said, still looking for the other journals.

"Yes, sounds like a tried-and-true method for getting rid of competition. Neda was really happy, talking about seeing Uilleam on walks and running with him as wolves in the woods, and then she didn't write for several days. When she did, she said John MacQuarrie, scribe for the clan, had told her about discrepancies in the accounts."

"Neda's husband, Gideon, was supposed to have died on the battlefield. Was it true?" Grant asked.

"Clan battle, she says. Looks legit."

"Aye, unless one of his clan stabbed him in the back and made it look like it was the enemy's doing."

"True," she said.

"Here's the one for the time period when my father died." He handed it to her. "I'm still looking for the one when my mother died."

Colleen read some from the first one he'd handed her, then said, "Nothing else in this one. Just a lot of praise for John and how glad Neda was that she had installed him as the new manager. Wait, okay, here is when he was murdered. She was horrified, swore it was Uilleam who had been behind the killings. She…yes, she'd had spies learn the truth. Then she sent men to hunt him down."

"Good. Bastard."

"Then she installed your father." Colleen opened the journal that Grant had handed her. "Okay, she loved your father just as she had his mate, Eleanor. But when Robert died, Neda suspected foul play because it was too much like when Eleanor had died years earlier. She couldn't learn who had done it." Colleen skimmed through page after page after page. "Wait, here we go. She learned that Archibald's father, Haldane Borthwick, had been visiting Theodore the day Robert died. She'd been away at her aunt's sickbed and stayed for the funeral, then got word that Robert had fallen from the cliffs to his death. She was furious. Some had said he might have committed suicide. She didn't believe it for a minute. You boys were away at college and she… *Holy* cow."

"What?" Grant asked, setting down the journal he was holding and joining her. He rubbed her back as he looked over her shoulder.

"Neda learned Archibald's father had killed Robert. She and Darby went to pay Haldane a visit. *She* killed him, she says. Haldane never expected her to do it, though Darby was there to aid her if she needed him to."

Grant's jaw dropped. "I can't believe it. That's why Darby would never say. We thought he'd gone missing for a day and done it and that Neda was away shopping. I never knew." He let out his breath. "She was a remarkable woman."

"I'm sorry," Colleen said, taking Grant's hand. "I wish I'd met her. Ever since I got here and learned so much about her, I've hated my father for ensuring I never saw her and hated myself for not seeing through the deception."

"You couldn't have known, lass," Grant said, pulling her into his arms. "Come, let's look at more of this later. I didn't find the one for the time period when my mother died yet. But let's take a break. Why don't you tell me what you're doing for your hen night."

"Ha! That's a secret," she said, knowing he only mentioned it to keep her from feeling so sad about what had happened to his family and her own. "What about you and your bachelor party?"

"You think I would tell you about the stag party when you won't tell us what you're up to? Where are you having yours?"

She chuckled. "If I told you, you might crash it."

The guys might think they would crash the girls' party again, but she had every intention of the ladies storming the men's affair.

Chapter 22

AT DINNER, GRANT AND COLLEEN NOTICED THAT Frederick, the lad who was taking care of the dogs, seemed upset about something. He kept avoiding looking at her—or at Grant.

Colleen suspected what the matter was, but wasn't about to approach the boy. He needed to come to her and tell her what he'd done.

"He's been avoiding you ever since we returned to Farraige Castle," Grant said, seeing her look again in the boy's direction.

"He has. I've gone out of my way to show there are no hard feelings, but I won't come right out and put him on the spot."

Grant turned his attention from Frederick to Colleen. "What has he done?"

She shook her head. "Nothing of consequence. But I believe he's feeling guilty about it, and he needs to take the first step to make things right. I have no problem with the lad." She wanted to say it was all Grant's fault the boy had pulled the prank on her.

Grant chewed on his ham, then said, "I can talk to him."

"No. He needs to do this on his own." She furrowed her brow at Grant. "I'm serious. Don't you go asking him what this is all about. It's no big deal."

She sighed. She shouldn't have told him anything about it.

"As you wish," Grant said.

But he sounded like it nearly killed him to comply in the matter. And she hoped he really would do as she wished instead of being his usual pack-leader self and attempting to deal with it.

———

Colleen returned to the study to make a budget for the upcoming year. Though Grant had every intention of letting the situation go with Frederick, he couldn't. His job was to see to his pack members' needs. And if one had a problem, he wanted to help.

Not only that, but if Frederick had done something with regard to Colleen that he needed to apologize for, Grant wanted it done sooner rather than later.

Grant headed to the wall walk and watched the sunset, the clouds purple, while swaths of red-orange colors blazed across the sky. He phoned Enrick. "Have Frederick meet me up on the wall walk at the northeastern tower."

Enrick asked, "Is this about his moodiness?"

"Aye." So Grant and Colleen weren't the only ones to have witnessed the lad's unusual behavior.

"Do you know what it's about? I've asked, but he just shrugs me off like there's nothing wrong. I'm worried that maybe he's feeling bad about losing his mum again," Enrick said.

"That's what I'm about to find out," Grant said.

"Okay, he's at the kennel. I'll fetch him." Enrick ended the call.

Grant leaned against the wall and watched the sunset, thinking he needed to bring Colleen up here on a night like this.

Before long, he heard Frederick climbing the steps inside the tower, and when he opened the door, the teen looked like he was about to be beheaded.

"Come. Talk to me," Grant said gruffly.

The lad complied, getting close enough to satisfy Grant. "I asked you earlier if something was bothering you. You said no. However, Colleen believes you need to speak to her about something. She said she isn't upset with you over whatever it is."

Frederick's dark eyes rounded.

Grant frowned. Seeing the boy's reaction, Grant knew he was guilty of something. "Aye, women tend to know things before we do even. So I suggest you speak with her and clear this matter up." He hadn't intended for the lad to tell him of his transgressions, just that he wanted to let Frederick know he was aware there was a problem and the lad needed to deal with it.

"My laird, I...I do wish to confess something," Frederick said.

He studied Frederick who now fidgeted with a piece of hay. "What do you have to confess about?"

"The lady. I didn't mean to make anyone mad, but you...were so nice to me when my mum died and put me in charge of the dogs." He looked at the wall-walk floor.

"Aye. Frederick, say what you have to say." Grant couldn't help his stern expression or gruff voice. If the lad had truly done something onerous, he would have to pay for his actions in some manner befitting the crime. Colleen might not want him to, but just because Frederick was a lad of fifteen didn't mean he could get away with some form of devilment and not have to pay the consequences.

Frederick looked up at him. "I'm so sorry, my laird. I really like the lady, and she's been so kind to me. She's showed me all kinds of tricks on how to get the dogs to mind. And it's really working. But…"

Suddenly a thought came to Grant. "This isn't about the dog getting into her room that second night she was here, is it?"

The lad's eyes widened. Then he nodded. "Aye, it is."

Grant laughed. "Then it's no big deal and the lass isn't upset with you."

"I overheard you speaking to your brothers and saying she would be like her father and that she would not be good for the clan. You told me to release the hounds in the great hall at mealtime after you finished sparring with Ian and his men after she first arrived. So I thought when she made you leave your own chamber…" Frederick swallowed hard. "I thought you wanted her gone. Everyone said so. No one should have told you to leave your own chamber."

"Nay, lad. The lady had every right. The castle is hers."

Frederick looked again at the floor. "Well, I truly believed she was bad for the pack, like you said. Until she started teaching me how to handle the dogs. And then she saved Ollie. And well, everyone signed the petition to ask her to stay with the pack. And you acted like you wanted her for a mate. Then she became your mate. And I knew everyone would be angry with me for what I did. You and her included."

Grant was fighting a smile. "I understand your reasoning, but you should have spoken to me before about this. And you should have apologized to her long before this."

"Aye."

"As your pack leader, I make the decisions, and then if they're wrong, I'm to blame and no one else."

"You mean everything you did to try and make her leave was your fault?" Frederick asked.

Grant smiled. That was one way to put it.

"She's going to hate me," Frederick said sulkily.

"It's up to you to make it right with her," Grant said.

"You mean I have to tell her. Myself."

"Aye. She's in the study working on new charts. Why don't you go in and make your peace with her?"

Frederick swallowed hard. "I will."

Grant felt a little bad that the boy had taken his lead in doing what he had done, though he doubted Colleen would be upset with the lad. Still, Frederick had to make amends for his own past deeds when he was in the wrong. It was all part of growing up.

Not that Grant was going to let him do this *all* on his own.

In the study, Colleen had just finished creating one of the budgets when she heard a light knock on the door. She thought everyone in the whole pack knew by now that when she was working, she didn't mind anyone coming in. They didn't have to obtain permission to see her.

"Come in," she said.

The door opened slowly and Frederick stood there, head bowed a bit like a beta wolf, looking like she planned to execute him on the spot. She smiled brightly at him, trying to diffuse the tension in the air. She wondered if the only reason he came to see her was because Grant had talked to him. She would talk with her mate afterward about that. She really hadn't wanted him interfering.

"Come in, Frederick. To what do I owe the pleasure—"

"I came to apologize," he said, eyes downcast, not moving from the doorway.

"Come in and shut the door, why don't you?" she said in a motherly way. "Have a seat," she said and sat across from him near the windows in the little reading alcove.

"I let Hercules into your chamber. I didn't make him get into your bed. I just…well, the door to his laird-ship's chamber was already ajar. And I peered in and saw your door to his room was open. I just thought Hercules would startle you, but I didn't think he'd get into your bed."

"I see. Why did you do it?" That was all that mattered to Colleen.

Frederick didn't say anything.

"The notion was yours alone?"

"Aye, well, I got the idea from his lairdship when he asked me to let the dogs loose in the great hall for the meal."

She smiled at the memory. Someday she would tell her own children about their father and how hard he had tried to chase her off.

She couldn't help being amused that the boy most likely thought taking the initiative to leave Hercules in her room would have pleased Grant. Admiring Frederick for wanting to please his pack leader, she couldn't fault him.

"So I believed he would be delighted with me if I

let the dog in your room. I thought it was really quite brilliant of me," Frederick continued.

"I totally understand. But now you're sorry."

"Aye. You've been so nice to me and taught me how to train the dogs and…" He swallowed hard. "You're Laird MacQuarrie's mate now and our pack leader, too, and well, I just had to tell you the truth. Even if you hate me for it."

She took a deep breath and let it out. "Let me tell you a little secret. I already suspected as much."

"You did? And you didn't say anything to me about it?" He sounded and looked awed as he raised his brows and his eyes grew big.

"No harm was done, except it cost me a little more sleep."

"I'm sorry," he said, but he looked somewhat relieved. "How did you know?"

As if she couldn't have determined what had happened with just a little sleuthing. "You said you tucked the dogs in for the night. You mentioned they weren't 'locked' in, as if saying anyone else could have let one out. But you were responsible for them, and I suspected you had brought Hercules into the keep that night.

"You also willingly mentioned he had to have used the wolf door, but he hadn't. I checked. He used the side entrance after someone opened the door for him. Of course, a lot of smells circulated around the door at the time, but yours and Hercules were also present. Not one of the other dogs, though. And from what I've seen, the dogs aren't ever inside the keep except for the special occasion when they were allowed to sit at the meal with us. True?"

"Aye, my lady. I'm sorry."

"Since you were also responsible for bringing them in to dine with us, I assumed you had also brought him to my chamber." Not to mention it seemed like something a boy would do. "You are forgiven. Besides, it was all Grant's fault."

"Why is it Grant's fault?" Grant asked, entering the study, a smile curving his mouth as his darkened eyes focused on Colleen.

She felt a little thrill at the sound of his deep, dark, and very sexy voice. His tone wasn't angry, but more—he wished to pay her back for saying what she did to the lad.

Frederick jumped to his feet, tangling his shoes in the rug, and caught himself by grabbing the chair's high back before he fell.

Colleen wondered how long Grant had been eavesdropping. She'd been listening so intently to Frederick that she hadn't even heard Grant open the door and slip into the room. Quietly. Like a wolf on a hunt.

"Because you gave him the idea in the first place," Colleen said sternly. When Grant opened his mouth to speak, she raised her hand to silence him. He cast her a small smile. "Not by giving him an order to do so, but by your actions earlier. Therefore, the responsibility is yours."

"So you wish to punish *me* for it, then?" Grant asked, looking like he enjoyed the idea.

"Yes." In a most agreeable manner. She couldn't help it. Grant brought the wild wolf out in her. To Frederick, she said, "You are free to go. Thank you for telling me the truth."

"Thank you, my lady." Frederick beamed, but then he quickly glanced at Grant to see *his* take on it.

Looking pack leader serious, Grant shook his head. "In the future, remember what I said, lad."

"Aye, no more doing things on my own without your permission," Frederick said. He quickly dipped his head to both and hurried out of the study.

When the boy left, Grant approached Colleen. "You completely undermined me in front of my pack member." He pulled her from the chair.

"You completely deserved it." She wrapped her arms around his neck. "You weren't supposed to talk to him about it."

"I couldn't have him feeling bad about whatever it was, and he needed to apologize to you. Are you done with your budgeting?"

"Only for the farms and the household budget. What did you have in mind?"

"Hot sex." He released her and locked the study door.

"What…not in here."

He waved his arm at the rich, chocolate-leather, Victorian-style chaise lounge sitting in a far corner, a plaid blanket tossed haphazardly over it. It reminded her of a place a Grecian lady would lounge while a toga-wearing muscled hunk—similar to a kilt-wearing hunk—fed her grapes before she seduced him. She smiled.

Surrounding it, the dark oak paneling was softly lit by wall sconces, giving it a warm glow. The books lining the shelves and reaching to the high ceiling and the flickering of the flames in the fireplace added to the coziness. Everything was ornate, the crown molding around the ceiling decorated in Celtic knots. Beautiful.

It could work.

She took Grant's hand and led him to the chaise lounge and began kissing him. He wore jeans and a sweater, but not for long. The best part was that he wore the blue plaid boxers she'd displayed on the pirate's flagpole at Argent Castle, and that made her smile. Right before she reached down and cupped him.

"I knew there was a good reason to wear this for you," he said, his voice husky and his expression helplessly in lust.

"Yes," she said in a hot and eager way.

Grant hadn't planned *this*. He'd never imagined having his way with his mate in any place other than their bedchamber. As hard as he was, he'd never manage all the stairs to their chamber without being in some discomfort.

He soon had divested her of her soft sweater and jeans, smiling to see her wearing the bra he had so victoriously attached to the pirate's flagpole, and kissed her more insistently. He bared her breasts, then leaned down to suckle one, not expecting her to melt onto the chaise lounge.

She smiled up at him, wearing only her pale blue lace thong and bra now. "All we need is a cluster of grapes that you could feed me—"

"We have all the fruit we need right here." And then he slipped off his boxers and joined her, dragging her panties free and tossing her bra to the floor.

His hand curled in her silky hair. He kissed her mouth before he moved lower to suckle her breast again. This time, she couldn't escape him.

Both their hearts drummed hard as their lusty scents mixed—she-wolf with male wolf, sweetness and spiciness. His erection pulsed against her thigh as he licked and pulled at her nipples with his lips, loving how they extended with his touch, loving her heated flesh.

He knew before he reached between her legs that he'd find her ready and wet, eager to accept his rigid cock.

Everywhere her hands touched him made his blood run hotter. He throbbed for her, needed release, needed her.

He loved how she took him to task about the lad, yet at the same time teased him about it. They were perfect for each other, perfect as mates and leaders of his pack.

Oh, yeah, perfect, he thought as his fingers sought to give her pleasure while his mouth met hers. Her eyes were closed, her expression one of concentration as he played with her clitoris, working it, bringing her higher. He pushed one of her knees up and then the other, spreading her. She smiled at him, her eyes half-lidded, her body open to him. And then he stroked her again until she cried out, involuntarily closing up on him.

He pushed her legs apart again and entered her hard, heard her gasp, and meant to pull out, but she stopped him with a harsh, "No." With renewed vigor, he thrust into her with hearty and lusty need. She anchored her heels against his arse and thrust her hips, connecting with him forcefully.

"Lass," he groaned as she gave him a cocky smile, knowing just how fast she could turn him into a power-ful firestorm of craving, and just how quickly she could bring him to completion.

He continued to thrust, to prolong the glorious feeling of being tucked inside her hot, wet, velvety sheath.

Finished, but only for the briefest of times, he sank

against her, their hearts still pounding hard and furiously, their breathing rushed, the only other sound the crackling of the logs in the fireplace.

He toyed with a curl of her hair caressing her shoulder and kissed her cheek. "Now you were saying about this cluster of grapes?"

"Yes," she said, smiling, her hand stroking down his hip. "I envisioned you feeding me while I lay on the chaise lounge in a toga, one breast exposed, or maybe both. Then I'd seduce you."

His cock stirred inside her.

She chuckled and kissed his ready mouth. "You're insatiable."

"I can't help it if the notions you have and your sweet body make me behave so wickedly. I will have to ensure Maynard adds grapes to the grocery list."

"I noticed he added doggie treats so I wouldn't make mincemeat of another choice steak."

Grant smiled. "Tell me more about your Grecian plan of seduction."

She ran her hand down his arm. "You'd wear a kilt. I thought of a toga, but I'd rather seduce a kilt-wearing Highlander, chest fully bared."

He leaned down and licked her breast, his cock pulsing again inside her.

She laughed.

He started to kiss her lips again. "Keep talking about this seduction. Show me."

Colleen couldn't believe talking about her sexual fantasy would turn Grant into a raging inferno of love all over again. Then again, he'd really gotten into her being a pirate wench.

When they finally retired to bed that night, she vowed she'd have to come up with more sexual fantasies for her Highland warrior, who was one hunk of a wolf in the flesh.

Chapter 23

BEFORE GRANT AND COLLEEN VENTURED FORTH THE next day, they cuddled together in their bed. If anyone had told her she'd be doing this while she came for her yearlong stay, she would have thought him crazy—especially when she had believed Grant and his kin were human. She sighed, then smiled up at him. "So…what are you going to do for your stag party?"

"I'd skip it to be with you."

She sighed. "I've already promised the ladies, and they're all game to have the bachelorette party."

Grant had every intention of learning just what the ladies had scheduled.

After eating lunch, he met with his brothers in the study, while the ladies conversed in the great hall, discussing their secret schemes.

"In the history of *lupus garous*, I don't think I've ever heard of our kind having a stag party *after* the mating," Enrick said.

"I agree. Which is why we need to learn just where the lassies intend to go," Grant said, wanting to have fun with the women, but feeling a little out of sorts when he learned they intended to leave the property and possibly run into unsavory sorts. Not only that, but he worried the other women might encourage Colleen to kiss a male stranger, or hug him, as a silly last farewell to single life. But their kind didn't do such things—not once they were mated, which for *lupus garous* was more binding than any wedding ceremony.

"Wait," Lachlan said. "I thought we were talking about a stag party."

"Our job will be to ensure that we can participate in the lasses' party like I did with Ian's kin last time. We just need to learn where the women are going and—"

Darby poked his head in through the study doorway. "They are headed for Kelton's Pub, my laird. But first to Lily's bed and breakfast."

Grant smiled, glad his valet was so capable of spying on the ladies without their knowledge. Then he frowned. Unless they knew very well that he'd overheard them speaking of their schedule.

"Uh-oh," Enrick said with a twinkle in his eye. "Does Colleen know about Lily?"

"There's nothing to know. She was a one-night stand and never anything more. And human. As for the pub, we'll arrive before the lasses get there," Grant said, not about to be thwarted. But he and his men wouldn't go to the B and B. The pub was where they'd have their fun. "I want ten men to follow them without their awareness, purely as a precaution to watch over them."

Lachlan said, "Enrick, you'd better watch out. Heather MacNeill already stole your trunks. Never know what she might do if you show up to harass her."

Enrick gave him a look that said he was game, which surprised Grant, but he had more pressing concerns in mind. Such as getting to the pub before the women arrived, and ensuring the women had no troubles along the way.

The bachelorette party was in full swing as Colleen

and the rest of the ladies dressed in their clan plaids—
MacNeill for some and MacQuarrie for others. Calla was
wearing the Stewart plaid. The younger women wore
minikilts. The older women's skirts reached their ankles.
Colleen felt so deliciously naughty. She was told in no
uncertain terms that the lasses went regimental also. Not
so much that it was a military or guy thing, but in the very
old days, women went without. That was when the fashion was to wear long gowns—easier to use the bathroom.
And, of course, if a woman chanced upon her lover in
the glen and no one was about, that made things…easier.

But even so, she felt absolutely scandalous wearing a
minikilt and no underwear.

Not that they had any intention of meeting up with
the guys tonight. They had their own stag party going
on somewhere.

No matter how much Colleen protested not wearing
underwear, Julia said, "When it comes to bachelorette
parties, propriety goes out the window."

Colleen suspected Ian wouldn't agree with her decision, and she was certain Grant wouldn't, either.

The men had been so busy talking in the study that
she and the ladies had managed to slip out without their
knowing. Someone would be sure to tell them eventually. But the ladies would be off on their adventure before that happened.

In a caravan of several cars, the ladies stopped to take
pictures of themselves by the green hills and sheep, their
skirts blowing in the chilly breeze. Colleen posed for
pictures with her friends and several of the MacQuarrie
women who were her new kin now. No wedding was
needed to make it so.

They dropped by the B and B owned and operated by Lily, Grant's former lover—or one-night stand or whatever she had been to him. Colleen knew she needn't have bothered, but she wanted to make sure the woman knew Grant was now strictly off-limits.

Lily raised her brows when the thirty women entered the small lobby of the B and B and then spread out into the living area.

"Grant and I are getting married, and we're having our bachelorette party tonight. So if it would be all right with you, we wanted to take pictures in your B and B since you are friends with Grant. We'll be posting the pictures around, so you might even get some business," Colleen said in a she-wolf got the he-wolf sort of way.

The woman didn't appear happy about Colleen's claim to Grant, but the chance at free publicity had her hopping to, in an effort to take the best pictures of the group inside the inn and out.

And then everyone chanted, "Pub! Pub! Pub!" and they were off again, only this time to enjoy a bit of brew.

As soon as they arrived at the pub, they knew they were in trouble. Grant and his male friends and kin had parked their vehicles there. Colleen hadn't meant to crash his party this early in the night or to do so at the pub, thinking more in terms of doing so at the castle, privately. But this *was* where she and her friends intended to go for *her* party. So it wasn't *exactly* crashing his. Only she was certain that as soon as he got a look at her tiny kilt, he would insist the party was over.

Shoulders straight back, Julia opened the door for Colleen and then she stepped in, followed by the rest.

The men in the pub quit talking and laughing and

turned to see all the women enter. But they didn't look quite as shocked as she had expected. Well, maybe a little, as they eyed the women's short tartan skirts. Then they smiled as if they'd pulled a fast one on the women. Had the men known the ladies' plans?

She suspected so. The cads. "Grant, what are you and the rest of the men doing here? Who told you we were going to be here?"

"The castle walls have ears, lass," he said, reaching for her arm.

The crowd of men took up virtually every seat. The ladies would have to go outside and use the benches on the patio if they wanted to sit down. Grant patted his lap to offer her a place to sit, up close and personal.

She smiled down at his wolfish grin. "You're being a gentleman and offering your seat to me, right?"

"Aye." He patted his lap again.

She laughed and shook her head.

"Scottish hospitality, lass," he said. Before she could let him know she was all for sitting on his lap and in his arms, he seized her arm and tugged her down. She laughed as she sat rather hard on his lap. He groaned a little, and then she wiggled to get comfortable and made him groan some more. Served him right.

Grant set the tone for the party, and ladies squealed as Ian and his brothers collected their mates and pulled them onto their laps. Others did the same.

Calla ended up on Guthrie's lap, but Colleen wasn't sure if Guthrie offered her the seat or she had claimed him. Colleen glanced around to see where Heather had ended up. She was sitting on Enrick's lap. Colleen wondered if Heather's request for her to grab a pair of his trunks so she could display them on the pirate's pole meant there *had* been something going on between the two of them before this—despite her denial.

"You really aren't here because you knew we planned to come here, are you?" Colleen asked Grant. She couldn't believe he'd really want to crash her party again.

"You don't think I'd want my mate off running around, being with other men for any reason, even just to tease as part of a hen party prank, do you? And certainly not dressed like this." He slid his hand over her bare leg. "Besides, you'll catch your death in something so skimpy."

"No, which is why I'm not hugging men for pictures or anything. You would likely hunt them down otherwise, do them bodily harm, and ruin a fun party."

"Aye, you have the right of it, lass."

"You know this was supposed to be our last hurrah," she said, smiling up at him as Julia took their picture.

"*Before* you were mated. Not that I would have agreed to that, either. Once we were mated, any stag parties or bachelorette parties became unacceptable, unless we're together at them. Besides, you have more fun when we crash your girlie parties."

She had to agree he added a lot of spice to the affair. "Fine. But it's all chick flicks when we return to the keep and…"

Grant kissed her full on the mouth. He was so right. They didn't need the crazy parties to say they were free one last time. Not when they were already mated. That didn't mean ladies' night would be a thing of the past. On the contrary.

"We'll watch them with you. As your mate, I want to know everything you enjoy doing," he said agreeably.

Colleen patted his thigh. "Are you up to baking decadently delicious chocolate treats?"

"I am. And eating my fair share, too."

She smiled and hugged him soundly. "I think I'll keep you as my mate."

"I couldn't be happier with our sleeping arrangements. I do have one question for you, though."

"Oh?"

"You didn't send those pictures you took of me while I was sparring with Ian to some other lassies, did you?"

She smiled.

"Darby said he swore the man showing off his arse on Facebook was wearing one of our kilts, and the man he was fighting was wearing the MacNeill tartan. Seemed like too much of a coincidence to us."

She laughed. "What are girlfriends for?"

"I knew it. You said you wouldn't share them." He squeezed her tighter against his chest.

"Well, at least not the identity of the person bearing that sweet ass."

"And now who's baring her sweet—"

"I am not."

He laughed. "With as windy as it is, lass? I'll have my cell handy when we leave here."

She'd hold her skirt down, then. She shook her head at him, but he was grinning wickedly and she knew he would, too. Not to share it with anyone, though.

When the whole party of stags and hens headed home, it was pouring rain, the first she'd experienced since she'd arrived. A shuffling of who rode in which cars followed. Ian and Julia grabbed a ride with Grant and Colleen, and they could barely see their way to the castle in the downpour.

That night, after watching romance movies and sharing popcorn and some crazy chocolate concoctions, Ian and his family left for Argent Castle with plans to return in two days for Colleen and Grant's wedding. The forecast looked like intermittent rain. But it wouldn't put a damper on the festivities, as excited as everyone was.

Everyone else headed for their respective beds. Grant had wrapped Colleen in his spare plaid while they snuggled and watched the movies, ensuring she didn't show off her legs or other unmentionables in the short minikilt. As soon as he carried her to the bedchamber, he set her on her feet, then ditched the plaid wrapped around her.

"I want you just like this," he said, running his hand over her bare leg. Still dressed in his kilt and her in her minikilt, they got into bed together. He pulled her back against his chest, his hand reaching down to feel under her minikilt.

She smiled. A questing finger quickly found its way inside between her slick, hot folds, and she groaned with the sensual assault.

"You should have told me you were already wet for me. You don't know how much it killed me to touch all that silky flesh and not be able to lift that tiny kilt and bury myself inside you while I waited for everyone to retire for the night. From now on, you only wear it for me in the privacy of our chambers."

She smiled, happy to do so, not willing to have a breeze lift her kilt and show off her buttocks. He stole her breath when he began nibbling her ear and rubbed his hard body against her backside.

His phone gave an annoying jingle, making them both tense. It was close to three in the morning, and she couldn't believe anyone would bother them at this hour. Unless it was something serious.

Grant kissed her cheek and withdrew his finger from her feminine folds. "This better be damned important." He pulled out his cell, still holding her close, moving his hips so he could connect his hard cock with her mini-kilted buttocks. She obliged him by wriggling against him, providing friction, too.

"Aye," he growled into the phone. He slipped his hand up her sweater to cup a breast, his fingers softly pinching a nipple, making it tingle with need.

She heard Enrick say, "Archibald's men are here. Ian said they saw five of them in the woods prowling the perimeter near the castle, and Baird is with them."

Her heart skipped a beat. Grant stiffened against her. His sexy scent subtly changed to anger.

Grant swore. "I'll be right down." He gave Colleen a tight embrace. "Stay here, lass. Don't get undressed. I'll return," Grant said, still dressed only in his kilt.

She knew then he would shift if he needed to chase the men or wolves down. He kissed her cheek, then stalked out of the room with the cell in hand.

"Did you see any of Baird's cousins? Any of the rest of his men? What about Archibald?" Grant shut the door to the chamber.

Colleen slipped out of the minikilt in a flash, kicked off her boots, and hurried to throw on her jeans and boots again. At the very least, she wanted to watch what was going on from the ramparts.

Before she could grab a rain jacket, the bedchamber door opened. Thinking Grant had returned for something, she turned. And gasped.

To her horror, a soaking wet Archibald rushed into the room. Before she could scream, he struck her in the temple. A sharp pain registered, and a sprinkling of white stars against an inky black night followed. And then? Nothing.

Chapter 24

THE NEXT THING COLLEEN WAS AWARE OF, HER head throbbed, her hands were tied together, and her mouth was gagged as she lay on the soft mattress. What had happened to her? Then she remembered in a flash of horror. *Archibald*. He was here, and she was in grave danger.

How had he gotten inside the keep?

She kept her eyes closed, listening to movement, trying to determine where he was in proximity to her. She was lying on her side of the bed, her feet unbound. That was good. She planned to kick him, though what good that would do, she didn't know.

Archibald moved toward her, away from the window. "Wake up or I'll kill you where you lay," he said, his voice soft but filled with threat.

Her eyes popped open.

He offered her a cold, calculating smile. "You don't appear happy to see me," Archibald said, sneering at her. "Here I thought we were getting along so famously. I imagine you wonder how I reached you so easily. Through the old sewer pipes, where we're going now. Do you mind?" He yanked her from the bed.

Her wrists burned from the rough hemp rope. She jerked away from him to free herself. She fought him, trying to kick him with her boots, but he growled low, "If you fight me, I'll knock you out. Your choice."

She stilled her efforts, knowing she could do nothing if she was dead to the world, and he could easily kill her somewhere else. She was certain that was his intention. He dragged her down the hallway until they came to a door. He jerked it open and forced her inside, then shut the door. The room was a tiny water closet, never used, from the looks of it. Boards had been pulled free from a hole in an antique-looking toilet—nothing more than a box, with a couple of boards nailed to the top of it to form a toilet hole. Or that had been at one time. She smelled the faint odor of mold and mustiness.

"Hasn't anyone told you about the Welsh princess Nest, a former mistress of King Henry I? A prince from her homeland, a second cousin, Owain, learned how she'd been enslaved by the robber chief Gerald of Windsor. Owain sought to dine with her and was so struck by her beauty that he was determined to have her for his own and free her from her despicable husband.

"The story goes that he and fifteen of his men invaded the castle at Christmastime and she left willingly with him to protect her husband and children. They, her husband and children, meanwhile, had gone through a toilet hole very much like this one. Only theirs had been in use. This hasn't been used for several centuries. You can count yourself fortunate. Can you imagine being married to a man like that who would hide in the sewage pipes underneath the castle while his wife was taken away?

"Just a quick slide down the pipe and you will be where I want you to be," he added.

Stuck beneath the bowels of the castle, she feared. But someone could still rescue her, she hoped.

He lifted her and dropped her through the toilet hole. Her heart skipped beats as she slid through the pipe, fearing she'd be deep in the bowels of the castle with no way to get out for hours. What she didn't expect was to feel the chilly outdoor sea air just before she landed on the rocks below the seawall, the gag muffling her frantic screams.

The Irish wolfhounds barked in the distance, excited, wanting to join the men in their search out front. But it sounded like they had been confined to the kennels. Which was understandable. Though wolfhounds were named such because they had killed wolves in the distant past, she doubted they would do well against a pack of wolves.

The chilling rain drenched her, soaking through her sweater and her jeans.

Oh…my…God, she was certain the pipe was dumping her into the frigid sea, and with her hands tied, she would drown right away. This was bad, but she thought she still had a fighting chance as she squirmed and wriggled, trying to loosen the rope that bound her.

Archibald landed beside her before she could scramble to her feet, her bound wrists making it difficult to maneuver, the rocks even slipperier than before with the rain and wind pelting them at a slant. The whitecapped waves stood out in contrast to the black water, forcefully crashing against the moss-covered boulders.

"That wasn't so bad, was it? Before the inhabitants cared anything about conservation or sanitation, they just let it all dump out to sea," Archibald said, grabbing her arm and hauling her to her feet. "But they removed the section of pipe that actually fed into the water, so these now end on the rocks. Your father showed them to me when I was a boy. We practiced entering the castle in that manner. Other cases exist where an enemy force breached a castle in such a way. Only who would ever do such a thing today? Eh?"

He yanked off her gag. "No one will hear you down here while everyone is beyond the castle walls looking for me—including your mate. Wouldn't he be surprised to learn you decided to take a swim in the cold, black sea at my urging? Only he'll never know I had anything to do with it."

"You can't mean to kill me." Yet she knew he intended just that.

"Centuries earlier, my grandfather should have owned this place." Archibald pulled her down the path leading to the breakers.

She balked at being moved, but she knew he could just as well toss her over his shoulder and then take care of her before long anyway. The thought that both Grant's mother and father died in the same manner chilled her to the core. Somehow she had to prolong this so Grant or one of his men would realize she was gone. They could trace her scent and, hopefully, realize she'd ended up in the sewer pipe and then landed on the beach, and not that she'd walked into the room and then left. She belatedly realized Archibald had no scent. Why wouldn't he? They wouldn't know that he'd forced her to leave with him and that she was in trouble. She feared they'd never learn of it in time. She had to stall him.

"Your grandfather Uilleam killed mine on the battlefield, didn't he? He wasn't cut down by one of the enemy clan's swords, but by his own loyal man," Colleen said, sure of it now as chilling raindrops ran down her face.

"Sometimes a fine line exists between your enemies and your friends. Gideon Playfair fought bravely in battle and died. That's all anyone needs to remember," Archibald said.

"He died at your grandfather's hand," she said, trying to yank her arm free of Archibald's fierce grip as he moved her closer to the breakers. The aspect of being in that icy water was all the more terrifying since she'd already felt its chilling pull when she and Ollie were swept away. She never wanted to experience that again. She kept telling herself she'd read about people winter-swimming in frigid water, believing it was healthy for the body. But doing it all tied up with the threat of being smashed against jagged cliffs? She didn't believe that would be good for anyone's health.

"Then John MacQuarrie had to learn of the theft in the accounts and tell Neda. Uilleam explained to her that John had lied about the figures, but she still believed John," Archibald said.

"Because John hadn't lied, and Neda knew it. Uilleam must have broken her heart."

Archibald shrugged. "All in doing business."

"So he never really loved her. She was just a means to an end. What are you planning? Why kill me?"

Fury in his expression, he scowled down at her. "My father was a good friend of your father. If Theodore hadn't been such a bloody—"

She slipped and fell on the rocks, freeing herself from Archibald's steel grasp for an instant and landing on her butt.

Archibald immediately dove for her and jerked her to her feet, his breath unsteady. "Well, they got rid of

Robert's mate, figuring as much as he loved her, he'd neglect the estates or kill himself. He did neither. The first opportunity Haldane and Theodore had, they helped him join his beloved mate. But Neda still wouldn't install Theodore as a manager of the estates. She knew him too well—his drinking problem, his lack of caring anything for the properties, his inability to handle money. He would have bled the estates dry. He hated Robert MacQuarrie, and he hated Grant and his brothers for the affection your grandmother doled out to them."

"If Theodore had become manager, how would that have helped your father?"

"Haldane and Theodore were the best of friends. They would have found a way to rid themselves of Neda Playfair. That was the plan. But Theodore was too much of an arse and was so furious that his mother didn't let him run the properties that he left for America and abandoned my father. And after all they'd done together, too."

"So when my father did inherit the castle, you thought you could convince him to let you take over management, but what happened? By that time he didn't care?"

"Aye. The bloody sot was too fond of his bottle. Then I had the idea that if he died, you would inherit. But damn if you didn't take up with Grant. I never expected that. He'd made it well known he wasn't happy that Theodore's daughter was coming here to tell him how to run things. I figured I'd step in and be your Highland hero. Take him to task. Protect you. It was working so well. But I never expected you to stoop so low as to give in and go with him. I still didn't believe you would fall for him. In the past, you'd always ended up mating betas."

"You're not a beta," she said.

He smiled, albeit the look was pure evil. "You're right. It was killing me not to be like Grant was toward you. I figured the time would come when I could be myself around you—after we were mated."

"Only he's my hero," she said, chin up, glowering at Archibald. "And my mate."

"So where is your hero now, eh, lass? He will lose you, like he lost his mother and his father. Maybe he won't manage your loss as well and will join you in the deep, briny sea."

Even if she didn't make it, she knew Archibald wouldn't, either—her only bright side to this deadly situation. "They'll kill you. You won't be able to escape."

Archibald waved his hand at the darkness. "A raft. How do you think I got here in the first place? I have no plans to die today or any other. And I've left no hint of my scent anywhere."

The notion that he could get away with murder made her sick to her stomach. She saw the black rubber raft tied up against the rocks, black as the water, and she could see how Archibald had managed to make his way here without anyone spotting him. Though in ye old times, men serving guard duty on top of the wall walk probably would have noticed if a wooden boat had ventured to the cliffs, but it surely would have been dashed against the sharp-edged crags.

She thought the raft looked half-waterlogged, between the rain and the waves, and drooped a little on one side. Losing air? A hole or two in the rubber sides?

He would drown, she hoped, if she had to.

Chapter 25

THIS HAD TO END NOW, GRANT VOWED. NO MORE Borthwicks would harm his family. As soon as he realized Archibald wasn't with his other men out front, Grant returned to the bedchamber to check on Colleen. He didn't believe any harm could come to her there, but he still felt wary about leaving her alone. Partly because he was afraid she might have tried to follow him—as alpha as she was.

He stalked into the room and discovered she was gone right away. Her minikilt sat on the chair. She'd changed. Unless...she'd shifted. Her raincoat was on the floor. She had to have shifted into her wolf form.

Was she on the ramparts, watching for him? He pulled out his cell and called one of his men on watch as he headed out the door and realized the most recent scent she'd left was fearful. And not headed for the stairs to leave the keep.

Fearful for his safety, aye. But why would she be going this way? His heart thundering, he couldn't help the fear escalating in his blood. He kept telling himself she had to be fine.

He tracked her scent to the small water closet that contained the old sewage pipes. His heart nearly stopped beating. What the hell? He knew she wouldn't have just gone exploring the various castle rooms, considering what was happening outside the keep.

He yanked at the door. Bolted. Horror swamped him as he yelled, "Colleen!" and jerked again at the door. Then he began to kick the solid oak, determined to break it down.

Maynard came running. "I heard you yelling from down below. What's happened?"

"Colleen was here. The door is bolted."

Maynard helped Grant kick it open and found no sign of the lass in the small water closet, long since shut up, the boards covering the toilet hole torn aside and thrown on the floor. Grant swore. "Alert the men Colleen may be down at the cliffs."

"Aye…aye, my laird." Maynard hurried out of the water closet and raced down the hallway.

Grant kicked the boards out of the way, careful not to step on the exposed rusty nails. He peered down into the pipe and smelled Colleen's sweet scent mixed with the mold and earthy smells of the pipe. *Bloody hell!* He couldn't believe anyone could have forced her down them. Especially when he smelled no other wolf's scent in here. Had Archibald come for her?

He would kill him. Grant stripped and shifted into his wolf form. Without a moment's hesitation, he slid down the pipes, hoping he didn't break a leg when he landed on the rocks below.

He tumbled out of the pipe onto the rocks and saw Archibald dragging a hand-tied Colleen down below to the breakers. His heart hammering his ribs, Grant knew tackling the bastard that close to where the sea was coming in could mean his and Archibald's deaths. Maybe even the lass's if he couldn't stop them before she got just as close to the sea.

He would do anything to save his mate's life. He knew

his brothers and his pack would take care of Colleen as soon as he could free her from Archibald's grasp.

Grant raced down the path in the driving rain, slipping a little, and lunged for the cur, praying he didn't slide with him and pull them off the edge of the cliffs. Using his wickedly sharp canines, he grabbed Archibald's arm and sank his teeth deep. The man cried out. With his free arm, Archibald reached for a knife in his boot. Before Grant could let go of him and jump back, a wave curled up over the rocks, threatening to take them both out.

Grant prayed Colleen had gotten back away from the breakers. The wave swept him and Archibald off their feet. His heart in his throat, Grant felt himself and Archibald being carried out to sea as he heard Colleen scream.

—∾∾—

Colleen had heard the deep-throated growl that sent a shiver down her spine right before she saw the wolf dash for them. Grant. Even though she knew the threat was not directed at her, the sound was enough to curdle her blood.

A flash of gray fur lunged at Archibald. As a powerful, raging wolf, Grant grabbed Archibald's arm, chomping down, forcing him to cry out and release her.

Heart somersaulting, she fell against the slippery rocks. Archibald swore and fumbled to get to a knife sheathed in his boot, the wooden handle sticking out for her to see, but Grant yanked him back toward the breakers.

Chilled to the core of her being, she moved toward them, unable to do anything with her hands tied.

A wave rose behind them, large enough to knock them down, and she screamed, "No!"

She dove toward them, not that she could do anyone any good, but the wave swept wolf and man into the sea before she could reach them.

"No! Colleen!" Enrick shouted as he hurried to reach her.

She barely heard the men scrambling down the rocks. And then strong arms pulled her away from the threat of the sea.

"No!" she screamed. "Let me go! Grant!"

The seawater and rainwater drenching her, she struggled to return to where he had disappeared. She wanted to help him in any way that she could, wanted to see the men bring him out of the sea. But Enrick and Darby hauled her back to the seawall.

"Lass, we will do everything we can to rescue Grant," Enrick assured her while he cut the ropes binding her wrists. Then he lifted her over the wall to Lachlan.

She knew they could do nothing. Not in the dark in the roiling sea. Not when Grant was a wolf.

Lachlan had hold of her arm with a titan grip and hurried her to the keep.

She shivered and shook and couldn't stop agonizing over wanting to return to find Grant. She didn't remember everything that happened after that. She thought she hit Lachlan in the eye. She might have cursed a few choice words. How could they give up on him now? How could they keep her from him?

"We don't want you to catch your death, lass," Lachlan said, moving her against her will to the castle and trying to reason with her. "Grant would have our hides."

He spoke as if Grant would survive, that he wouldn't see it any other way.

Men hollered for Grant from the top of the cliffs.

"Others will head down to the rocky beach beyond the cliffs. We'll find him," Lachlan assured her again, sounding more this time like he was trying to convince himself it was true.

Had any of those living here over the centuries survived the sea, either in their wolf forms or human, other than she and Ollie who had been fortunate enough to have been seen and rescued in time? She didn't want to ask for fear she'd hear no one had.

She fought to control her emotions. They *would* find him alive. They had to. He had been a wolf when the sea had taken him. He would be warm enough, but had he been injured? Could he fight the tide's relentless pull? Could he keep from being dashed against the rocks?

When they reached the kitchen, Maynard prepared hot tea for her. "Here, drink this," he coaxed. He was dripping wet like she and Lachlan were, and she assumed then he'd run back inside ahead of them to fix the hot tea for her. She wanted to cry.

Lachlan said with a stern word of warning, "Watch her. I'll get a blanket for her."

She wanted to return to the seawall, but she didn't believe Maynard would let her take one step toward the door. She took a sip of the tea and choked on it. Whisky dosed the tea to a good degree, and she felt the liquid burn her throat and all the way down to the pit of her stomach.

"Drink up, lass. You'll feel better."

Numbed, she thought. Alcohol wasn't good for making an ice-cold body warmer.

When she finished the tea, Lachlan returned with a white blanket covered with pink roses. She recognized it. The blanket had been on the little girl's bed in the room that her grandmother had set aside so lovingly for her, hoping she would someday visit. And now her grandmother was lost to her forever. A couple of tears rolled down Colleen's cheeks as she clutched the blanket tightly around her.

"We have to find him. We have to save him," she gritted out between shivers.

Darby quickly joined her, and Lachlan slipped away while Maynard filled her teacup with more of that god-awful whisky laced with tea.

"We will," Darby said. "I'm to see you to your room."

Grant's room. She burst into tears.

———◦◦◦———

Grant struggled to swim against the swift tide, to free himself of the never-ending, swelling waves that threatened to bash him against the rocks.

Splashing wildly with his arms and legs, Archibald thrashed around, trying to keep afloat in human form. He would never last, not without someone's help. He would succumb to the cold before long.

Grant's fur coat kept the chill out, and he tried to swim away from the rocks, against the strong currents. But they pulled him in close to Archibald. Seizing the opportunity, Archibald grabbed hold of Grant and tried to use him as a flotation device. Grant swung his head around and bit into Archibald's arm—his good arm. If he hadn't, the bastard would drown them both. Archibald cried out, released him, and was swept away. That was the last Grant saw of him.

Grant continued to wolf paddle against the strong

currents in the direction of the rocky beach well beyond the castle cliffs. The only way he'd manage was if he could swim away from the cliffs. Had either his mother or father been in wolf form when the sea had taken them, they might have survived. One thing he knew, he couldn't make it back up the cliffs on his own.

Colleen. He couldn't quit worrying that she hadn't moved sufficiently away from the breakers after he knocked Archibald's grip loose of her. What if she'd ended up in the sea with them?

His kinsmen had to have rescued her.

He heard his brothers shouting for him. They weren't calling for Colleen. Which had to mean she was safe with them. Grant couldn't howl in the water to let them know he was still working his way past the rocks. Sheer cliffs prevented him from seeing the shore or the area on the rocks where the trail led to the breakers below the castle.

A hint of beach finally appeared. Relief swept through him. Lights wavered all along the water's edge. Barely keeping his head above water, he knew his kinsmen couldn't see him in the black sea with the rain still falling in torrents.

Yelling for him, nearly twenty of his men watched the sea. Others, running as wolves, looked for any sign of him along the rocky beach.

Desperately, he wanted to call out to learn about Colleen. Was she safe and warm? Was someone watching over her? He refused to consider that she had ended up in the frigid waters with him.

When he got closer to the shore, Lachlan shouted, "Thank God! Grant! He's there!"

Flashlights all angled in his direction as men ran to reach him.

One of the men in wolf coats howled. As soon as Grant reached the shore, bedraggled and worn out, he shook the cold water from his fur and howled, too. A chorus of howls chimed in. Some came from the cliffs on the other side of the keep. Others came from the beach as the wolves hurried to greet him.

Grant gave Lachlan a stern look, asking in a silent wolf way about Colleen.

"She's fine. Upset, of course. Fearing the worst. Maynard gave her hot tea, and Darby's escorting her to your chamber to get a hot shower." Lachlan smiled. "She gave me a black eye and a few choice words when I wouldn't let her stay on the cliffs to watch for you."

Grant gave him a wolf's smile. He loved her. Not that he had wished for his brother to have a black eye or that Colleen had given it to him, but he loved his feisty mate.

Then he barked with joy that she was fine and raced up the long climb to reach the closed portcullis, hoping he wouldn't encounter any of Archibald's men on the way there. He didn't want anyone to sidetrack him from seeing Colleen as soon as he could.

Wearing their wolf coats, ten of his pack members raced outside the gate as soon as it was lifted to greet him. No sign of Archibald's men or Baird and his kin. It appeared it had all been a ruse so Archibald could reach the keep. Grant suspected they'd all left, planning to meet up with Archibald later after he'd drowned Colleen.

Lachlan was still climbing the steep stone steps up the cliffs, the rest of the men in human form following him.

As soon as Grant entered the inner bailey, Enrick hurried to join him. "The lass is safe and sound, thanks to you, Grant. Darby's guarding the chamber to ensure she doesn't leave it. I was about to run up there to tell her you were on your way, but thought you might like to have the honor. We found the raft Archibald used to reach the cliffs. The rocks had torn holes in it. He would never have survived the return trip home if you hadn't taken him out already."

Glad Colleen would be all right and that Archibald would have perished no matter what else had happened, Grant nodded and raced for the keep and entered it.

When he reached his chamber door, Darby grinned at him and opened it for him. "Let us know if you require something hot for the two of you to eat and drink. I know it's late, but if you need anything, Maynard and I will get it for you. Just let us know." Then he closed the door for Grant.

Grant shifted and stalked across the floor to reach the bathroom. The shower was running and he heard Colleen crying. He hated to hear her so distressed.

"Lass, it's me, and you should know by now you can't get rid of me that—" he said, about to reach for the clear shower door, the steam misting the glass so that all he could see was her delectable outline.

He didn't finish speaking as Colleen jerked the door aside and threw herself into his arms, dripping wet, smelling of peaches and cream and...*whisky*. He smiled.

He swept her up and carried her back into the tiled shower and shut the door.

"I thought you never wanted to drink our whisky again," he joked, trying to lighten the dark mood.

He thought she told him to shut up. He wasn't certain, as she ravished him with kisses, her hands grasping his wet hair, and her body pressed hotly against his.

He wanted to tease her out of her distress—as she was still crying—happy tears, aye, but still...

He wisely thought better of trying to make light of his dunking in the sea and said, "I am fine, lass. And I love you with every fiber of my being."

"Oh, Grant," was all she said as her whisky-flavored lips and tongue stroked his.

He rather liked the taste on her as he hugged her tight and kissed her reverently, passionately, possessively. He stroked her hair in a loving, reassuring way, then said, "Next time you wear that sexy minikilt, nothing is stopping me from having my way with you."

She smiled. "I will hold you to that."

Gladdened to the depths of his soul that she was safe, he ran his hands over her slippery skin and felt every soft inch of her. His fingers worked down to her center and stroked between her legs. She panted and moved against his probing fingers. She closed her eyes and leaned her head back against the tiled wall out of the water's spray as he let the warm drops wash away the sea collected on his skin.

God, how he loved her. She appeared to revel in his touch, lost to it. He wanted more than anything to chase away all that had happened to her in the last hour or so, to warm her, to love her. They were together, mates forever. Nothing would take that away from them.

He brushed his mouth against hers, meaning to be gentle, but she didn't seem to want gentle. She clung to him, kissed him boldly on the mouth and cheeks, his throat, his chest.

And piercing awareness struck him. She was the owner of the castle, the estates, and of him—his heart, his body, his soul. She owned him outright. He loved the knowledge that the she-wolf had claimed him, just like she had claimed her beta mates.

He threaded his fingers through her wet hair, glorying in every aspect of her, from the way her silky hot body molded to his to her soft curls hiding a wealth of feminine treasures and tickling his leg as she rubbed herself against him.

Her breasts rose and fell against his chest, her nipples taut with need.

Her breath was as ragged as was his. His raging desire to satisfy both their needs pushed him to kiss her deeper. His fingers tangled in her hair and his body caressed hers, wanting more. Her tears had long ago subsided, and she was wrapped up only in the love they shared.

He trembled with the pent-up need to have her as he leaned down to kiss one wet breast, his fingers lowering to stroke her sex.

Colleen thought she would come apart as they kissed and suckled and rubbed against each other. They were meant for each other. The sea could not separate them.

He was stroking her and licking her nipple, making her arch up, wanting him to satisfy the wild desire cascading through her. He glanced up at her. She saw the turbulent look in his eyes, the concern there, and she loved him all the more.

"Keep going," she whispered, her voice husky.

He grinned at her, though he couldn't hide the concern still there. But he did continue to rub her into climax, and before she could fall from the exquisite torture of the moment, he centered himself and entered her. He filled her and stretched her to accommodate his rock-hard erection as her inner muscles quivered with climax. She wrapped her legs around him, and he plunged all the way, deep, demanding, and needy.

God, he felt so good. She wanted to keep him like this inside her forever, never letting go. Never scared to death she'd lose him again.

She tightened her legs around him as he held her buttocks in his hands and continued to push into her. Being joined like this with her mate felt so right. So complete.

The friction between them, the way he tongued her mouth and deepened the thrusts, awakened the need to climax again. The sweet ache between her legs burned for it. She felt it coming, felt the giddy sensation of sexual fulfillment, and fell over the edge just as he let loose with a heartfelt growl. He released his seed deep inside her, bathing her womb in heat and love.

He continued to thrust and rock against her as their mouths melded with renewed kisses.

Somehow, they managed to turn off the water, dry themselves, and climb into bed.

"Did you want to eat anything, lass?" Grant asked, wrapping his naked body around hers, not only his arms, but his legs also, as she nestled against his chest and groin. "Anything to drink?"

"You," is all she murmured against his chest. It had to be around five that morning or later already. Even if she'd wanted anything, which she didn't, she would not have asked anyone to get it for them. "You're okay? Not injured? Not bruised?"

"A Highland warrior doesn't tell his lassie about bruises he might be wearing."

She smiled against his chest.

He caressed her back with his rough hand. "He might mention in passing that he sustained a sword wound if it was very deep."

She chuckled, caressing his waist with the same tender touch.

Then he grew serious, his voice filled with regret. "I should never have left you alone, fool that I was."

"You did what any sane man would have thought was right. Who would ever have suspected Archibald would do something so crazy?" Colleen asked. "Or even know that he could gain entrance in that manner?"

"I can't believe he intended to kill you. He had to know he wouldn't have lived once we found him."

"He had a raft. He said he intended to use it for his escape. That he had no intention of dying this day or any other."

"His raft was not fit to use, from what Enrick said. He wouldn't have made it."

She nodded. "I didn't smell his scent. I assumed he used something to disguise it. If he had gotten away with murdering me…"

"He wouldn't have," Grant said, his voice a deep growl.

"If he had, would you have known it was him?"

"Aye, I would have. Our men saw him at one point, but then he disappeared. So we knew he had been in the area, but none of us could track his scent. Now I know why. But his attempt to kill you didn't make any sense. What good would it have done him?" Grant asked, kissing the top of her head reverently, tenderly.

"His actions all had to do with taking me away from

you. You might have the run of the castle, but he would have taken away something from you that—"

"I want more than life, lass." Grant held her tighter, not wanting to let her go. He'd nearly died when he saw what Archibald intended to do with her, fearing he would not reach her to rescue her in time.

"Why were the pipes still there?" Colleen asked, sounding puzzled.

"Neda wanted to keep them for nostalgic reasons. Part of the history of the place. Something to show her grandchildren and their grandchildren. I told her we should have sealed them off for good years ago for safety's sake."

"I understand her thinking, but if we have any more enemies lurking out there, seems to me the pipes should be sealed off at once. I agree with you. First thing, when we have a chance. But for now, all I want to do is rest up for the wedding."

Grant smiled at that. As crazy as things had been and as excited as his people were, he assumed this was the only bit of rest they could indulge in. Which meant he didn't intend to let Colleen out of his sight for a good eight hours or longer. To sleep…or whatever else they had in mind to do.

Chapter 26

THE WEDDING PREPARATIONS WERE TIRING, AND HER cousins would be arriving soon. Needing a respite before the celebration, Colleen finally slipped away to Neda's room and sat on her grandmother's bed. Tears formed in her eyes as she ran her hand over the blue bedspread embroidered with gold threads in the pattern of the tree of life. "Thank you for raising Grant and his brothers to be the men they are today. I love you, Grandma, even if I never was able to meet you. I wish I had. I wish I hadn't listened to my father."

She took a deep breath and sighed. "I'm marrying that Highlander you raised like a son and made your manager. He's all I ever needed in a mate. He and his kin won't ever lose their place at Farraige Castle. I just wanted you to know that, because I know you loved them as much as I do."

She glanced at all the journals sitting in stacks and remembered they hadn't finished looking for the journal for the time period when Grant's mother had perished.

Knowing this wasn't the time to search for it, she couldn't help it. She wanted to know what her grandmother had thought about Grant's mother's death.

She sorted through the remaining journals and finally found the one. As she suspected, Neda had been beside herself with grief. Water, probably from her tears, had made much of the ink run on several pages as

Colleen envisioned her grandmother writing down the events of what had occurred. Neda had loved Eleanor, whom she'd considered her daughter. And she'd loved Robert like a son. Much more so than her own son, Theodore, whom she suspected had murdered Grant's mother. And then Neda had taken solace in raising Grant and his brothers as her own grandchildren, caring for them, teaching them to read and write, and keeping them in line.

Colleen smiled through her tears, loving her grandmother all the more.

Then she heard someone enter the room and turned to see Grant studying her. "Calla and Julia were worried about you, lass. Search parties have gone out. Some thought you escaped the keep to avoid wedding me, though you have no chance at that."

She smiled and sniffled.

"But I thought that you might be here." He glanced down at the journal in her hands. "About my mother?" he asked gently, probably afraid Colleen would burst into tears. How would that look when she was about to get married?

She nodded.

He closed the distance between them and pulled her from the bed. She quickly set the journal down and wrapped her arms around his waist.

"She adored you and your brothers," Colleen said softly.

"Aye, what's not to adore, eh, lass?"

She laughed. "I have to agree."

"Are you ready for this?" he asked.

"Yes. Yes, I am."

"Good. Your cousins will be here any minute, and

Calla and Julia want to get you into your wedding gown, or I'd take you back up to our chambers and have my way with you."

She loved him. "I'm ready. For the wedding, that is. I'd never straighten my hair out in time if we returned to our chambers first."

"All right." He called Calla on his cell and let her know where they were, and then with one lingering kiss, he waited for the ladies to arrive before he left Colleen alone.

She knew he did so to ensure she didn't get all sentimental and burst into tears before the ladies could deal with her emotions.

"Ohmigod, here you are," Julia said.

Calla nearly ran into her, attempting to enter Neda's room at the same time as Julia, wedding gown and veil in their hands.

"We thought for sure you'd run off or something." But Julia said it with a twinkle in her eye. She knew Colleen better than that.

An hour later, Colleen paced the inner bailey, dressed in her white organza and lace-trimmed wedding gown and veil, looking like a fairy-tale princess, with her hair piled high on her head, tendrils curling down about her ears and neck, and pearls placed in several coils of curls. She was anxious to see her cousins, Edward and William Playfair, who were going to arrive at any moment. She would not let the ceremony begin until they arrived.

Edward was darker haired like Colleen, his brother blonder, and both looked uneasy as Lachlan and Enrick escorted them from their rental car to meet her. The MacQuarrie and MacNeill clans had all dressed in kilts

and the men carried swords to the wedding, traditional
for them as in centuries past.

She smiled at her cousins and hurried to greet them,
the wolfhounds also racing to meet them.

Thankfully, both her cousins loved dogs as much
as she did and knew how to make them mind. William
pulled out a pen and clicked it. Just like he'd taught
her. All three dogs sat before him, and then he hugged
Colleen. Edward did the honors next, looking much relieved to see her.

"Lachlan MacQuarrie said we were just in time for a
wedding," William said, eyeing her in her white gown.
"He said nothing about our cousin marrying anyone. He
wouldn't say who was marrying whom. We thought it
was one of his clanswomen. Not our own cousin."

"Who are you marrying?" Edward asked.

Both sounded shocked to learn she was getting married. Well, she hadn't called them about it and hadn't
thought to. She never asked their opinion when she
embarked on a mating. She didn't feel she had needed
to this time, either. Of course, part of their surprise
was probably because she never actually had a wedding before.

Grant stalked out of the keep to join them, looking
like a warrior on the battlefield. Her cousins looked like
they wanted to take a few steps back, but they stood
their ground, even though Grant appeared to be a threat.

Colleen tilted her head at her mate, giving him a look
to play nice. The men were only her cousins. She suspected his alpha male posturing had to do with greeting
new males to a pack and showing them that no one—not
even her family—had any say in what she or he did.

She made introductions and Grant shook both their hands, then said, "Welcome to the pack."

She was glad Grant had said so, except he wasn't offering but telling them, and she loved him even more for it. Her beta cousins might have tucked tail and run if given the choice after seeing all the kilted men armed with swords and *sgian dubhs* tucked in their socks and just as fierce-looking as Grant was while they checked her cousins out.

Grant offered his arm to Colleen. "We have our wedding to attend and you're just in time."

"You're marrying Grant MacQuarrie?" Edward asked, hurrying to catch up to them.

"You didn't ask us what we thought," William said. "I mean, ask for our permission."

She almost laughed at the idea. She loved them. "Well…what do you think?"

Grant gave them each a look that said they'd better agree with this, or else.

"Oh, sure. We agree, if you're happy," William said, glancing at Grant's sword.

"You can live here if you'd like," Colleen said. She wasn't sure if her cousins could manage on their own without her to watch their backs. Here, they'd have a whole pack watching out for them. And she'd really prefer it that way.

William and Edward shared looks, then smiled. "We thought we were just making a visit here. But…yeah, sure," Edward said.

"Sword practice in the morning," Grant warned. "The two of you will have a lot of catching up to do."

They nodded, looking a little as though they weren't sure what they were getting into.

"And you'll wear kilts," he added, his voice gruff, brooking no argument.

They glanced down at Grant's kilt. He gave them an evil smile. All men of the clan wore kilts on special occasions, Grant more often than the rest—and for that Colleen was grateful. She wondered what her cousins would think of the practice when they weren't supposed to wear anything under the kilts and it was a bit breezy around the place.

Grant squeezed Colleen against him. "You are the most beautiful bride."

"You are the handsomest kilted Highland wolf a woman could want for a groom."

He smiled down at her.

Guthrie opened the door to the keep for them and said, "You couldn't delay the wedding for another month or so, could you?"

"Guthrie," Colleen said, "When you and Calla are back at Argent Castle, you won't even notice she's there."

Guthrie didn't look like he believed her.

They entered the chapel and Shelley's Uncle Ethan offered his arm to Colleen to walk her down the aisle while Grant made Edward and William join him to serve as a couple more groomsmen, even if they were dressed in only jeans, sneakers, and sweatshirts.

She swore Ian's mother was ready to burst into tears, as if Colleen was her daughter, too. Colleen fought her own tears at knowing that her best friend's clan was taking her in just as much as Grant MacQuarrie's.

Frederick took all three wolfhounds in hand, though they wanted to follow her down the aisle, and made them stay with him at the back of the chapel. When the minister asked for objections, Hercules barked, letting her know he wanted to join her up front. Everyone laughed.

"Sorry, Hercules," Grant said. "She's all mine."

Which meant absolutely no way was Grant sharing his bed with anyone but her.

Before long, the ceremony was over and Colleen tossed her bouquet to the eager women, not knowing her own strength. The roses flew up and way over their heads.

Uncle Ethan caught the roses as they headed straight for him, and he blushed crimson. She was trying to send it to either Heather or Calla. Guthrie looked much relieved.

Everyone roared to see the older man holding on to the bouquet, his face the same color as the red roses.

"You're supposed to let a lass catch the flowers," Ian's mother said, scolding him and taking the flowers away from him.

More laughter ensued.

And to a shocked audience, Uncle Ethan said, "All right, ma'am. I accept." He took Lady Mae's arm and tucked it under his own.

"Accept what?" she asked crossly.

"A mating. Marriage. Whatever you'd like," he said, looking down at her with an adoring expression.

Cheers went up and Colleen swore Ian's mother looked like she would expire on the spot.

Ian and his brothers were clapping hard and whistling and cheering, showing their approval for their mother's mating with Shelley's uncle. Now, whether their mother would agree was another story. She probably wanted to sock him for saying so at Colleen's wedding, but Colleen loved it.

Grant had the privilege of removing the garter from Colleen's leg, running his hand over her bare thigh a little too intimately, and several of the men teased him about the show. Then he tossed the garter to a groom-to-be. It hit Guthrie in the chest, and he caught it, turned red-faced, and tried to hand it off to one of Colleen's cousins, who both shook their heads vehemently and wouldn't touch it.

Laughter resounded and then the music started and Grant and Colleen had their first dance, followed by everyone else, mated wolves and singles. Ian's mother and Uncle Ethan even danced at his coaxing and he held her so tenderly that Colleen assumed they were in for a mating.

The reception was buffet style, and though they knew they should stay longer, Grant and Colleen had another mission in mind. They went up to their bedchamber, and he removed her gown, then ditched his kilt and shirt. Both of them shifted into wolves, then ran through the castle while everyone hailed them with toasts of champagne.

Three of the men had to grab the wolfhounds to ensure they didn't chase after Grant and Colleen. Guthrie opened the front door for them. The mated couple ran out and through the inner bailey and then beyond. They ran and ran until they reached the glen where the sheep grazed on the green hills and the white, foaming burn rushed under the wooden footbridge.

The weather had turned colder, perfect for their fur coats, a wet mist draping over them as they reached the place they had shared their first kiss. On top of the hill as the sky turned yellow, orange, and pink and the sun began to set, Grant nuzzled Colleen's face in a wolf's way of courtship and she licked his face. And for a brief moment, they shifted, embraced each other tight, and kissed again.

Only this time they were husband and wife and mated wolves.

"God, I love you, Grant."

"Hmm, lass. You are my one and only love. Are you ready to return to the keep and our chamber?" he asked, rubbing her chilled arms.

She smiled. "I thought you'd never ask."

And then they shifted and raced off across the glen, in love with each other, with their home and their pack. Not in a million years would Colleen have ever thought she'd inherit a castle and a mate and his family all in one fell swoop.

Grant had run as a wolf through this glen so many times that he couldn't count the number, but seeing Colleen ahead of him, her tail wagging in delight, and knowing just what they were in for when they returned home, he couldn't have been happier.

He still wondered: if he'd been chivalrous and welcoming when Colleen had first arrived, would they be where they were today? All he knew was he was damn glad that the she-wolf had captured his heart and made him see the error of his ways.

Note to Readers

I gave my character Colleen the family name of Playfair, as I have done with Roux, the MacNeills, and the Campbells in previous works. I've done so much genealogy work and I've enjoyed including the family in the wolf packs for various reasons. MacNeill and Campbell because they had a love for one another that couldn't be denied in Scotland. Roux, because that means redheaded, and she's a red wolf. And now Playfair, because they were Scots as well.

The Playfairs truly are famous Scots, so that's why I wanted to base this story on their family. John Playfair was a brilliant mathematician and geologist. Craters on the moon and Mars were named after him. James, his brother, was a famous architect. When James died, John raised his young nephew, Andrew, who became even a more famous architect. The brother I'm descended directly from was William, the youngest and a twin, who was the inventor of statistical graphs and an engineer. He studied under a famous Scot—James Watt, engineer and inventor.

Acknowledgments

Thanks to Loretta Melvin for her invaluable research and keeping me straight on names and such, to Loretta, Donna Fournier, and Dottie Jones for being my beta readers, and to Brooklyn Ann for being my critique partner. Thanks to Deb Werksman for helping to make the books even better, and to Danielle Jackson for all her help with guest blog tours and tons of other promotions. And thanks to the cover artist gods and the models and the photographers who create real wolf works of art.

Silence of the Wolf

by Terry Spear

USA Today Bestselling Author

———

Life for the Silver pack just got wilder...

Elizabeth Wildwood has been a loner all her life, ostracized because of her "mixed" half-wolf, half-coyote blood. When she ventures into gray wolf territory on a dangerous quest of her own and is thrown together with the sexiest shifter she's ever met, she begins to wish for the first time that she could be part of a family.

When this unusual shifter female comes into his pack's territory, it's Tom Silver's job to protect her—if only she would let him...

———

"Ms. Spear brings her characters to life, both old and new, and you will find yourself invested in the story."—*Night Owl* Reviewer Top Pick, 4.5 Stars

"Nobody does werewolf romances like Terry Spear. The romance sizzles, the plot boils, the mystery intrigues, and the characters shine."—*The Royal Reviews*

For more Terry Spear, visit:

www.sourcebooks.com

Jaguar Hunt

by Terry Spear

USA Today Bestselling Author

Two deadly predators...

As a feline Enforcer, Tammy Anderson has one objective: locate the missing jaguar and return it to the States. She doesn't have time for distractions, and she definitely doesn't have time for sexy shifters with more muscles than sense.

One hot mission...

Everyone and their brother has warned JAG agent David Patterson that Tammy is Ms. Hands-Off...which only makes him more determined to get very hands-on. But things heat up in the steamy jungles of Belize and their simple mission gets a whole lot more complicated. Now it's going to take everything David's got to protect the gorgeous she-cat who somehow managed to claw her way past his defenses...and into his heart.

Praise for *Jaguar Fever*:

"Readers will enjoy this thrilling tale as love and danger collide."—*Midwest Book Review*

"Spear's writing style, as usual, is very detailed and descriptive. A must-read for lovers of paranormal romance."—*Romancing the Book*

For more Terry Spear, visit:

www.sourcebooks.com

About the Author

Bestselling and award-winning author **Terry Spear** has written more than fifty paranormal romance novels and four medieval Highland historical romances. Her first werewolf romance, *Heart of the Wolf*, was named a 2008 *Publishers Weekly*'s Best Book of the Year, and her subsequent titles have garnered high praise and hit the *USA Today* bestseller list. A retired officer of the U.S. Army Reserves, Terry lives in Crawford, Texas, where she is working on her next werewolf romance and continuing her new series about shape-shifting jaguars. For more information, please visit www.terryspear.com, or follow her on Twitter, @TerrySpear. She is also on Facebook at www.facebook.com/terry.spear.